The RISE of TEHH

THOMAS EDISON HAMILTON HANCOCK
The Boy Who Rebuilt A City

BETTY COLLINS SMITH

WESTBOW®
PRESS
A DIVISION OF THOMAS NELSON
& ZONDERVAN

Scripture taken from the King James Version of the Bible.

WestBow Press books may be ordered through booksellers or by contacting:

WestBow Press
A Division of Thomas Nelson & Zondervan
1663 Liberty Drive
Bloomington, IN 47403
www.westbowpress.com
1 (866) 928-1240

ISBN: 978-1-4908-7938-3 (sc)
ISBN: 978-1-4908-7940-6 (hc)
ISBN: 978-1-4908-7939-0 (e)

Library of Congress Control Number: 2015907184

Print information available on the last page.

WestBow Press rev. date: 5/28/2015

This Book is dedicated to my family.

My Lord, Jesus Christ, for putting this story in my heart.

My mother, Mathey Hamlett. My husband, Rev. Morgan A. Smith. My daughters: Zerqueenna S. Sanders and husband Travis, LaMorgan A. Smith. My granddaughter: Jordan R. Shular. My brothers and their wives: Wade and Donna, Toney and Gloria, and Victor Hamlett. My sister Earnestine and husband Paul Mumford, Sr. My nephews and wives: Paul and Leslie, Patrick and Christie Mumford, and Christopher Hamlett. My nieces and husbands: Shakeya and Quindarius Bennett, Gloria and Quincey Harville, Davida and Jamaine Spann, Jessica and Andrea Hamlett. Uncle Eugene and Charlotte Naylor, and Aunt Gwendolyn Naylor.

Thank you all for your encouragement and listening ears as I shared this story with you a thousand times.

My brothers and sisters of my father, James Collins in Detroit, Mi. Calvin, Joe, Sonny, Henry, Jeanette, Barbara, Arlene, and Alsline.

My Smith family: Ms. Arstella Smith, Frankie, James Lee, Johnny, Eddie, Jason, Anthony, Vashie, Barbara, Joy and Stella Mae.
My dear friend, Beverly Harris
First Missionary Baptist Church, Pratt City
Mount Zion Missionary Baptist Church
Mount Hebron Baptist Church
The Jefferson County District Association -
The Minister's Wives, and all of my students.

Special thanks to Sister - Beatrice Y. Augustus
For loving and believing in me.

CHAPTER 1

For man also knoweth not his time: as the fishes that are taken in an
evil net, and as the birds that are caught in the snare; so are the sons
of men snared in an evil time, when it falleth suddenly upon them.
(Ecclesiastes 9:12)

I heard the preacher talking about this one Sunday in church, and I didn't
know what in the world he was talking about until I grew older. I finally saw
the evil that snared men and women, boys and girls, rich and poor, colored
and white, the dumb and smart, rendering them helpless. People who at one
time had the potential to make this a great city instead chose to throw it away
because of the choices they made. Rich men chased after money, alcohol,
drugs, and prostitutes until they were destroyed by them. I watched pimps
and gangs turn parts of our city upside down and ravish the inhabitants.
They turned already depressed communities into cesspools, and the stench
filled the air.

I asked myself, *Why am I so concerned about all of this? Why does all of this
bother me so?* I was just a child and a poor one at that. What could I do about
it anyway? Even though I felt like I too was trapped in this sinkhole of life
like a bird caught in an evil net, I saw many people who were worse off than
me. They were held hostage by their own ignorance and the thoughts of their
imagination, rendering them helpless until they couldn't dream of a better
day. For them life was all shades of gray. Hopelessness became a way of life
for them but not for me. I saw things differently, for some strange reason, and
couldn't understand why. In my heart I saw myself rising above all of this to
become somebody one day. I just didn't know how. I came to realize that in

every city God has His savior of the people to bring them out of darkness into the light. Sometimes it can be a child like me.

Somewhere in a forgotten place called Box City, among gangs, thieves, thugs, prostitutes, pimps, pushers, and all the filth, you could find me. I was a handsome young boy named Thomas Edison Hamilton Hancock, "Tehh" for short, pushing my wagon around town. My mother gave me this name because she had high hopes for me. She told me that she felt deep down in her heart that I would make a difference in this world. She wanted me to have a powerful name that commanded respect. She didn't want to be like the other mothers who named their boys after pimps, pushers, thugs, and bad boy singers. So many of those children ended up dead or in prison. She didn't want that to happen to me. It was like evil spirits were attached to those names. So she chose to name me after men who made America great—men like Thomas Edison, inventor of the light-bulb; Alexander Hamilton, the first secretary of the Treasury of the United States (and whose picture was on the ten-dollar bill); and John Hancock, whose signature stood out on the Constitution. Since her last name was already Hancock, that made it even better. She was going to make sure I had a name that wouldn't kill me.

To see me you wouldn't believe I had the potential to be anything because of how society labeled me. I was the opposite of everything my mama believed for me at first. I was a good kid to a certain degree, but trouble always seemed to find me. In spite of all she hoped for me, I was doomed from the start. If people weren't cursing me out, they talked about me like I was a dog or just picked on me. Some even told me that I would be nothing but a burden on society. For some strange reason something on the inside of me wouldn't let me believe that. No one knew my inward struggle to break free of the stigmas people had piled upon me. These stigmas can become heavy weights for a young boy like me, but they didn't. They made me aware of the world around me and how cruel people could be. They made me more cautious, stronger, and more determined to be somebody one day no matter what. I learned the power to rewrite your life story was in your own hands. Mama was actually right. I did make a difference in this world, and this is my incredible story.

Most people considered me to be strange or special growing up. I mean the short school bus special for not-so-bright kids. To them I was dumb and unreachable, as if I was actually from a distant planet or something. How could my mama make fun of me like that by saying I was going to make a difference in this world? Folks said I couldn't even read, write, or think for myself. Not only was I dumb to them, but I was also stupid. What they didn't know about me was I could actually read and write very well. They just never saw me doing it. I loved to read. I read everything behind closed doors. I read the financial section of the newspaper, money magazines, accounting books, antique books, cookbooks, encyclopedias, dictionaries, and law books. If it was a book, I read it, even though it was determined by doctors and psychologists that I couldn't read. I especially liked to keep up with the stock market since I had a few pennies riding on some new computer software that was going to take off one day. I found out about something called penny stocks in a book and decided to try them.

The doctors, school, and everyone had misdiagnosed me and told the world I was a dummy and there was little help for me. Each morning I got up, hid my intelligence behind ignorance, and hit the streets collecting newspapers, magazines, financial information from bank dumpsters, and old office equipment, putting them in my homemade wagon. This may sound strange, but for me ignorance had its privileges too. It gave me access to some strange places and people. If I couldn't read or reason, as they said, then how was I to know that I wasn't supposed to be there?

Because of my access, I would find people and money in places you wouldn't believe. I came upon a businessman in a shack with a prostitute. Surely he could have afforded a motel. He gave me twenty dollars to get out of there, and I did just that. One day I found two hundred dollars in a stocking stuck in a shoe in an alley behind a motel that said, "Keep Out." I hated to think about what happened to the girl who came up two hundred dollars short. One day they were cleaning out one of the rooms in another motel and threw away a box of clothes and stuff on the trash pile. I was looking through the stuff and found a bra stuffed with ten- and twenty-dollar bills. That was definitely a padded bra.

Most people would look at my wagon and smile when they saw all the books, newspapers and magazines I had in it. Most of them knew I couldn't read or reason. They had classified me as a dummy, but my job paid and sometimes very well, and I had enough sense to know it. I learned that people will believe whatever folks say about you, even if it wasn't true. Most of them will rarely take the time to find out the truth for themselves. They just go with the flow. If they had asked me an intelligent question, I would have given them an intelligent answer.

Even though I had this powerful name, Thomas Edison Hamilton Hancock, it was not enough to keep me from getting kicked out of school permanently. It was finally determined that I could never, and I quote *never,* learn because I was supposed to have had a severe learning disability and emotional problems. I was thirteen years old when the school psychologist and doctors said I had the attention span of a three-year-old and recommended that I should be institutionalized to get the help I needed. Thank God for my mama, Meyel. She wouldn't let them take me away because she loved me so much. She fought to keep me out of that institution and said she would take full responsibility for my actions. She was the only one who actually knew the real me. She was my rock, but she would slap me upside the head in a minute. I didn't play with my mama.

She was sixteen years old when I was born. She and my daddy were married for five rocky years. They fussed and fought all the time. There was no such thing as peace in our house that I could remember. My daddy was a tall, skinny man with an afro. One day they were fighting, and I got caught in the cross fire. He missed Mama and knocked me up against the dresser. I hit my head hard and passed out for a few minutes. They never took me to the doctor to make sure I was okay. After that I started acting strange and having a lot of headaches. Some were very bad. Mama would give me an aspirin and tell me to go and lie down.

One day Daddy told Mama he was going to the store for some cigarettes and never came back. He just disappeared, leaving her with three children to take care of all by herself. I loved my daddy, but he changed that when he took all the money Mama had for us tucked away in a jar under the bed. It was like he didn't care if we lived or died. There was hardly any food in the house. She had to ask the neighbors for help. She had already dropped out of school to help him care for us. After he left, she worked in kitchens and motels and did laundry for people. I often wondered what he was doing or if he even thought about us since he didn't have to care for us anymore. I promised myself that I would never be like him.

Mama had several disappointments with men and didn't bring them to the house anymore after what almost happened to Diamond. One of her ex-friends came to the house drunk one day while she was at the store, and

Diamond let him in. She didn't know any better, because she knew him and thought it was okay. She was just six years old at the time. I was out back and didn't know he was there. He tried to rape my little sister. Mama always told her that if anyone tried to touch her in the wrong way to scream as loud as she could, and she did. The neighbors heard her screaming, and we all came to her rescue. Big Jim and another man from across the street came and beat the stew of out him. We never saw him again. All of that began to affect me and Mama as time went on. She became very protective of us, and I became very protective of her, Diamond, and my brother, Benjamin, in spite of my so-called disability. Mama said I would always be the man of the house. She told us that she would never trust anyone else with our lives like that again. I asked God to please help me to make my mama's life a little easier if I could. I just wanted her to be happy and safe.

CHAPTER 2

One day I was looking for stuff on the streets and saw a "Help Wanted" sign in the window of Ricko's Bakery. It wasn't that far from the house, and I thought that job would be perfect for my mama. She wouldn't have to work so many different jobs to take care of us. Mr. Ricko would leave me some leftover cakes and cookies in a box with a red string on it sometimes when he saw me coming his way. I went in the bakery and thanked him for the cookies and asked him about his sign in the window? He told me that it said help wanted. I asked him what kind of job it was and what you had to do to get the job. He smiled, cleared his throat, and told me he needed someone to help him make cakes. They needed to know how to read, know measurements, know how to follow instructions, and have very good communication skills. The rest he would teach them. Then he told me that I was too young for the job, and I had to know how to read. Like everyone else, he knew that I couldn't, and I just played along. I asked him if he had any old books around on baking that he didn't want. He told me he did and gave them to me. He was going to throw them out anyway. I kindly thanked him and went on my way.

As I was leaving, I heard him making fun of me saying, "Did y'all see that? What's that boy going to do with those books? He can't read. Look at the pictures? Most of these colored folks round here don't know how to read. That's why that sign is still in the window. And, if they could read, they still wouldn't. I tell you, if you want to hide something from 'em, just put it in a book. They sure won't look there."

The joke was really on him because I read him loud and clear. That made me so mad. I went on out the door like I didn't hear him. I heard what he said all right, and I was going to prove him wrong because I could read and understand very well. He told me everything I needed to teach my mama. While walking away, all I could think of was helping my mama get that job. That would be fifty more dollars a week for us. We could save two hundred extra dollars a month and twenty-six hundred a year based on those bonus Fridays. I knew she could do it if she just had the chance. All I had to do was hope that I could convince her to try. My mama was nearly thirty and looked fifty because she worried about us and worked so hard.

I went home and began reading all the books that Mr. Ricko gave me on baking and tried to find simple ways to explain it so Mama could understand. I don't know how or when it happened, but I learned to read really fast and remember everything I read. All I had to do was focus and think of the book, and then everything came to my mind. It's still kind of weird to me. When Mama came home she was so tired that she just dropped down on the couch. Sometimes she would even fall asleep. I gave her a cold glass of water and sat down beside her. I was so excited. I asked her, "Mama, how would you like a better job?"

All of a sudden her energy came from somewhere and she rose up and said, "Baby, I sure would. All of these jobs now are just killing me."

I said with enthusiasm, "Ricko's Bakery needs someone to help make cakes. What you think about that?"

She said, "I don't know anything about working in a bakery. You have to have experience for that."

She made it clear to me that she didn't have any experience. Well, I took that big leap of faith and said, "What if I can teach you all about baking, Mama?"

She turned and looked at me like I was some kind of fool and told me I didn't know anything about baking because I couldn't even cook. Then she said, "Now what can you teach me about baking, huh?"

I begged her to please let me at least try. She knew I had never begged her like that before and wondered what was wrong with me. I just felt deep down inside that I could actually teach her. All I needed was a chance. Then I said, "Have I ever let you down before, Mama?"

She thought about it and said, "Well no! What do I have to lose?"

For three hours a night, for two and a half weeks, I taught my mama the art of baking from the books Mr. Ricko gave me. She caught on so quickly, and she was just amazing. She learned the measurements, decorating tools, terminology, the various baking pans, their uses, and the temperatures for baking. She proudly made an "A" in my class. Each day I went by the bakery to see if the sign was still in the window. It was still there. One evening I came home, and Mama surprised me. She had actually made a cake that looked like the ones in the bakery window at Ricko's, and it tasted so good. I was so proud of her and myself too. I learned that I could make a difference in somebody's life, even if it was my mama. Diamond and Benjamin ate cake like they were going crazy and told Mama how good it was. You should have seen my mama's face. She was so proud, so confident, and she was so happy. I cried and thanked God for the opportunity to help her in that way.

A few days before she went to apply for the job, I was looking through a box of books I had found on a trash pile. I saw a book that told you what to do when you looked for a job. I didn't know what an interview was at the time, but the lady on the cover caught my attention. After I read the book, it made a lot of sense. I thought I would teach Mama some of what it said just in case. Looking back, Mama said those were the hardest two and a half weeks of her entire life, but it was worth it. She even told me that I was a great teacher and that she was sorry for saying I couldn't teach her anything.

That Monday morning she got up and went to Ricko's Bakery with confidence. She applied for the job and got it even though she had never worked in a bakery before. I learned that *if you can read and follow instructions,* you could change *your* world. If you are teachable, you can always learn something new. She came home that day happier than I had ever seen her before with tears in her eyes. She gave me a big hug and told me she got the job and that she would start the next week. She told me with joy that she didn't have to work all those different jobs anymore. She would make more money at the bakery than she did working the three other jobs. Then she asked me what I had done to her. I paused and asked her what she meant. She said, "The manager was so amazed at my knowledge of baking. He asked me what cooking school I attended, and if I had ever thought about management one day." She said at that point she could have fainted. She started crying and told me that she couldn't have done it without me, not in a million years. She smiled and said that she thought she could never learn something new like that because she had dropped out of school. Then she frowned and looked at me sadly and said, "How come no one else can see your abilities, Tehh? How come? You are a genius, honey, and I know it."

Well, if no one else knew, my mama certainly knew that I was no dummy. With her limited education, she depended on me for just about everything. When it came to money, I was the man. I did the banking, helped her manage the finances of the house, made out the grocery list, and clipped the coupons. That was one of the reasons for all the newspapers. We had to save every penny we could to survive. The store clerks were always amazed to see this colored woman with the exact amount of money in her hands with the coupons, rarely making a mistake before they totaled her up. It's wasn't that Mama couldn't learn do some of those things. She just chose to let me do them. I guess that was one less headache for her.

CHAPTER 3

I said all of that because I want you to understand why my mama decided to take the risk of letting me stay home with her. All she ever wanted was for me to be what I was born to be. She believed I would make a difference in this world. She just couldn't understand why I would just shut down at school and let people think that I was dumb when I wasn't. The truth is the school system didn't work in my favor. It worked against me because of my diagnosis. People refused to recognize my true potential. They sided with the school psychologists, teachers and folks who didn't even know me. For them I was just a case study. When it came to my teachers, if I passed a test, they accused me of cheating and gave me a failing grade anyway. How could I win? It was right there staring them in the face, but they didn't want to recognize it. I was from the wrong side of the tracks. They threw me into a category of under-achievers and troublemakers because I fit the profile. That was actually where they want me to stay. Most of the troublemakers and underachievers came from the same geographical area as me. We all lived in the worst part of Box City. According to them, I was in the class of the hopeless with no chance of escape. I refused to accept that. I didn't have a severe learning disability at all. I was just a misunderstood genius that stuttered when I was scared or nervous and suffered from some very bad headaches. I guess you could say that I was so far ahead of my time that the schoolteachers couldn't relate to me. Many of them didn't even understand what they were teaching sometimes. They just made up stuff as they went along. After all, who was going to know - they were wrong? They were the teachers. I knew and it made me sick. If I had given each of them a test, most of them would have failed it. Over time school made me a nervous wreck.

They just bored me to death and I didn't care anymore. So, I simply shut down and tuned them out since I had to go to school any-way. Over time I just became good at playing the dumb game a little too well.

Little did I know that one day in my history class at the age of thirteen my life would change forever. I had one of the worst headaches of my life that day and went to the office to get permission to go home. They wouldn't let me go. They thought I was just putting on an act. They gave me a pass and sent me to my class anyway. My head was pounding so badly. I was scared and didn't know what was going on with me. I had never felt like that before. All I wanted was peace and quiet, and for the class to hurry up and end. I laid my head on my desk to get some relief. I felt like a ticking time bomb getting ready to explode. Then the teacher asked the class to explain why it was necessary to have the Constitution of the United States. Rather than the class talking about the Constitution, they turned around and started making fun of me and my name, especially the Hancock part. That made me so angry that I got up and went off, throwing chairs and stuff. I told the teacher that she needed to learn how to take control of her class and stop making fun of me. I asked her if she understood what the Constitution was. I certainly was not the Constitution. I felt like something was leaking inside my head. I couldn't control my actions. I was trying to, but I couldn't. I was totally out of control. Then I began holding my head and saying, "My head hurts. Oh, my head hurts." I became so loud and angry that two male teachers from nearby classes had to come and hold me down.

One of the teachers, Mr. Nelms, told me that I was too old to be acting like that. He said, "You could hurt yourself or somebody else. Calm down! What you did is going to definitely get you put out of school for good now." In all of my pain, he said, "You are just wasting our time by being here." Then before I knew it, my head jerked, and I passed out on the floor. The whole class was so scared. I was rushed to the hospital and released a few weeks later.

I heard that my mama was terrified. She didn't know what she would have done if something else had happened to me. Mama told me later that all she could do was pray and cry at my bedside. When I opened my eyes, I asked, "What happened, and why am I in the hospital?"

She told me the story as best as she could—at least what the school told her.

After a series of test doctors discovered that I had a small tumor or something on the right side of my brain that had ruptured. The doctors said that it was unusual, but they were glad that it happened. One doctor said it was a miracle. If it had continued to grow, it would have killed me. Mama told me that it was the side where I had hit my head on the dresser when I was a little boy. The doctors said no surgery was necessary at that time from what the X-rays showed. They would treat it with medicine first to see if it would eventually go away. That was what caused my headaches and aggression. However, there were still questions about the severe learning disability. As they looked back over my school records, doctors saw that I had never made higher than a D average and asked, "How in the world did you ever get to the seventh grade?" Then he told Mama I needed to go where I could get special help and recommended a place for me. Mama quickly told that doctor that she had already been through that. She pleaded with him to let her take care of me unless it became difficult for her to do so. It was this strange and violent behavior that caused me to be expelled from school and discover my true genius.

As time went on the tumor disappeared, and I began to function much better. The headaches went away, and so did the violent behavior. My head felt as light as cotton, and I could really think for the first time in my life. I don't know what kind of thinking I was doing before. I grew bored being out of school and had a lot of time on my hands. I saw an old man pushing a wagon on the streets collecting stuff, and it stuck with me. One day I made myself a wagon and began collecting junk and stuff off the streets to. After I did it for a while, I learned what to look for. I made some nice money sometimes from the stuff I sold at junkyards and collector's shops, not counting the money that I found. It was enough to start my mama a savings account at the bank and add to it regularly. That's when I realized one man's junk can become another man's treasure.

I was never raised to be a lazy child. That's why I could get up and out early each morning. Out of all that I went through in my life, my true genius was never affected. My mind was sharper, and my observation skills were better than ever. My hearing was excellent. I could see things of value a mile away, and every now and then I would discover a real miracle.

CHAPTER 4

My life changed for the better one Tuesday evening while I was searching through a junk pile behind an old vacant building on East 57th Street. It was a huge, ugly abandoned building that sat between two hills. The area was all grown up with tall trees, grass and bushes. People threw all kinds of junk out there. As I searched through the rubble, I made a strange turn. Out of the corner of my eye, I thought I saw a door to that ugly building. I tried to shake the thought off, but it wouldn't let me. Something kept telling me to go and take a look. Well, I looked and discovered a door behind stacks of wood covered by years of heavily grown bushes. Under normal circumstances it would have been impossible for me or anyone to find it. You can say it was a miracle that I found it that day. I hid my wagon behind some bushes and decided to check it out. I carefully gave the door a few shoves and it opened and revealed to me a whole new world.

The light peering through from some of the dirty windows above allowed me to see very clearly all the hidden treasures below. It was awesome. It appeared that at one time it may have been an underground city for businesses and entertainment until something happened. *What happened?* I thought. *Maybe a major disaster, a riot, gang violence, or other ills of society that made it dangerous for people to come back here.* My mind ran ninety-nine miles a minute. For some reason I checked out the wiring and where the lines ran. I checked for lighting and light switches. I went into each room to see what was there. It was as if my mind clicked into a building inspector's mode as I surveyed everything. Everything was covered by years of thick dust and spiderwebs. It was like a ghost town. There was something special about this place because I had no fear. It was like there was a special connection between it and me. I just couldn't understand it. It was so weird.

I wandered into what may have been an old underground bank. There were teller windows everywhere, a huge bank vault, and all kinds of banking equipment still there. Then, as I walked across a certain part of the floor behind the teller windows covered with a dirt-filled mat, I heard a loud squeak. I walked over it again and heard the same sound. I was curious then. I pulled back the mat and noticed a covered hole in the floor worn by time and lifted up that part of the floor. To my surprise, it was a kind of secret floor safe. There were a lot of bags covered with a thick layer of dust, and I pulled them out one at a time. Some of the bags were so heavy it took two hands to pull them out. When I opened the bags, *my, oh my!* I couldn't believe what I saw. My heart jumped within me, and I broke out in a sweat. It was well preserved money. It was real money and lots of it. I had never seen that kind of money in my life. I couldn't believe my eyes. There were thousands of dollars, maybe hundreds of thousands of dollars, gold coins, silver coins, some very old, stocks, bonds, jewelry, small guns, you name it. Then I wondered again what could have happened that would cause them to leave all this money and everything and never came back for it. Whoever hid the money in this safe in the floor with a huge vault nearby had to be dead by now. I put some of the money under my shirt, wrapping it with some rags tightly that I found in one of the rooms for safe keeping. It must have been about ninety thousand dollars I had on me.

I looked around to see where I could hide the rest. I found the perfect spot. There was a place where some bricks had fallen out of the wall of what may have been some kind of store. There was a lot of space inside the wall, and I hid everything in there and put all the bricks back in place. I pulled an old counter in front of it without leaving marks on the floor just in case someone found their way into the place. I also found some strange banking papers that really intrigued me with a list of names, addresses, and special notes. I took some of them with me, along with all the stocks, bonds, and investment papers to look over later. This looked like a case for a great mystery detective. I continued to look around after that and found a huge room with all kinds of gambling equipment. It seemed this was secret money, gambling money, and no one was supposed to know about it. My mind clicked, and I wanted to learn everything about this place and the banking industry.

The light was fading fast in the building, and I found my way out of there. I made it up the stairs and to the door. I slowly peeped out, scanning the area to make sure there was no one around. I closed the door tightly and got out of there. I knew I would have to make the door secure so that no one could get in. I would come back later and get the rest of money a little at a time and hide it. I got my wagon, put the papers and stuff in the bottom of it with some of the money, and made my way home as fast as I could. I thought that I had found a gold mine. Grandma always told me the Lord was going to bless me one day. I didn't think it was going to be like this. That was the kind of blessing that could kill a man. I could have had a massive heart attack down there, and no one would have known where I was. I was so glad I didn't die. I thanked the Lord, and I thanked my grandma who was in heaven.

Time had gotten away from me, and I knew Mama was going to be upset. I was trying to make it home as fast as I could. On the way home I thought, *Little old me, Thomas Edison Hamilton Hancock, Tehh, Meyel's son, the brother of Benjamin and Diamond, society's dummy, what have I gotten myself into now?* I thought all the way home, breathing hard. Sometimes my legs would go limp as I thought and pushed my wagon. I would sweat and think some more. I got happy and scared at the same time and thought some more. Then the what-ifs came to my mind, and I would try to shake them off. What if I got robbed right now, or what if I got stopped by the police and they searched me? What if the gangbangers caught me and beat me down and ninety thousand dollars started flying everywhere? My mind was driving me crazy. I started humming to calm my nerves. Then I asked myself the ten-million-dollar question. *Why is it that when you don't have any money, nothing bothers you, but when you come into a lot of money, it scares you to death?* I was scared to death. My heart was pounding, and I thought I was going to have a heart attack at fifteen years old. I wasn't ready to die yet. I was one poor, rich, colored boy scared to death at that time. All I wanted to do was get home in one piece.

As I walked along the streets, all I could think about was all the money I had on me. This was a secret I had to keep to myself until I could figure things out. Then I got excited and thought, *Of all the people in Box City, I had to be the one that found it. A little colored boy like me that people said couldn't read, write, or understand.* Then a moment of sadness came over me. It was like a tiny part of me died for a second. What if I couldn't read as they said, and I found all of that money and didn't know what it was or what to do with it? How sad that would have been? I looked up to heaven and thanked God again. I asked the Lord, "What do You have up Your sleeves for me?" This thing was much bigger than me, and I needed Him to help me with it. I begged Him to please let me get home alive first.

As I headed home as fast as I could, Mr. Naylor yelled to me to hurry up and get home before it got too late.

"Your mama gonna tear you up, boy," he said.

Mama must have called him, looking for me. He knew Mama was going to be really upset if I didn't get there soon. I thanked him and asked him to call her and let her know that I was on my way home. I tried to get home as fast as I could. This was one day I didn't need another beating because having all of that money just wore me out. Finally there was a sigh of relief. I could see my house up the street. I had made it home alive and in one piece. I sat on the steps to catch my breath and calm my nerves. I felt like I had been in the ring with a mighty boxer. I was truly beat.

I put up my wagon, hid the money, and went in the house. Mama was napping on the couch in front of the television. I quietly went over and kissed her on the cheek, and she woke up. "Hey, Mama," I said, "how you doing?"

She told me she was fine and that my dinner was in the oven. Then she said, "You two hours late getting home. Is everything okay? What happened?"

I told her I was okay and that I had gone farther than I thought. "You should have seen me trying to get back here before it got too late, Mama. I nearly had a heart attack. It seems like everything start coming out in the evening." I even told her that I didn't like the dark on foot and that I was a day man, strictly nine to five. She just smiled and told me to not let it ever happen again.

CHAPTER 5

A month or so later something wonderful happened. I came home, kissed Mama, fixed my plate, and sat down. I was eating my dinner when she called me. She said, "When you finished eating, I needed you to look over the bills and explain this strange letter I got from the rent office in the mail."

I said, "Yes, ma'am," and finished my dinner. Then a strange feeling came all over me. I told her that I was going to make her proud of me one day and thanked her for believing in me when no one else did.

Mama got up with tears in her eyes and came over and puts her arms around my neck and gave me a big hug. She sat in the chair beside me and said, "I'm proud of you now, baby. It's you that help me keep the roof over our heads by the grace of God. You are my money man, my financial adviser. You know I'm not good with numbers at all. You taught me how to read when folks said you couldn't read. You taught me baking and helped me get a better job. Baby, I thank God for you right now. If you don't do anything else, you have done more than enough. He couldn't have given me a better son. I am proud to trust you with my life and every dollar I make. I couldn't ask for anything more." She got up and then sat back on the couch saying, "God is going to bless you in a mighty way, Tehh. You just wait and see."

I smiled as she spoke, looked up to heaven, and said, "He already has, Mama. He already has."

I finished dinner, washed my plate, and sat on the couch by her. I picked up the mail from the table and asked her which one of the letters she was talking about. She took the letter from the stack in my hand and said, "This one, baby." Then she leaned over, smelled me, and said, "Boy, you need to hurry up and take a bath."

I began to read the letter. "Wow, Mama, I can't believe this. The family of Mr. Zorbinski, the man who owns this building, wants to sell it for fifteen thousand dollars cash to the first person with the money."

Mama jumped up and said, "What?"

I said, "They want to give you the opportunity to buy this building."

She said, "What do you mean, Tehh, buy this building?" Mama could get a little elementary at times.

"Mama, this building is now for sale. If you want it, we have thirty days to let them know something. The owner died, and the family is selling everything he has, including all of his real estate." Mama started rubbing her head like she had a headache. "Are you okay, Mama," I asked.

"Tehh, I don't have that kind of money, baby. I don't know what we are going to do. I can't afford a larger place for the four of us on what I make if they go up on the rent. Ricko's don't pay that much." She sat down on the couch with her face in her hands, saying, "I just don't know, honey."

Then suddenly it came to me why God had allowed me to find my secret treasure at this appointed time. I jumped up and said, "Mama, don't worry," as calmly as I could. "We have some money in the bank."

My mama took her face out of her hands, raised her head slowly, and looked at me again like I was one of the biggest fools she had ever seen in her life and said, "What? Did I hear you right, Tehh? We have money in the bank?" Her tone scared me. I had never heard my mama sound like that before in my life.

"Well, yeah, Mama," I said, backing away to put some distance between us. "Maybe not that much, but we have some." Then she changed before my eyes. She was steaming like a bull getting ready to charge. That hand was getting ready to slap me upside my head if I didn't say the right thing.

"Tell me right now how much, Tehh," she said.

I said, "Right now, Mama."

"Don't play with me, boy," she said angrily.

I didn't know if I was talking with my mama or the devil at that moment. She was getting pretty upset with me. I figured I'd better hurry up and tell her something before she knocked me out. You see, when people are not use to having more than five hundred dollars in the bank, you have to be very careful how you say things. "Right now, Mama," I said softly and calmly, "I believe we have about $16,576.37 in the bank."

18

She dropped down on the couch and froze for a few minutes with her eyes and mouth wide open. It scared me. I didn't know what to do. She was speechless. Then she got up, looked at me, and began shouting out the numbers, "$16,576.37!" I had to hurry and put my hand over her mouth to quiet her because our walls had ears. To some people that was like a million dollars in these hard times. Then she calmed down and asked me, "How in the world did we get that kind of money in the bank, Thomas Edison Hamilton Hancock?"

When she uses my whole name, I knew I was in big trouble. "Well Mama," I said. "You see, I read all these money magazines and stuff, and they tell you what to do with your money. I thought I would try it to see if they were telling the truth."

We sat down on the couch and I said, "When I made out your checking deposit slip, I also did a savings deposit slip and added money to both accounts."

Then she said puzzled, "I don't have no savings account, Tehh."

I calmly said, "Yes, you do, Mama. I opened up a savings account for you about two years ago."

She said, "Boy, you were just thirteen years old then."

I said, "I know, Mama. I call it our rainy-day fund in case something happened and we needed money. And see, Mama, we need the money right now."

Then Mama told me she just couldn't believe all I was saying. I tried to explain it as best I could. "When you got the job at Ricko's, I put all of your increase plus twenty percent in the savings account. We continued to live off the same amount of money or less before you got your job."

She frowned and said, "What!"

I told her that most people fail financially because they don't prepare. Putting away a little each week adds up over time. Then she told me she could understand it a little. I told her that I had her put away a little of her paycheck each week and most of the money from the stuff I sold or the money I found. Then she smiled and said, "Boy, here I was thinking we were barely making it, and we had money in the bank."

Suddenly she changed on me again. She jumped up, grabbed me by the shirt, and said, "Boy, I could just kill you for not telling me that. I could have bought me a new dress every now and then, Tehh."

Even the good I tried to do would cause trouble for me. I apologized to Mama and asked her to forgive me. Then she returned to her normal self and said, "You were looking out for our future because your daddy sure didn't." I told her that I was looking out for our future and that if she wanted to buy the building, she could. My mama's skin color changed before my eyes again. She began jumping around and saying, "Yes, yes, yes, sugar, yes! Thank You, Lord Jesus. Thank You for my son. I won't have to pay rent no more."

I said, "That's right, Mama. They will have to pay you if we get the building."

She just jumped around, saying, "Thank You, Jesus. Thank You. Thank You. Thank You, Jesus."

Unexpectedly she caught me by the neck in her jumping and almost chocked me to death trying to give me a hug. "Okay, Mama, you are killing me. Let me go, Mama, please."

She released me and told me she was sorry. I told her that I would fill out the bank withdrawal slip before she went to work. Then she could go to the bank, get the money, and call the people about owning our building. I told Mama that we couldn't wait because they had given thirty days. It was the early bird that got the worm. I asked her to not let the real estate people come to us. We would go to their office so that nobody would know. "Boy, listen at you," she said. "Sounding like a real businessman."

I told her there was another piece of property I wanted her to check on when she talked to the people. I said, "Please promise me, Mama, you won't tell nobody about this, okay? We don't need any trouble right now. Let folks think somebody else owns it if we get it until we can figure something out."

My mama gave me a big hug and said, "I promise, honey, whatever you say. Diamond and Benjamin are probably already asleep. Now let's get to bed." It was at that very moment that I asked God for a girl like my mama one day. Then she said, "Honey, please hurry and take a bath before you go to bed because you stink."

I got up early and filled out the withdrawal slip for Mama. I was so excited I couldn't sit still. Things like that didn't happen to people like us any day. I had to do something with my time. Too many things were going through my mind. I decided to do what I had never done before. I would make breakfast for everyone. I guess teaching Mama about baking began to kick in. Boy, things were looking good. The smell of the coffee, bacon, eggs, grits, pancakes, and cinnamon muffins woke up everyone. My sister Diamond was the first one in the kitchen rubbing her eyes. "Good morning, Tehh," she said.

"Are you going to die, Tehh?" This child was serious. "Please don't die," she begged with tears in her eyes and everything. "You don't ever cook. Please don't die, Tehh."

I said, "I'm not going to die, Diamond. I just felt like cooking this morning."

Then my egghead brother, Benjamin, came into the kitchen with a big, greedy smile on his face, rubbing his eyes. "Oh, no! Tehh, you okay, man? You are not going to die, are you? I have never known you to get up this early and cook anything. Mama always cooks. You got to be sick or something. Wow, it sure smells good, and I'm so hungry too." Then he called Mama with his big mouth, scaring her. "Mama, hurry up and come in the kitchen. Something is wrong with Tehh. I think he's dying, Mama."

Mama rushed into the kitchen, drying her face with a towel. "What is going on in here? Tehh, are you okay, baby? What is all this? I have never known you to get up and cook breakfast."

I said, "I'm fine, Mama. I was excited. This is a great day! Today is the beginning of a brand-new life for us. I just wanted to do something special."

Mama looked at me, smiled, and said, "Thank You, Jesus." We all sat around the table, eating and talking. Diamond and Benjamin kept thanking me for a great breakfast. Then Diamond asked me, "What are we having tomorrow?"

"Steak and waffles," I told her. "Steak and waffles for the princess." She had seen a steak and waffle commercial on television and said that was her favorite breakfast, even though she had never had it before.

Diamond and Benjamin got ready for school, and Mama got ready to go to work. I gave her the withdrawal slip and a few instructions on what to do. I asked her to be very careful with her purse when she left the bank. To put my mind at ease, I decided to meet her when she got off the bus. With everyone gone, I ate the last of the breakfast, washed the dishes, and followed my normal routine. I got my wagon and started down the street to collect my papers and find hidden treasure. I decided I wouldn't go to my secret place but would stay close to the bus stop area to meet my mama when she got off the bus.

CHAPTER 6

As I was leaving the apartment, someone threw wash water from the upstairs apartment and almost drowned me. "Hey," I yelled, "I'm down here. Watch it!"

It was Mrs. Richards. Her mind wasn't too good. "I'm sorry, sugar. I forgot to look. Are you okay?" she asked.

"Yes, ma'am Mrs. Richards." It was stinky dishwater full of all kinds of stuff. I smelled like a toilet. I went back in the house, took a shower, put on a new set of clothes, and started out again, taking a different route this time.

I was walking past Mr. Johnson's hardware store when he called me. I went over to see what he wanted. "How you doing there, Tehh?" he asked.

"I'm fine, Mr. Johnson," I said.

"I see you got some stuff in your wagon already. I got some stuff out back if you want it. I just put it out this morning," he said.

"Thank you, Mr. Johnson. I sure would." Then he asked me if I had heard about the folks selling all these buildings around here. I said, "Yes, sir."

He told me that the owner died and the family was selling his estate. "Do you know what an estate is, son?"

I said "Yes, sir." He told me he didn't know what some of the people were going to do because most of them didn't have that kind of money to buy the building they were in. He knew he couldn't. He said they sent everybody a letter, and asked me if my mama got one. Then he made another stupid remark by saying, "You probably wouldn't know if she did or not because you can't even read. Seems like they should have a place to help people like you, son."

I just stood there, looking stupid, never saying a word, thinking, *I'm going to make sure I buy your building, Mr. Johnson, and go up on the rent.* "You watch yourself and tell your mama what I said now, okay?"

I just said, "Yes, sir." I left him and went around the back to see what he had put out. A lot of old stuff. I noticed some old money bags at the bottom of one of the boxes he threw away. One of them felt like it had something in it. I was hoping it was money. I started to peep when I was interrupted by an old man looking for scrap metal. I put the boxes in my wagon to check later along with some other stuff. He spoke, and then I went on down the street, collecting newspapers left on benches, magazines, and old telephones from the trash. Nobody knew, but I got two dollars a phone at Mike Hoshkin's shop on 19ᵗʰ Street. He fixed them up and resold them.

As I went along, a man called me and asked me if I would help him take some stuff off his truck and put it in his shop. I told him I would. I moved all kinds of chairs, tables, lamps, boxes, pictures, beds, and stuff. I was so tired. I worked like a dog, and all he gave me was ten dollars and told me that it was twenty. I was so mad, but I said thanks anyway. Why do people like to take advantage of people like me? They should be more willing to help. I was going to certainly check on buying this building for sure, and go up on his rent. I was disappointed and tired. I decided to take a rest. I thought, *I really hope Mr. Zorbinski owns this building.*

I went across the street and bought myself an ice-cold strawberry soda from the store and sat on some bricks outside to enjoy it. It was so good. I looked up the street and saw two bankers sitting on the bench across from the bank, eating their lunches. I was interested in hearing if they had anything to say about all of the buildings for sale. As a dummy, I was already invisible and harmless to them anyway. So I decided to take my wagon and move in closer to hear what they were talking about. I pretended I was looking through the trash as usual. It's amazing how much you can learn just by listening. Some folks can't hear because they just talk too much. One of them said, "I tell you these people don't have the money to buy up these buildings. They are barely getting by as it is. If they can't buy them, we can. The bank can buy them at a good rate and go up on the rent by twenty-five percent and make a killing."

The other banker said, "Some of these buildings are a risky investment for the bank. That's why they haven't jumped on it yet. You got to consider the maintenance expense. They need too much work. You can pay fifteen thousand dollars for the building and then ten to fifteen thousand dollars to fix them up with all the new laws. Even if you raised the rent, you still wouldn't make enough to break even. You would come out better to buy the properties, demolish them, and rebuild."

The other one said, "Look around. Who do you think wants to put up a new building in this area? They will just destroy it like they did before. When I was a young boy, I remember my father telling me a whole section of this town was shut down because of them." I guess he was talking about us colored folks. He said, "You would have to reprogram these people for that kind of change. This is a low-class area. Low-class people will never have a high-class mentality. They only want a handout or a temporary fix. Look at that one in the trash." He was speaking of me. Then he said, "All he wants is something for nothing."

The other one said, "Yeah, I guess you are right. We leave our nice neighborhoods to work in a place like this."

The other one said, "Yes, but the pay is worth it. Let's get back to work." The men got up and walked across the street into the bank. Then I wondered if the bank had bought the bank. I wanted that too if they hadn't.

Walking along the streets, the banker's words rang loudly in my head. "Low-class people will never have a high-class mentality. You will have to reprogram these people for that kind of change." Little did the bankers know that they had given me some very valuable information.

It was about 12:30, and I noticed two men putting stuff from a building on the street. I went over and asked them if it was okay for me to take stuff off the pile. They said it was okay, and I began looking through the pile, putting stuff back in place neatly. I found an old can stuffed with a rag and put it in my wagon. The can looked like one I had seen in an antique magazine. I found tons of magazines and comic books and put them in my wagon. I found old books, unusual dishes, and shoe boxes stuffed with envelopes. I found phones, clocks, radios, fans, typewriters, phonographs, rolled-up documents and more. I found an unusual chair that I thought Mama would love. I could easily get it upholstered one day. My wagon was so full that I couldn't get anything else in it. I took stuff home and came back for more several times.

With that finished, I began collecting more stuff off the streets along the way. Mr. Jacobs was walking his dog and stopped to talk to me. He said,

"Tehh, where did you get all of those muscles from, son?" I smiled and told him I had gotten them from pushing my wagon. He said, "If you were in school, you sure would make a darn good football player." I thanked him and walked on, checking out a few more trash piles. It was getting close to the time for Mama to come home. I stopped and got me a burger and soda, and sat on a bench and ate. I finished eating, got my wagon, and headed to the bus stop. I was so excited to hear what Mama had to say that I couldn't hardly wait. I parked my wagon under a tree and waited for the bus.

Waiting there, I saw one of my greatest fears. A drug dealer name Ray James Booker who was always trying to get the kids to sell drugs and do other bad things for him. He had cornered me several times, trying to get me to join his gang, but I was too dumb for him. It was by the grace of God that I got away from him. I was praying that he would go the other way this time, but he didn't. He came over and looked at my wagon, checking out what I had in it. I really hated that man with a passion. He thought threatening and hurting people made him somebody. He looked at me with that ugly face and said, "Boy, is junk all you want out of life? Ain't no money in junk, stupid! I can show you right now how to make some real money." When he moved in front of me, looked me in my face, and showed me his gun, I wanted to faint, but I didn't. I just stood there, trying to be strong. Then he said, "I bet you don't even know what real money looks like." He went in his pocket and pulled out a small roll of money and showed it to me. I did what I do best. I just stood there, looking stupid. What he had couldn't compare to what I had come into. He said, "Now you take a good look at all this money and remember what it looks like. Cause a dummy like you will never see money like this in your life." Then he looked in my wagon and asked, "What is a dummy like you going to do with newspaper? You can't read. What you going do, huh? Use it for toilet tissue?" Then he pushed my head real hard and walked away, pointing his finger at me like he was shooting a gun and laughing at me. I held my peace. I didn't want any trouble with him. I was glad to be a dummy at that moment.

For the first time his insults didn't bother me. I had a plan, and Ray James was no part of it. I could even afford to pay someone to wipe him off the map now if I wanted to. I wished I could rid Box City of all the leaches like Ray James. I would round them up and drop them all in the middle of a shark-infested ocean and watch the sharks have a feast. I knew I wouldn't really do that, but it felt pretty good thinking about it. After that little episode I started thinking about all the things I wanted to do for my mama and Box City. So many things were going through my mind while I was waiting on the bus that it was hard to keep up with them. I knew I would have to find a way to write them down without being seen.

The bus pulled up, and Mama got off. She was so surprise to see me standing there. She gave me a big hug and said, "Let's go home, sugar." I got my wagon, and we walked on home, talking. I asked her if she got everything done at the bank, and she said she did. She told me all day long she worried because she thought she would have to carry all that money in a big bag down the street. She was surprised because it all fit so nicely in a small envelope in her purse. Then she said, "You just don't know how much better that made me feel. All I could think about was getting robbed." Then she smiled and said, "Honey, you won't believe this. The teller asked me if I wanted large bills or small ones. I said large bills! You hear me, Tehh? Large bills! I have never been asked that before in my life." She was so happy. She told me that she had called the real estate people and that they want us to come to their office on Saturday morning at 11:30. I told her that was just perfect. Then I asked her how she felt at that very moment. She smiled and said, "Baby, I feel just wonderful. You changed my whole life today. I felt like I was somebody for the first time in my life." She stopped and put her hands on her hip and said, "I went to my bank with dignity and withdrew thousands of dollars from an account that I didn't even know I had. You see how much I trust you, Tehh. That teller gave me the money and said, "Thank you, Ms. Hancock. May I help you with something else?" It felt good. She treated me with respect. You hear me—respect! And if the Lord is willing, we will be the owners of an apartment building and whatever else you have in mind one day."

Walking along the streets in our own little world, Mama asked me to tell her about the other building I was interested in. I told her that it was on East 57th Street near downtown. It was completely vacant, but I believe it had lots of potential if we could afford it one day. She smiled and said, "Listen at you talking like one of those real estate people."

I said, "Mama, I read a lot of books about this kind of stuff, and I think it would be a good investment for the future. I want to invest in something for Diamond and Benjamin, so that when they finish college, they can own their own businesses."

She frowned and said, "You can see college for them, Tehh? I sure hope you are right because that sounds good to me. It's amazing how God has allowed you to see what no one else can." Then she stopped again and said, "You know college is still my dream for you, Tehh."

I said, "I know Mama, and in five years I can see this place starting to boom again."

Suddenly I saw my Mama's countenance fall. She said, "Baby, my memories of what my mama told me about East 57th Street were not good ones. That was the part of town my mama said colored folks couldn't go into. She kept a close eye on us. White folks would kill you if you were caught over there."

I said, "That was a long time ago, Mama. Things have changed now." She said that when she was a young girl, her mama told her that the white folks had a secret underground city locked off from everybody. It only opened at night and on weekends. Cars would be parked everywhere. They had clubs with strippers, go-go dancers, gambling, prostitutes, and everything. Some of colored folks sold them moonshine back then. The colored maids would overhear what the white folks talked about and told everybody when they got home. No one ever found the underground city because they said it was underground somewhere. Between the riot and TB epidemic most of the white folks left Box City and never came back to it. I asked her, "What caused the riot?"

She told me they said some white men killed three colored children who had wandered into the area. They were all less than eleven years old. Their little bodies were found in an alley in our area of town. The parents told the police, but nothing was ever done about it. Over time that angered the colored folks. They all got together one day and fought back. Tears were in Mama's eyes. She said the colored folks nearly burned this whole city down because they were so mad and scared at the same time. They caught the white folks off guard. "It was a bloody time for us and them in Box City back then. Many colored folks were killed and white folks too. A lot of white folks were scared. They packed up their families and left this place forever. Many who were killed owned a lot of the businesses that were not destroyed."

Her mama had said that some of the colored folks got so caught up in the fight that they even burned their own communities. They had gone stone crazy. What was so funny was that they were looting the few stores that were not burned, but had no place to take the stuff they took. Some of them had to live on the streets because they burned themselves out of their own houses. Over the years a few white folks took interest in Box City again and started opening up businesses here a few at a time, but times were hard. Our people could never get enough money to open up anything. We were barely surviving. We always had to depend on them for just about everything.

I thought about what the banker said while Mama was talking. "Low-class people will never have a high-class mentality." Then it hit me hard why there was no vision. Our colored people had been down so long that they couldn't see things getting any better and didn't even try. They just passed that hopeless mentality on to the next generation. That's why so many of our people lived on the streets and it didn't bother them. They had nothing else to look forward to. I remember reading in the Bible where it said, "My people are destroyed for a lack of knowledge." I didn't understand it then, but I do now. The banker was right. All they want is a handout or a temporary fix. That's why they don't believe they can do anything. When we looked up, we were at the house. I thanked Mama for telling me all about East 57th Street. I put my wagon away, thinking about the things she told me. Then I asked God, "What can I do to make a difference in Box City?" When you don't have any friends, you spend a lot of time talking to God. *This is going to be a great adventure*, I thought.

CHAPTER 7

Saturday morning came, and I got up early and fixed breakfast. Everyone got up and came into the kitchen to eat. No one asked me if I was dying this time. They all said good morning, fixed their plates, and ate. Since it was a Saturday, Diamond and Benjamin went in the living room and watched television. Mama and I got ready to go to the real estate office. She told Diamond and Benjamin to do their chores and stay in the house until we came back. I made sure we had all the money we needed, and we started out.

It was a beautiful day, and we tried to act normal like we were going to the store. We didn't want anyone to know what we were up to. We had to walk about six blocks to catch the bus to go to the real estate office across town. We got on the bus, and I took the window seat. I began to notice how the scenery changed as we left one side of town going to the other. I had never gone to that side of town before. I saw beautiful parks, clean streets, and families walking together, and there were visible policemen. There were no clothes or underwear hanging on clotheslines from apartment buildings. There were no boarded-up windows or piles of junk on the streets. Everything and everywhere was all clean. Then I thought about the banker's words again. "Low-class people will never have a high-class mentality." We were now in a high-class area, and they were well represented. The banker was absolutely right to a point. Then I thought in spite of what people called me, *Why don't I have a low-class mentality? Why does all of this stuff bother me and no one else? Why am I now the richest person in a poverty-stricken, low-class area?*

The bus finally reached our destination. We got off and walked a block to the real estate office. It was a beautiful building. We went inside. Mama went up to the desk and said, "I am Meyel Hancock. I have an appointment." The lady told her to have a seat and that someone would be with her shortly. This was a first for us. The office was really nice and clean. The furniture looked very expensive. They had pretty pictures in frames on the wall like the ones you see in a museum on television. We took a magazine from the rack, sat down, and began looking through it. A little while later a tall man came out of his office and asked Mama to follow him. She asked me to come with her. We went in, and he asked us to have a seat. He said that he was Mark Hinkle and he was glad we wanted to buy the building. He said we were the first ones to come forward to buy anything.

He began telling Mama about Mr. Zorbinski's death and how the family was selling all the real estate. He asked Mama about our apartment building and if she had had any problems with it. She told him that we had never had any problems. He said that was good. The reason they were selling the property cheap was because the person who bought the building would be buying it as is. They would be totally responsible for the entire building maintenance. The family would no longer be responsible for it, and he asked if she understood that. Mama looked at me. I nodded my head, and she told him yes. He asked her, "Do you have the money?"

She said, "Yes I do." My mama opened her purse and pulled out the envelope with the money and counted out fifteen thousand dollars and took a deep breath. Mr. Hinkle looked surprised. It was like he had never seen a colored person with that kind of money before. Perhaps he was surprised that she could count. Little did he know that he hadn't seen anything. He had Mama sign some papers, which I carefully read with her and gave her the okay to sign. She smiled, and he gave her the deed to our building with some other papers. He talked to us about insuring the building to protect our investment. My mama was now officially a landlady. I asked Mr. Hinkle if the people in our building could continue to pay them the rent as usual. He said that they could, but there would be a yearly fee for the service. That's the way it was with Mr. Zorbinski. I asked him to keep our identity a secret and told him how to contact us when needed. Then I nudged Mama in the side for her to ask him about the building on East 57th street. Quickly she said, "By the way, Mr. Hinkle, has anyone bought the building on East 57th street, yet?"

He said, "No, not yet."

Mama said, "I was wondering how much they were asking for it?" He looked at a sheet of paper on his desk and said. "They want thirty thousand dollars for it."

I quickly asked, "Can we buy it today?"

Mr. Hinkle was knocked off his feet and said, "Yes, give me a few minutes to draw up the paperwork."

Then I asked, "What about the bank? Have they bought their property yet... and Ricko's Bakery and the other buildings there."

He said, "No, son, they haven't."

I was so excited and asked, "How much are they? He said, "The bakery is about fifteen thousand with the other buildings, and the bank building is twenty-five thousand with the other buildings. It had some recent renovations."

Quickly I said, "We want to buy them too."

Impatiently I asked if I could use the restroom.

Mama looked at me and said, "Tehh are you okay, honey?"

He said, "Yes, down the hall and to your right. Outside the door."

I rushed out as fast as I could as if I had to actually use the restroom. The restroom for colored folks was on the outside of a door on the back of the building. I had to tell myself it didn't matter now. I had gone back to my secret place and got some extra money just in case I didn't have enough. I went in the restroom to get the money. I had it wrapped on my body for safety. I came back in the office with the money in a bag. "Boy," he said with a frown. "I mean Mr. Hancock, do you know that is about seventy thousand dollars cash for everything? You can't possibly have that kind of money on you?"

With a smile, I said, "Yes I can."

"What grade are you in, son?" he asked.

My mama quickly said, "He's out of school for now." I looked at Mr. Hinkle's face and quickly put the money on his desk. That kind of money instantly changes the way people see you. I knew he was wondering where we had gotten that kind of money. He probably thought we were into drugs or something illegal. So I made up the perfect lie. Sadly I said, "My daddy and grandma died together in an accident, and we were the beneficiaries."

Mama looked at me like she was she was going to pass out. Mr. Hinkle told us he was sorry to hear that and drew up all of the papers. I signed all the papers with Mama and gave him seventy thousand dollars for all the properties, and he gave us the deeds with some other papers and the keys to the East 57th Street building. I was jumping for joy on the inside. He told us to have them insured to protect our investment. My mama actually passed out for a few minutes, but she was quickly revived. Mr. Hinkle gave her some water from a real glass. I asked him to allow the bank, the bakery, Mr. Johnson, and all the other tenants to continue to pay them the rent but to keep our identity a secret, and said that we would collect monthly.

The deal was done, and we left as proud owners of real estate just like the book said. While we were leaving, I heard Mr. Hinkle say to someone, "That's an extraordinary young man she has for a son. I wish I had a son like that." Having money changes the way people see you. I wasn't dumb to him but extraordinary, and that made me proud. I told Mama on the way out that we would have to get safety deposit boxes for all of the papers and money, and a post office box too. I didn't want any business mail coming to our apartment because some of those folks were so nosey. She never said a word. Here I was talking business, and she paid me no attention. In my heart I thanked God for letting part of my and Mama's dream come true. I wanted to make my mama happy, and she believed that I could make a difference in this world.

After a few minutes reality set in, and then it hit me. Fear came all over me. I knew that when I got outside that door, Mama was going to kill me dead. I never told her about all the other money. After we left the building, Mama still didn't say anything on our way to the bus stop. I was really scared and about to wet my pants. I didn't know what she was going to do to me. In my heart I prayed every step of the way. "Lord, please don't let my mama kill me."

We finally reached the bus stop and sat down to wait on the bus. Suddenly Mama took a deep breath and came back to life. I almost jumped out of my skin. I saw the red in her eyes. "Tehh," she said, "what bank did you rob, boy? You'd better tell me right now! I don't plan on going to prison for you and no one else. Do you hear me, Tehh? I will kill you first." She was getting loud, and I looked around to see if anyone was looking. "Do you hear me, boy?"

I said, "Yes, ma'am."

She said, "I will kill you dead and bury your body where nobody can find you, not even the Lord." Mama was mad, and I knew she was serious when she said the Lord wouldn't be able to find me because He knows everything! "I have two other children at home that needs me." Then she started crying. I felt lower than a snake at that moment. She said, "I trusted you, Thomas Edison Hamilton Hancock, with my life, and you go and do something stupid like this to me? Where did I go wrong with you, boy? Tell me—where did I go wrong with you?" Then she got up and stood right in front of me and said, "Boy, you really had me fooled."

Several people began to come out of their businesses to see what was going on. I told her people were looking at us and to quiet down some because we were not at home. She said loudly, "Shut up! I don't care who is looking. I never thought the child I gave birth to would do me like this. It was hard labor too." I was afraid to touch her, fearing she would actually knock me out.

I softly and calmly said, "Mama, you didn't go wrong. I didn't rob a bank, and no one is going to prison." Finally she moved from in front of me. I was so thankful. She slowly sat down and listened to me. "Everything was all legal," I told her. "I love you too much to hurt you, Mama. You raised me better than that. I wouldn't hurt you for nothing in the world. You know that."

Then she said in that evil voice, "Tell me where you got seventy thousand dollars. I want the truth now!"

I said, "God gave it to me, Mama."

Before I knew it, she slapped me upside my head and said, "Don't you play with the Lord, boy!"

I thought to myself, *I sure hope my tumor don't come back after these slaps upside the head.* "Mama, what I tell you … you can't tell anyone."

Then all of a sudden she put her hands over her mouth and said, "Oh no, you killed somebody, didn't you, Tehh? Tell me right now."

I said, "No, Mama, none of that. Remember that building on East 57th Street I was telling you about. The one that we now own."

She said, "Yes."

I told her how I accidently found it a few months ago. How I was looking through a trash pile and strangely saw a door behind some bushes. I didn't know how I saw it because you can't see it. It was like God revealed it to me. I told her that I went and gave the door a few shoves, and it opened. It was that lost underground city that was hid in plain sight, and no one ever saw it. I told her how it had everything, including a bank down there. Then I said,

"Mama, you want believe this. In the bank under the floor I found over six hundred thousand dollars in cash, jewelry, and coins, not counting some other stuff. It had been there all those years, and no one knew it. It scared me to death when I saw it." I explained to her that was the day I came home late. "Mama," I said, "I know it was nothing but the Lord that had me find it." I told her that the $16,576.37 was actually what we saved. I just added about twenty thousand from the money I found. That's why I just had to have that building if we could get it. Everything in it would belong to us, including all the money.

Mama stood up, put her hands on her hips, and said, "That's why the teller was so nice to me. I still had money in the bank." She thought she had taken everything out. I told her there was no telling what else was down there in that building. Then the color came back in my mama's face, and she began to smile again. That's when I realized I would live to get slapped upside the head another day. She asked me to forgive her for what she thought. She told me that all of that information at one time was just too much for her. Then she moved close to me and whispered in my ear, "Tehh, we are rich! We are rich, Tehh!" I had to break her heart softly.

I whispered back, "Not yet, Mama. Not yet. We have to be very careful. We can't let anyone know right now." Again I thought about what the banker said, "All they want is a handout or something for nothing." I said, "Mama, folks would be at our door every minute of the day begging or trying to rob us. We will have no peace. We are going to have to act as usual for a while. Do you think you can do that for me, Mama, until I can figure things out?" Mama looked at me sadly, then smiled, and said okay. "One thing I can say, Mama. You can buy a few dresses every now and then, and take a real vacation every year."

She said, "I like that. Now can I possibly get a nice used car?"

I smiled and said, "You sure can, Mama." I told her that I believed everything that had happened to me like being misdiagnosed with a sever learning disability and getting put out of school was all part of God's plan. He had to camouflage me. I know it sounds crazy, but if I had not been collecting junk that day, I never would have found the underground city that changed our lives. We will no longer be the same. I believe God has a plan for us and Box City.

The bus arrived. We got on, and I took the window seat. As soon as the bus drove off, it wasn't long before Mama fell asleep. She was exhausted. I can imagine a woman with three children and an eighth-grade education doing the best she could to take care of her family. She goes from renting an apartment to owning a twelve-unit apartment building where people were paying from two hundred and fifty to four hundred dollars a month for rent. Going from being poor to secretly being rich in a matter of minutes can be overwhelming. I really must have been crazy because it didn't excite me. Well, I was a little excited but not the "I am rich" excited. I didn't want a fancy car or a big house or even nice clothes. All I wanted was a better Box City and for my mama to be happy.

Looking at the beautiful buildings, clean parks, and nice schools, I wondered if Box City could ever look like that. Then I heard the banker's words again in my head, "You would have to reprogram these people for that kind of change." *How do you do that?* I thought. How can you reprogram a city filled with gangs, thieves, thugs, prostitutes, pimps, pushers, dropouts, and people who have made hopelessness their best friend? How can you change them? Then I heard the voice in my head say, "One person at a time."

Mama woke up and began to look around. "You mean I slept the whole trip, Tehh? We are just about home."

I said, "Yes ma'am, Mama. It was like the sweetest sleep you had in a long time. You didn't make a sound." Mama told me she guessed that was the sound of peace within. The bus pulled up to our stop, and we got off. I realized that we were not the same people who had gotten on the bus. We were now the first colored people in Box City looking at buildings we actually owned, and it felt good. I still had a few dollars in my pocket and asked Mama if we could stop by the store and get some groceries so we could celebrate. I had a taste for some fried chicken, and I asked Mama to make one of her cakes. Mama asked me if I had any money left because she didn't have enough on her for groceries. I smiled and told her I did. She smiled and hit me on the arm. We got the groceries along with a few surprises for Diamond and Benjamin, and headed home. We laughed and talked all the way home about the way things were and the way things were going to be for us now.

We made it home and found Diamond and Benjamin watching television. They had done all their chores and mopped all the floors. I was so proud of them. "Mama," Diamond asked, "what took y'all so long? Seems like you been gone all day."

Mama said, "It was a long bus ride to the other side of town."

Diamond continued, "Well, Mama, can we go with you the next time you go? We would like to see what the other side of town looks like too."

Mama went over and put her hands on the side of Diamond's face and gave her a big kiss on the forehead and said, "Yes, you can. All of you can go the next time." We were all so excited. Diamond and Benjamin started putting up the groceries. I told Mama to go and take a short nap. We would start cooking later.

CHAPTER 8

I went and sat on the front porch and looked around, thinking. While I was sitting there, Toe Joe came over. I don't know how he got that name, but it kind of grows on you. I hadn't talked with him in a very long time. He was kind of like me in a sense, labeled as dumb, a troublemaker, and a person who would never amount to anything. The mind-set of the people around here was sad. They could easily see you going to prison or even getting killed by the time you were eighteen, but they couldn't see you finishing high school, going to college or doing something good with your life.

"Hey, Tehh, what's going on, man?" he said and sat on the step.

I said, "Nothing much, man. What's going on with you?"

Then he started telling me about the news on the streets. He said that the man who owned all these buildings had died and his family was selling everything. They were giving the folks in these apartment buildings the opportunity to buy their building. I asked him if they were going to buy their building. He laughed and said, "Man, you crazy. My mama don't have that kind of money." Curiously I asked what he did with his money. He said, "Man, I ain't got no money. Where did you hear that from?"

I said, "You work at the grocery store every day and you don't save anything?" He told me that by the time he got through helping his mama pay the bills, there wasn't much left for him. Then I said, "What about your stepdad?"

What did I say that for? He began to get angry and said, "He ain't no stepdaddy to me. He's just one big leach sucking the life out of us. The man won't work in a pie factory." He started rubbing his head and said, "He wants to beat up on my mama likes she's a punching bag and then try to demand

37

everybody's respect. Man, I know she can do better without him. I tell you, Tehh, some days I just want to—"

I quickly grabbed his shoulder and said, "All right man, let it go for now. Let it go. You are getting upset."

He said he was sorry and told me that people just didn't know what folks go through around here. Then he asked, "Is your mama going to buy your building? She works at Ricko's Bakery. Don't they pay good money there?"

I said, "No, man, not that good. We are just hoping that whoever buys the place don't go up on the rent."

I asked Toe Joe, "Why is it that after all these years we don't own anything in this city?"

He said, "I don't know, man, but I do know that I don't want to live like this. Man, you don't know how many days I wish I was back in school trying to get my education. School is our way out of here, man."

I asked, "Why did you drop out of school anyway?"

"Man, I had bad grades and anger problems. You see, my stepdad would come home drunk and start fussing and fighting with me, and I couldn't study. He would call the police on me for nothing. He just got on my nerves. I stayed mad all the time because I disliked him just that much. I couldn't fight him back because of my mama. She was trying to keep me out of prison." He told me that one day a guy started a fight with him at school. Sadly, Toe Joe caused him to break his arm and leg because he was so angry. They put him out of school for good. He said the other guy started the fight. He had a knife and almost pushed him over the stairs to his death, but he was the one who was put out. He said that wasn't right and that the guy was nothing but trouble from the start. Then he smiled and said, "He's dead now, but I am still alive."

As I listened to Toe Joe, I realized his problems at home. The school system had failed him too, and he was trapped in a place where he didn't want to be. Time was getting away and I had to go in and help Mama fix dinner. I told him that it was good talking with him and said, "Let's talk again soon." I heard that voice in my head again say, "Start with one person at a time."

I got up and went in the house to fix dinner. I peeped in on Mama, and she was sleeping like a baby. I decided to let her sleep on. I called Diamond and Benjamin into the kitchen and told them that we were going to fix dinner together. We would let Mama sleep and surprise her. They were so excited and said, "But we don't know how to cook."

I said, "Don't worry. I will teach you."

Diamond told Benjamin that if I could teach Mama how to cook, I could teach them how to cook too. I showed Diamond how to season the chicken for frying. I showed Benjamin how to make the mac and cheese. The green beans were easy. They were in a can, and all I needed was a little ham seasoning for them. Diamond put the rolls in a pan to heat in the oven. Mama had created a quick cake recipe that was out of this world. I decided to try my hand at that. We were all in the kitchen preparing dinner like we were on an assembly line. Since Diamond had the task of frying the chicken, I had to make sure the grease was hot enough. I showed her how to drop each piece without burning herself. The kitchen smelled so good, and we were so proud of ourselves. Mama slept through it all until the cake started smelling. She jumped out of bed and ran into the kitchen and said, "Umm, what is that smell? Is that my cake cooking?"

We all looked at her, smiled, and said, "Yes, ma'am."

She said, "You children never cease to amaze me, especially you, Tehh. Why didn't you wake me up?" We told her that we wanted to surprise her. She went over and washed her hands and checked out the pots on the stove and said, "This looks and smells so good. I can't believe y'all did all of this without me."

There was a knock at the kitchen door, and Mama went to see who it was. It was Miss Emma in the apartment next door. Miss Emma kept an eye on Diamond from time to time when there was an emergency and Mama had to work late.

"Meyel," she said, "Girl, what are you cooking in here that's smelling so good?" She told Mama that the smell was all in her apartment and she just couldn't take it anymore. Her stomach was tightening up in knots. Then she said, "Girl, if it's okay, can I come over for dinner?" Mama told her she could. Miss Emma said, "Thank You, Lord." She rushed out the door and said she would be right back. Miss Emma is a character. She keeps us laughing all the time. The world needs more happy people like Miss Emma.

Dinner was ready, and we all sat at the table, enjoying our food. Miss Emma said, "Meyel, I know you are proud of these children. I didn't know they could cook like this. Girl, this food is better than some of those restaurants I been to. This cake, I have never tasted anything like it. It is so good. You need to have your own bakery with food like this and give Ricko's Bakery some competition." Miss Emma never stopped talking and eating. "And you say Tehh made this cake and he can't read? Girl, you are a good teacher." Mama looked at me, and I shook my head for her to let it go.

Mama said emotionally, "Thanks, girl. He's getting much better. I thank God for my children every day. You'd better believe it, Miss Emma, when I tell you I am so proud of my children. They are all I have in this world." After dinner Mama and Miss Emma went and sat on the front porch and talked and talked and talked about everything. Diamond, Benjamin, and I cleaned up the kitchen, cracking jokes on one another. We had so much fun.

When we finished, I went outside to empty my wagon and get ready for the next day. Looking through the stuff I found the other day, I saw the old can stuffed with a rag and pulled out the rag. That rag was really stuck in that can. "Wow," I said when I pulled it out. There were four huge diamond rings. I looked inside them, and they were all twenty-four-karat gold. I had never seen that before. All I could remember seeing was ten karats in a ring. They all had to cost several thousand dollars. I had been reading up on how to tell the difference between real diamonds and fake stones, and these were real. There were about thirty old silver dollars and some real old pocket watches from the Civil War. They had to be worth a pretty penny. I cleaned up the old can, and I saw that it was one of those in the antique book. The ones in the book sold for up to three hundred dollars. I really had to find out how much this stuff was really worth. That was a very valuable camouflage. It looked like an old oily rag in a can fit for the trash. Whoever put it there knew exactly what they were doing. I had fifty old comic books that were very rare. I knew they could be worth something too. I found the old dirty moneybags from Mr. Johnson's Hardware store that he put on his trash pile. I open them and found money in one. I had to go in the house and get me a glass of water because I couldn't believe what I found. Now that I didn't need money it was coming from everywhere. I found two thousand dollars and a five-year-old deposit slip. The money never made it to the bank, and they never missed it. I thought, *What were they doing five years ago to make that kind of money here in Box City?* It was as if all the stars in the universe were lined up in my favor. The antique and collectable books that I found and studied really came in handy. It was sad to say, people didn't realize they were throwing away lots of money. I looked in the shoe box and read a few of somebody's love letters to her mister. One read, "I hope you can get away from her soon so we can be together. I really miss you, darling. The baby is growing up to look more and more like you every day. I can't wait for you to leave her and be with me. I love you so much. Your darling, Judith." From the dates on the letters, I knew those people had to either be dead or too old to remember missing each other. I wondered if Mr. Johnson knew he was that baby.

I finished empting my wagon and took a few of those banking papers to look at. I went in the house, took a bath, and got ready for bed. After I looked over some of those old banking papers, it looked like even back then they were raking in a lot of money each night in the underground city before the riot. Different ones were getting a big cut of the action. They accounted for everything, even the prostitutes they kept in the back quarters. I discovered that the money in the floor was the secret cut money from the papers I read. The jewelry was from people who ran out of cash. I laid there across my bed, trying to imagine what actually went on back then from looking at the building. I wondered how all of that money had affected Box City's economy, if it had at all. Everything was going through my mind. My eyes were getting heavy. I fluffed my pillow, rolled over, and went to sleep.

CHAPTER 9

A few months later while I was collecting junk on the streets, I thought about having an antique and collectables shop for all the stuff I had found and stored. I would need someone to run it for me. I could work there part-time or something. I had all of those buildings and all kinds of ideas of what I wanted to do with them. The thing that ate at my mind the most was how was I going to fix my life? I am a genius, but society thinks I am dummy. I needed to get an education first. I couldn't afford to go back to that school and fall into that same trap again. I needed to get a good education quick.

I overheard a white lady talking to a white guy at the bus stop about getting something called a GED one day. I hung around long enough to get an understanding of what they were talking about. Colored folks didn't talk about anything like that. Then I thought, *That was some real good information. Maybe I should try for my GED. That way if I passed, I might be able to go straight to college and learn so I can manage our business empire.* I learned that it didn't matter where good information came from. Get an ear-full and run with it. That was exactly what I did. Being a genius was one thing, but having the proper credentials to back it was another. I want to gain the respect of Box City for my accomplishments one day, not because I had money. *Tomorrow, I'm going to get up and go find out more about how to get my GED.* The thing about determination is that it won't let you sit still no matter how you try. It's like someone who's invisible is always pushing you to do whatever is necessary right then. Some folks just won't move. They just sit there and let life pass them by. Not me. I am going to be somebody one day.

One morning I woke up feeling pretty good. I decided to fix breakfast again. There were still a few steaks left in the freezer. I made Diamond's favorite steak and waffles with scrambled eggs. Benjamin loved omelets with cheese and hot coffee, and Mama was easy to please. We still had some of Mama's cake left over, and I put that on the table. Before I knew it everyone was coming in the kitchen ready to eat. There was that knock at the back door. It was Miss Emma in her housecoat, ready to eat again. "What y'all got going on in here now. That smell was killing me," she said.

Everyone said good morning and thanks for breakfast. But my sister, Diamond, came over and gave me a big hug. She told me that she loved me and that I was the smartest boy in the world. That kind of got to me because I didn't expect that. It made me feel so good. Miss Emma looked at her with food in her mouth and said, "That's so sweet, Diamond, encouraging your brother like that." We all ate breakfast and began our day. Benjamin and Diamond went to school, and Mama went to work. I went and got my wagon and set out to find treasure.

As I walked along the streets, I took a good look at the buildings we owned. I discovered that I didn't like what I saw. I saw people throwing wash water from upstairs apartments on to the street. Trash was piled up everywhere. There were millions of flies in those areas where water was thrown, and it smelled so bad. The buildings had all kinds of writing all over them, and some were boarded up. Then I thought about the buildings on the other side of town and how they were all so clean and beautiful. What I saw right here were people who just didn't care, and it hurt. The banker was right when he said, "Who would invest in a place like this?" At that moment even I didn't want to invest money in a place where people were just going to destroy it again. *What can I do to change it?* I had a few tears in my eyes. I wiped them on my shirt sleeve and went on my way.

Low in spirit, I stopped and searched through several junk piles and didn't find much quality. I decided to look under a box in an alley near the barbershop, and it scared me half to death. There was a dead body. I went in the barbershop, shaking and stuttering. I told the first man I saw that I had found a dead body in the back under a box. He and all the people in the barbershop jumped up and ran out to see what I was talking about, knocking me out of the way. Somebody called the police, and in minutes there were policemen, a fire truck, an ambulance, and reporters. This was a good time for me to act like I had a little intelligence if they tried to talk to me. Before I knew it, I was the dumbest person in Box City. Everyone stole my three minutes of fame by saying, "He can't understand what you are talking about because he can't read, write, or understand." I guess I couldn't see either. I found the body. I told the barber about it, and he told someone to call the police. I sucked it up and went on my way. Later the barber was on the news, talking like he had discovered the body. He never even mentioned me. I was indeed invisible to everyone in this city, and it hurt. I thought I would buy the barber's building and go up on his rent.

I went on down the road a piece and found myself in front of a bookstore. I parked my wagon and went in. I asked the lady at the desk if they had any books on how to get a GED. She smiled and took me over to the books. As she was thumbing through the books, she asked, "Are you really interested in getting your GED?" I told her that I was. She told me that the library offered free classes to anyone who was interested. The classes were offered during the day to make it easy for people to catch the bus and not worry about being out at night. Then she told me that I would have to pass a test to qualify. I bought the GED book and several others. I thanked the lady and made my way to the library. I was so interested in the GED that I didn't realize I had passed several junk piles until Mr. Smith called me. He told me that he had several boxes for me. I went over to see what he had. Mr. Smith ran a clothing store with an alteration shop in the back. He told me he thought he was my first stop of the day because my wagon was nearly empty. He had found some clothes my size and hoped I could wear them. It cost him too much to send them back. I put the three big boxes of clothes in my wagon and thanked him for thinking about me. They really looked good. I had to hide them under some other stuff so no one would take them off my wagon while I was in the library. Mr. Smith had no idea that I owned his building and went up on his rent.

I finally made it to the library and went in. Since I was out of school, it had been a while since I had gone there. Most of the books I read I had found on the streets. I went in and asked the lady at the desk about the GED classes. She looked at me and asked if I wanted to register for the test. I told her I did. She scheduled me for the next Wednesday at 12:00 and told me to please be on time. I kept thinking, *If I am going to help someone else, I have to first help myself.* This would be the first step to a better life for me. I had to get my education even if I was a genius. I was determined to get that diploma with my name on it no matter what. I got my wagon and went on my way. It was a school day, and I noticed how many boys and girls my age and older that had dropped out of school. There were at least seventy in a six-block radius just doing nothing but hanging out. My grandma would say, "An idle mind is the devil's workshop."

I passed by a grocery store one day, and noticed they were throwing away canned goods and stuff. I went over and asked the men if it was okay for me to take some? They told me that it was okay and to take as much as I wanted. I put as much of it as I could in my wagon. I thought about the fact that there were a lot of people in my building who could use that food even if it was a little outdated. I had to make several trips. After I put all of that stuff on my wagon and took it home, I was so hungry and thirsty. I stopped by the café and got me a big burger, fries and a large strawberry soda. It was so good. I took a window seat to keep an eye on my wagon. As I sat there eating, I thought about my future and the future of Box City. *If I could get my GED, I could go right into college.* I was almost sixteen years old. If all went well, I would be graduating from college when most kids would have been there a year or so. I was going to need some people to help me operate all of those buildings I bought, especially the one on East 57th Street. "Lord," I said, "I need a plan." I finished my food and decided to call it a day. I went on home and put up my wagon and decided to watch a little television. The next thing I knew, I was waking up. I must have been really tired.

I went outside and sat all the can goods on a table and told the neighbors to come and get some. People came from everywhere. In a matter of minutes everything was gone without even a *thank you* from most of them. They were so ungrateful. Again, I thought about the banker. All they were looking for was a handout or something for nothing, and it hurt.

I went back in the house and started dinner. I thought about what Miss Emma told Mama about our food and decided to do something different. I pulled out one of Mama's cookbooks to see what I could do with what we had. I found chicken, cheese, spaghetti, onions, eggs, cabbage, sweet potatoes, and cornmeal. I flipped through the pages of the book to see what I could find and began cooking. I thought about my false diagnosis and all I would be missing out on if I couldn't read or understand. I would have never had the opportunity to cook. I began to get a little philosophical, waving a big spoon, walking around the kitchen like I was talking to someone, saying, "Where there is knowledge there is empowerment. Where there is empowerment you will find knowledge. If empowerment is driving the car, then knowledge is sitting in the backseat." As long as I knew what I could do, that was all that mattered to me. Everything smelled so good. Then before I knew it, there was a knock at the back door. I hid the cookbook and went to see who it was. It was Miss Emma again. I thought to myself, *Lord, please stop up her nose so she can't smell anything."*

"Tehh, your mama home?" she asked.

"No, Miss Emma," I said, "She's still at work."

"That smell is all over my apartment, and I can't stand it. Well, if she's at work, then who is doing the cooking?" she asked.

I told her I was, and she was speechless. I had to put her mind at ease quickly. I told her mama fixed everything last night and I just put it in the oven or did whatever she told me to do to it. Then Miss Emma said, "Oh, I see. Okay, sugar, tell your mama I will be over for dinner," and then she left.

It was just about time for everyone to come home, and everything was ready. Mama didn't have to worry because everything was done.

The first person home was Diamond, and she said, "Hey, Tehh, where Mama at?"

I told her she was at work.

Then she got all stupid, asking, "You fixing to die again, Tehh? You cook so good when you are dying, Tehh."

I told her I was not dying. I just wanted to help Mama out. She is always so tired when she comes home. We need to do all we can to share the load.

She said, "Okay, what do you want me to do?"

I told her that she could set the table and put the flower I had gotten in the center. She looked at the flowers and told me that they were so pretty and they smelled good too.

Then she said, "Tehh, you know what?"

I said, "I know … you love me."

She smiled and said, "I wasn't going to say that, but I do love you. What I was going to say is that when I am old enough to have a boyfriend. I want him to be just like you."

Then I thought to myself, *This girl is killing my emotions. She just has a way of making me cry.* "I am a guy," I said to myself. "Guys don't cry." I thanked her and gave her a big hug.

Then the door opened, and it was Benjamin. "Mama home?" he asked.

"Nope," Diamond said, "Tehh is just dying again, and that's why he's cooking."

He said, "I don't care! I'm as hungry as a bull, and it smells so good in here."

I quickly said, "Y'all go wash up. Mama should be here in a few minutes."

Before I could get the words out of my mouth, she came through the door. She played me real good, smiling. "Hey, Tehh, are you dying again, honey? It smells so good in here." She put down her purse, gave me a big hug, washed her hands, and began checking out everything on the stove. "Tehh," she said, "I am so proud of you, honey. Can we eat now because I am so hungry?"

I said, "Yes, ma'am, and Miss Emma will be over too." I gave a big bang to the wall, and Miss Emma was at the back door in a flash.

We all sat down, fixed our plates, and enjoyed dinner. Then Miss Emma had to open her big mouth, as she was chewing. "Girl, this food is so good. Tehh told me you fixed everything last night and all he had to do was just put it in the oven." She just wouldn't shut up. "Girl, you have your children trained. I am not trying to be funny, but Tehh is a quick learner even if he can't read. He didn't let anything burn or dry out. This chicken tetrazzini is excellent ... and the glazed cabbage, wow, and girl, the stuffed sweet potatoes. I ain't never had anything so good, not to mention the corn bread." Miss Emma made one of the funniest faces I had ever seen and said, "Meyel, please don't leave me. Take me with you wherever you go so I can continue to enjoy this good food."

Mama looked at her and said, "Miss Emma, you are so crazy, but I love you." Mama and Miss Emma went out on the front porch and talked. Diamond, Benjamin, and I cleaned up the kitchen and put up the leftovers.

Diamond fixed the table and placed the flower back in the center and said, "I really liked the way the table looks. It makes me feel like we are not poor anymore." Then I thought, *If a flower makes her feel like that, I can do that all the time.*

After we finished the kitchen, we all went to our rooms. I picked up the GED book and began looking through it. Then I heard Mama calling me. I went outside to see what she wanted. It was Toe Joe and three of his friends. Since Mama and Miss Emma were on the front porch, we went on the back.

"Hey, man, these are a few of my friends. This is Jason, Mad Dog, and Brock. I was telling them about how I enjoyed talking to you the other day about our future and how the school had failed us. They said it failed them too."

I asked Jason why he wasn't in school. He told us that he kept falling asleep in school. He tried to stay awake, but he couldn't and flunked all of his classes. Some days he couldn't even think straight, so they put him out. It turned out that he was a diabetic and didn't know it until he passed out and was rushed to the hospital. Even when he told them at school that he wasn't feeling well, they ignored him too.

"Man, I could have died," he said.

"What about you Mad Dog?" I asked.

He told us he just got tired of folks laughing at him. He would get so nervous when he read out loud that he stuttered. The whole class would laugh at him and call him stupid. He just couldn't take it anymore, so he just quit. I told him that happened to me too.

"What about you Brock?" I asked.

He told us that the teachers bored him to death because he couldn't understand what they were talking about. They were using too many big words for him. When he would ask the teachers what they meant, they just got smart with him and told him they didn't have time to explain everything. So he flunked out. Then Mad Dog asked me why I wasn't in school. I told them that I had been diagnosed with a severe learning disability and had the attention span of a three-year-old. They told me that I would never learn, and I had a violent behavior problem. It turned out that I had a tumor that was causing the problem. It burst, and I am better now. Then I said, "The real truth is … I'm a genius way ahead of my time, but they wanted a dummy."

Then Toe Joe said, "Yeah, right! Man, everybody knows that you can't read or write. Everybody calls you a dummy."

I thought I'd better be cool for now and go along with Toe Joe. "You right, man, but it feels good to think that I'm a genius. I'm tired of being called a dummy, and I'm going to do something about it."

They all laughed and asked, "What are you going to do about it? You can't read." I told them I was going to learn how. I told them that some people were giving some free classes at the library and I was going to take a few of them so I could go back to school. "They have people to work with you on your level. If I can do it, will you do it too?" I asked.

Toe Joe laughed and said, "Man, if you can do it, which I doubt. I will be there with bells on." Jason, Mad Dog, and Brock all agreed to.

"Okay," I said, "this is how it's going to go. If I do this and get my GED, then you will get yours. We will become a secret gang and recruit others to do the same so we can change Box City."

They all laughed and said at the same time, "Okay, man, we will get ours." I knew they all said yes because they thought I couldn't do it. I felt good, so I asked them if they were hungry, and they told me they were. I offered them some leftovers, and they were happy. They ate like they had never eaten before, asking what is this and what is that. They were so funny. We all sat around talking about our lives and the state of Box City. At about nine o'clock everybody left and went home. I was so excited because I knew that I would pass the test and begin my GED. They just didn't know it. I can't wait to see their faces when I tell them I did it. After I learn everything about this GED thing, then I can teach it to them. If Mama can learn to be a baker, and Diamond can fry chicken, and Benjamin can make some of the best mac and cheese you have ever eaten, they can get a GED easy.

CHAPTER 10

I went to sleep one night and had the strangest dream. I was running this huge company called the Hancock Corporation from my wagon. I had a huge private office on the top floor with secretaries and many office assistants, and my wagon was parked over in the corner. I was at the construction site of another Hancock building going up and there was my wagon in its designated parking space. There was no crime in Box City, and children were playing and pulling their wagons everywhere. Other corporations were making Box City their home office, and there were wagons in each parking space. Box City was no longer a colored and white city. It was a people city where colorful painted wagons filled with flowers were in every yard. I was drawn into a gorgeous mansion with a beautiful king-size wagon bed where I was sleeping. The bed was so comfortable. I turned and rolled over to the other side, and *bam!* I hit the floor. I quickly woke up. It was a dream. Man, I fell off the top bunk bed. I could have killed myself. Benjamin woke up and said, "What's wrong with you, man? You peed in the bed or something? You scared me to death."

I said, "No, man, go on back to sleep. I just fell out the bed." I was so ashamed of myself. When I woke up, I had a sore leg, and it was hard for me to walk. I thought about the dream, and it actually motivated me. What I couldn't understand was why wagons were everywhere.

I couldn't wait for Wednesday to come so I could take the test for the GED. I rubbed my leg down with some alcohol to ease the pain. "No work for me today," I said. I laid on the couch thinking about putting some of those empty buildings to use. I picked up the newspaper off the coffee table and looked at the classified section for people renting office buildings to see what they offered and the amount of rent they were asking. At that moment I realized that even though I was a child, I had to take on the responsibility of being a man. Failure was not an option. There were several empty spaces in the bank building I had bought. That would be a great place to start. I could have them fixed up and lease them to compatible businesses. They could pay their rent to the real estate company. No one had to know who I was. Then I wondered what those bankers would say then about their new neighbors. It seemed like everything was going through my mind. The area where the bank was located was fairly clean. It was across from the park, the post office, and the police station. Then I figured I needed to go back across town and take a closer look at the businesses there. Mama, Diamond, and Benjamin would love that, and I could take some pictures.

I must have fallen asleep because I woke up and heard voices. I was kind of dazed, and I thought I smelled breakfast cooking. Or was I dreaming again? I got up and hopped in the kitchen. Benjamin was cooking breakfast, and Diamond was sitting at the table. I decided to do him like he did me. "Oh no! Not you! Are you dying, Benjamin? Please don't die, man. I have never known you to cook breakfast in your life."

He said, "No, man, I'm not dying. I just want to be like you and cook breakfast for everyone."

Then I thought, *What's wrong with these folks around here wanting to be like me? I ain't nobody special.* I just said, "Thanks, man."

Diamond asked me, "What's wrong?" I told her I fell out the bed and hurt my leg. Then all of a sudden she called Mama.

She ran into the kitchen saying, "Are y'all at it again? Benjamin, are you dying this time too, baby?"

Diamond said, "No, Mama, he ain't dying. He just wants to be like Tehh. Mama, Tehh fell out the bed and hurt his leg. You'd better look at it, Mama."

Mama came and looked at my leg and said, "Oh, my goodness, it's swollen. I'm taking you to the doctor right now. Get your clothes on, all of you." We all got in the car and went to the hospital a few blocks away. You would have thought I had been shot the way Mama was acting. I saw the doctor. He checked my leg and told me I sprained my ankle. He gave me some pain pills and told me to stay off of it for a few days, then it would be as good as new. Mama said, "Thank You, Jesus," and then she took us home.

Diamond said, "Now we can go home and eat Benjamin's breakfast. Tehh, I am going to be your nurse because I love you so much."

I thought to myself, *She is really trying to kill me with all this love.* I smiled and said, "Thanks, Diamond. I love you to." On the streets I was treated like dirt, but at home I was treated like a hero. We made it home, and Benjamin finished cooking breakfast. I was so proud of him. He was doing things just like I taught him. We ate breakfast, and Diamond cleaned up the kitchen. Everyone got ready and followed their daily routine.

Since I couldn't go anywhere, I decided I would just read the GED book. I got the book and made myself comfortable at the kitchen table by putting my foot on a pillow in a chair. I read and read and read, losing myself in the book. I answered questions, solved problems, did fractions, you name it. It was like I was in school at home. I had gotten halfway through the book when I fell asleep. I heard a knock at the back door and hopped over to see who it was. Oh, man, it was Miss Emma, and I had all those books on the table. I peeped out the door and said, "How you doing, Miss Emma?"

She said, "Okay. Your mama called me and told me to check on you and see if you were okay." I told her I was okay and thanked her for checking on me. She went on back to her apartment, and I was so relieved. I guess since she didn't smell anything cooking, she didn't have a reason to come in. *Today I will fix something simple for dinner since I have to stay off my foot.* I took out some hamburger meat to thaw out. *Hamburgers and fries for today with a nice dessert*, I thought.

I went back into the living room and sat on the couch and put my foot on a pillow on the coffee table and watched television. They did a special on illiteracy and showed the cities and communities that were affected the most. Ah, man, there we were! Box City was shown at its very worst for the whole world to see. I wanted to crawl under a rock. We were at the top of the chart for being illiterate. They even showed pictures of our community— girls with babies in their belly and one or two on the ground, men lying on street corners, others sitting around playing cards, folks hanging clothes from upstairs apartments, and me pushing my wagon. I had never seen myself on television before, but at least I was working. They pick the worst person in Box City to say something— Big Wooly. The man had missing teeth in his mouth and spoke with a slurred speech like he was drunk. The whole thing just made me sick. *I'm a child. Why do I care so much anyway?* I changed the channel to a cartoon to get that image out of my mind. I lived in the mess. I didn't need to watch it on television.

What was so sad was that the people were smiling as if they were happy. There was absolutely nothing "happy" about hopelessness. They were prisoners of their own imaginations and too blind to see it and break free. I got angry and said, "I refuse to accept that. I'm going to be the first to break free by getting my GED in this community. Let them come and write about that." Somebody has to break this curse. It is a vicious cycle that has to be stopped. Money wouldn't do it because all they want is a handout. I was getting so angry. I had to calm myself down. These people have to see a dummy like me get an education and rise to the top and become a millionaire. Then I thought, *What's the use? My plan may not even work.* I had even thought about asking Mama to leave this place and not wait four years to enjoy her life because now we could afford it. We had thousands of dollars with money coming in every day. But something kept telling me that if we left, I would be walking away from God's purpose for my life and Box City's. Even before I found the money, I had dreamed of a better Box City for me and my family.

I went back in the kitchen and read a little more, and then I fixed hamburgers, fries, and a tossed salad sitting at the table. I didn't have to stand at all. A hot plate is a good thing to have around the house when you can't stand. Mama had some pound cake left in the cake plate. I added whip cream, caramelized peaches and strawberries. It really looked good. I made sure Diamond's flower was in the center of the table. Everyone got home pretty close to the same time and was glad to see that dinner was ready. Mama said she didn't expect me to cook anything because of my leg. There wasn't a lot of smell in the apartment, but Miss Emma was at the back door anyway. Mama let her in, and she took her place at the table as usual, running off at the mouth. She began to get on my last nerve, and my leg started hurting again. I took a pain pill and went in the living room, sat on the couch, and soon fell asleep.

CHAPTER 11

Finally it was Wednesday, the day of the test for the GED. I got up early and made breakfast. I sat the table with omelets, blueberry waffles, ham, and hot coffee. No one got up, so I went to see what was going on. When I reached the hallway, everybody shouted happy birthday. I had forgotten my own birthday. I was sixteen years old, and now I could get a driver's license. But I was supposed to be a dummy who couldn't read or write. *When I get my GED, I'm going to get my license,* I thought. I thanked everybody and said, "Let's eat before the food gets cold." I thought I would just bang on the wall for Miss Emma. I knew she would be over anyway. There she was at the back door in a flash. Mama should claim her on her income tax the way she feeds her. We all ate breakfast, laughed, and talked about my sixteen years.

Diamond said, "Thanks, Tehh. The flower is beautiful. I don't feel poor today."

Miss Emma looked at her and said, "The nerves of that child."

Mama said, "It's okay, Miss Emma. I know what she meant."

Diamond and Benjamin went and got ready for school. Mama got ready for work, and Miss Emma went out the door. I hate it when people got all up in your family business uninvited. It can make you easily change your opinion of them. Everyone went their way. I cleaned up the kitchen, got my wagon, and hit the streets.

I really didn't mind collecting junk these days because I didn't have to anymore. Before, it was a necessity. We needed every penny I could scrape up to survive. Now it was a pass-time. It gave me something to do until I got my life together. I see things in a way that I had never seen them before now that we had money. I noticed someone putting some stuff out on the streets and asked if it was okay to take something. The man said ok. It was a lot of stuff from an old antique store that had been closed for a really long time. The man said they told him to clean out the building and throw away all the stuff. I guess someone bought it, or they were putting it up for sale. I thought I would check on that building too. It was a treasure chest to me. Dollar signs were bouncing everywhere. Everything was covered with dust and spiderwebs, but other than that, it looked like it was some very good stuff. It could bring in thousands of dollars. There were expensive oil paintings, glassware, beautiful plates, footstools, collectibles, and more. They just needed to be cleaned up—that was all. I learned that just because something was dusty or old didn't mean it had no value. I could see every item beautifully displayed in my store. I quickly filled my wagon with as much as I could and took the stuff home and came back for more. I made three trips home and back with the stuff from that shop, and I was worn out. The man said he would put some more stuff out tomorrow and told me to come back if I wanted to.

It was eleven o'clock, and I took a little time to rest before I went to the library to take my test. I was so nervous. I went in and gave the lady my name. She told me that I could have a seat and someone would be with me in about fifteen minutes. That was the longest fifteen minutes of my life. My mind went back to the school psychologist, who said I had the attention span of a three-year-old. I was really restless. The old feelings I had when I was in school began to sabotage me. I took a deep breath and got control of myself. *Failure is not an option*, I told myself over and over. *All of Box City is depending on you. Be a man! Sit up straight and focus. I will pass this test and begin to get my GED.* I repeated this thought to myself over and over until my fears were gone. A lady finally came out to get me and took me into a room. She sat me down at a desk and gave me several sheets of paper and a pencil, and told me to answer all the questions. She said that when the bell rang in an hour, I needed to stop. Well, I looked over the sheets and began to answer the questions. It was so easy I was through in fifteen minutes.

The lady noticed that I was just sitting there and doing nothing, and she came over. "Mr. Hancock, if this is difficult for you at this time, you can try again another day. I have had people come back several times." I told her that it wasn't difficult at all. I had finished with forty-five minutes left on the clock. She was stupidly shocked when I said that. "That is impossible," she told me. "How old are you?" she asked.

"Today is my birthday. I am sixteen years old," I told her.

"Happy birthday," she said. She took my paper and asked me to go back outside and have a seat until she checked my answers.

I thought, *I hope she don't do me like they did in school. I pass the test, and then they say I cheated and give me an 'F.*

I went and sat near the window so I could look out and think. The lady came back out and asked me to come back into the room. There were several other people with her. They wanted to know how I knew the answers. *Here we go again,* I thought. I was getting upset and said, "What are you trying to say? That I cheated?"

A man said, "Calm down, Mr. Hancock. We are not saying that, but we have never had a colored person pass this part of the test before the first time."

Angrily I asked, "Will I be able to start the class to get my GED or not?" I really wanted to walk out of that place and never come back. I felt like I was back in the school that had failed me. I had passed the test, but they didn't want me to pass the test because I was colored. They should have been happy that I did. I asked them if they all want to sit there and watch me take this test again. They all said yes. I felt like a monkey in a cage. The lady gave me another test, and I finished it in eleven minutes flat. All I was doing now was checking boxes, and then I was finished. They all look at one another and the clock. They asked me if I was sure I was through, and if I needed to go back and double-check my answers. How stupid did they think I was? They took my paper, and each one checked it. I purposely missed three the first time. This time I got them all right. They all scratched their heads, cleared their throats, and checked my paper again. Then they all apologized for what they called a misunderstanding and said that I could begin my class in two months. They told me that I was the first person, colored, white, or any race, who had scored 100 percent on this part of the test. They were interested in seeing how well I would do on the actual GED. Then I thought, *Why would you give a test that you didn't expect anyone to pass anyway?* That was crazy to me, but I was so glad to get out of there.

I realized that I was going to have to stand up like a man and not back down when people challenged me if I want to be somebody in this life. Getting upset and walking away wasn't going to change anything. I had to start acting like a man. I got my wagon and headed toward home. I stopped by the burger shop and treated myself to a big cheeseburger, fries, and a large strawberry soda. I took a window seat and looked out as I ate. I had to clear my mind of the people in the library and focus on something positive because it was killing my appetite. My burger was so good. I noticed two empty buildings across from the burger shop. *I think I might want to buy them. This area looks a little better, and it's across from another bank.* Later I asked Mama to call the real estate office to see how much they cost so we could buy them. There was no clothing store or antique shop there. That gave me something to think about. I was sixteen and getting ready to get my GED. It couldn't get any better than that.

I made it home and put up my wagon. I was so excited I was going to get my GED that I was running late. I knew Mama would be so proud of me. I hurried in to make dinner before everyone got home. I opened the door and was shocked out of my senses by a loud "Surprise" and the "Happy Birthday" song. They almost gave me a heart attack for my birthday. I would have died without my GED. Mama had invited a few of the guys and Miss Emma over to give me a birthday party. Mama made me a beautiful cake. She had everything I liked on the table. I gave her a big hug and said, "Thank you, Mama. I love you."

She said out loud so everyone could hear her, "I don't have a gift for you right now, Tehh, because it took all the money for the food. I just wanted you to have birthday party, honey, no matter what."

Money was definitely not the problem. She was just acting like it used to be before we came into money. Back then a party definitely would not have been in the picture. Miss Emma said, "Don't worry, Meyel. I have a gift for him." She gave me an envelope with twenty dollars in it and a big kiss.

"Thanks, Miss Emma," I said. Toe Joe, Jason, Mad Dog, and Brock gave me ten dollars each.

I gave them a man hug and said, "Thanks guys." Benjamin and Diamond had gifts for me too. This was another one of the best days of my life. We ate, talked, played games, and had a good time.

After everything was over, Benjamin and Diamond cleaned up the kitchen. Mama and Miss Emma went on the front porch and talked and talked and talked. The guys and I went on the back porch and talked about all the stuff that was going on with us. Toe Joe's dad and mom finally split, and man, was he happy. He said his mom got her joy back, and that was what he wanted. He could think now because that was one load off of his brain. "She looks like a new woman," he said.

Brock said his girlfriend was expecting, and we all said, "Expecting what?" at the same time.

He said, "A baby," and told us that he was going to be a man and take care of her because he loved her. He was looking for a job. Jason had gotten a part-time job at the meat-packing plant. He told us how bad it smelled. He said he spent the first two weeks throwing up. We all laughed and cheered him on. He said it had been nearly two months, and he was just now getting use to the smell. He asked Brock to come and apply, and we all laughed. Mad Dog told us he won fifty dollars on a scratch-off, and he was excited about that.

I asked him, "What did you do with the fifty dollars?"

He told us he lost it trying to win fifty more dollars and laughed. We all laughed with him. I told him to put it in the bank next time because money was hard to get around here. I thought to myself, *Mad Dog takes risks. He may not be a good match for me moneywise. He don't know the value of a dollar.* I wanted to include all of them in my plans, but I couldn't afford a gambler. Time would definitely tell. Toe Joe asked me what was up with me. Now was time to give them the big surprise. I told them I was going to start taking my special classes in two months, and they were shocked. "Surprise," I said.

Toe Joe said, "You got to be kidding, man?" He was actually shocked. I told him I was not kidding. I was going to be reading, writing, adding, spelling, and a lot of stuff. Folks around here will not be calling me a dummy anymore. They were speechless.

"We all still on, right?" I asked. They didn't say anything. "Just don't forget what you said guys. If I can do it, you can do it, right?"

For some strange reason, I thought they would be excited for me. They all dropped their heads, got up and left, saying, "See you, man."

Then I said, "Wait guys. If I can show you what they teach me. Will you try?"

They all nodded their heads and said, "That might work," and went on their way, never looking back. Something on the inside told me not to worry about them, and I didn't.

CHAPTER 12

A month later I got up early one Thursday morning, got my wagon, and hit the streets. I had a lot of stuff in the storage shed and needed to put it somewhere. I thought about an antique shop, but not necessarily an antique shop. I wanted it to be a place for curious seekers, offering things they could easily afford. I wanted to take a good look at the space in one of the buildings I bought near the bank. I couldn't go in as Tehh. So, I went over and stood outside, peeping through the window, trying to imagine what the space would look like. Before I knew it, a policeman came up behind me. He cleared his throat several times. I turned around, and he looked at me and asked, "What you doing here, boy? Let's move along before you cause trouble." That was one mean-looking policeman. That was my building. I owned it, but I did what he said and moved along. This was not the time for me to be stupid and reveal my identity. I had to get my GED first. I had seen enough and thought the building would be perfect for my first shop. All I needed was a plan to get things started, and no one would know who I was. Plus, I was going to need some help. Then I thought, *Maybe halfway through my GED class I could put the guys to work, and they wouldn't know that they were working for me.* This way they would get some early business training. If they finished college with me, they would never have to worry about a job again as long as there was no trouble.

I left and went searching the junk piles near the barbershop. I found a box of magazines and looked through them and found several men's magazines with wigs and beards you could order by mail. I took my wagon on the back of the building and looked through them and got a brilliant idea. I could make myself look ten years older and conduct my own business interviews and manage my businesses from a secret location, and no one would know that it was me. I had so much stuff going through my mind. *I just may have to write a book one day*, I thought. I checked a few more junk piles, picked up newspapers and magazines from benches, and made my way home.

I passed by an alley, and there was a prostitute asking me to come over. *I'm a dummy pushing a wagon. What can I give you?* I thought. I shook my head and started to walk away when she opened her shirt and showed me her big ... you know, breasts. Man, I took off running and sweating. The last time I saw some of those were on the dead body I found under the box. Wow, I couldn't believe it. "Does stuff like this happen to all the guys when they turn sixteen?" I asked myself.

On the way home I stopped by the grocery store to pick up a few things. I made a grocery list the night before since the people in the store knew I couldn't read and gave it to the clerk. She picked out all the items on my list and rang me up. I handed her thirty-five dollars with coupons, and she said, "You got it down to the penny like your mama."

As I was going out the door, I bumped into this cute girl with one of the prettiest smiles I had ever seen. I nervously told her I was sorry and just stood there frozen like a dummy. This had never happened to me before. She told me it was okay and that she knew me. She was in my class when they had to take me to the hospital that time. She always wondered what happened to me. I didn't remember any girls this pretty my class. I told her that I had been around and that I was sorry again. I said, "I had a tumor. But it's gone, and I'm okay now. They still won't let me back in school." She told me she was sorry and said to not give up. I thanked her and said I would see her around, and then I headed home.

I went on home and put up my wagon. I put the groceries on the table and went in the living room to watch television. The next thing I knew I was waking up. I went in the kitchen and fixed dinner and spent the rest of the time reading my GED book. By the time everyone got home, I was through. Then it hit me like a ton of bricks. I never asked the girl in the store her name. *Wow, how dumb could I be really?* Everybody made it home around the same time. We all sat down for dinner, and then there was that expected knock at the back door. Mama didn't even get up because she was so tired. She just said, "It's open, Miss Emma. Come on in."

"How is everybody doing?" she said and sat down. It was a spaghetti day with all the trimmings and pineapple upside-down cake. After dinner I asked Mama if I could talk to her about something important. She said okay and went out and talked to Miss Emma for a while. Diamond, Benjamin, and I cleaned up the kitchen. Benjamin seemed worried, and I asked him what was wrong. He told me his class was going to Washington, DC, and he couldn't go because he knew Mama didn't have the money.

I asked, "How much is it going to cost?"

He said, "Five hundred dollars."

I smiled and said, "Wow! Let me talk to Mama and see what she says. You might be able to go." I told him I had a little money saved and there were still a few month before then.

He smiled and said, "Thanks, man. You are the best." We all started cracking jokes on one another and having fun. I knew it wouldn't be a problem for Benjamin to go to Washington, DC, but we had to keep things a secret for now.

Later Mama called me out on the porch, and I went to see what she wanted. She said, "We can talk now."

First I told her, "Benjamin was upset because he couldn't go to Washington, DC. He thought you didn't have the money. I told him I had a little money saved and that I would talk to you." Mama told me that he never said anything to her about his trip. I told her that was probably because he felt she wouldn't have the money. I told her to ask him for the permission slip and details about the trip with the amount and just write the school a check.

Then she said, "Now that we have that settled, what did you want to talk to me about?" I asked her to come and look at the storage shed with me. She opened the door and said, "Oh my goodness! Where did you get all this stuff?" I told her about the man cleaning out the antique shop and throwing everything away. I brought it all home. She said, "Some of this stuff is really nice."

I said, "I know, and I want to open up a shop with it." I told her the building across the street from the burger shop near the Redwood Bank would be a good place. I had stopped by there today and peeped through the window. Then I said, "Mama, would you believe a policeman stopped and told me to move on?"

She asked, "What were you doing for him to do that?"

I said, "Just peeping through the windows."

Mama laughed so hard and said, "He told you to move from in front of your own building, sugar. What did you do then?"

"I moved, Mama. That's what I did. I didn't want any trouble."

She said, "Good for you. Now tell me your plan."

I told her I had found some books with beards and wigs and stuff. I thought I could disguise myself as a twenty-five-year-old man and hire someone to run the shop. They would know that Tehh would work there several days a week part-time. I wanted to hire at least two people to run the shop. I would need her to go with me to get the business license. I would have a truck come and get all the stuff and take it to the shop. I would go ahead and call the real estate office to find some people to paint and decorate it. First I wanted to go back to the other side of town to see their shops there. "What do you think about that?" I asked.

"I think you have been doing a lot of thinking about it," she said. "Do you want to take that trip on Saturday?"

I smiled and said, "Yes, ma'am."

Bubbling over on the inside, I told her the good news. "One more thing, Mama," I said. "I start school next month to get my GED."

As tears ran from her eyes, she said, "Oh, my God. Thank You, Jesus." She gave me a big hug and told me that she was so proud of me. She said this was the happiest day of her life because she wanted me to finish school and be what God wanted me to be. She just knew that I was going to make a big difference in this world because I had already made a big difference in her world. "All of the other stuff was good, but this tops them all," she said. Then I told her that if I got my GED, I could start college next fall. She grabbed me and hugged me again and said, "Now the world will know that you are truly a genius. I am going to sleep good tonight," and she went in the house. Suddenly she came back out and sat down and said, "You know, Tehh, I have been thinking about what Miss Emma said about our food and how good it is. What do you think about me opening up a restaurant with your recipes or a bakery?" I told her that I was just waiting to see how long it was going to take her to make up her mind. I gave her a big hug and told her that it was a wonderful idea. Now this is the happiest day of my life again. My mama was going into the food business. She told me to let her get all of her ideas together and that she would talk with me later.

When I woke up, I couldn't believe my eyes. Diamond was in the kitchen, fixing breakfast like a pro. She had the pancakes going. The bacon was on. The rice was on too, and she had the eggs in a bowl to scramble. I ran in and said, "Oh no, not you. Are you dying this morning too, Diamond?"

She just started laughing and said, "No, silly. I just want to be like you and Benjamin. If y'all can die, I can die this time to." Mama and Benjamin came rushing in the kitchen because the house smelled so good.

"Tehh, you cooked?" Mama asked.

"No, ma'am, Mama, it's Diamond. She's the one dying this morning," I said.

Mama just laughed and gave her a big hug and told us all how proud she was of us. "I can't believe you did this by yourself, baby," Mama said. She told mama that I was a good teacher, and then she finished scrambling the eggs. We all sat down and began to eat our breakfast. I noticed something was wrong. There was no knock at the back door and no Miss Emma. Mama went over and knocked on her door to see what was wrong. I hoped she wasn't dead. Miss Emma came to the door with a very bad cold. Her nose was so stopped up she couldn't smell a thing. Mama told her to stay in and that she would bring her some breakfast. "Thank You, God," I said. "We can enjoy breakfast for a change with our mama." Then I thought about the prayer I had prayed that time for the Lord to stop up Miss Emma's nose. I felt sorry for just a tiny minute. Then I thought, *I got to be careful what I ask in prayers from now on.*

CHAPTER 13

While everyone followed their normal routine, I decided to stay home and order several wigs, beards, eyebrows, sideburns, and mustaches. It would take three to four weeks for them to arrive, so I had to plan things around that time. I began to draw the design for the interior of the building for my first shop, putting the shelves in various places. I wanted an area for glassware, an area exclusively for plates, and an area for small furniture, etc. Pictures would be placed to accent the various areas of the store, and I wanted a special area for all the oil paintings I had collected. I wanted a wall area for books and magazines with a few chairs. This way people could sit and wouldn't be all up on one another. There would be display cases for jewelry and collectibles, and there would be a room in the back for items coming in to go on the floor. I wanted beautiful restrooms for men and women and beautiful curtains at the window to showcase what was inside and bring in all the different races of people in Box City. There would be a small kitchen with cabinets, a sink, a stove, a refrigerator, and a table with chairs for clerks to store and eat their food. Absolutely no eating would be tolerated on the floor. I want a professional staff. The service desk would be placed where the clerks could see every area of the store. One clerk would be at the register, and one or two would assist the customers. If business was good, I would hire a fourth person. I would work part-time two or three days a week at minimum wage, stocking and doing odd jobs after school. I believe I already had about fifty thousand dollars or more worth of free inventory that I collected off the streets. I have to estimate the utilities and what it would cost to make my drawings a reality. Tomorrow is going to be a great day. Mama was going to take us across town and look at some of the shops over there. We are going to have a good time. We may even spend the night.

I finished what I had to do and decided to hit the streets. I went a different direction this time and ran into a crowd of people gathered to hear someone speaking. I parked my wagon under a tree and moved up closer to see who it was and what he was talking about. A big sign said that he was M. D. Gafford. He was traveling the country trying to motivate people in low-income areas to educate themselves. He said he came to Box City because he saw us on television during a broadcast regarding illiteracy in our city. He said, "Most of you can't read. Why is that? How do you know if you are being cheated or if you are signing the right papers?" He held up a book and said, "Education is the key. It is the only way to a better life. The more you know, the farther you can go. If things are going to change in Box City, you are going to have to be the ones to change them. Do you want a better city with great jobs?"

Everyone shouted, "Yes!"

"Go back to school," he said. "Do you want better schools?"

Everybody shouted, "Yes!"

"Get involved now and do something to make them better. Do you want to live in better houses in communities that you can be proud of?"

Everybody shouted, "Yes!"

"Then take advantage of all of the educational opportunities available to you. Things don't just happen, people. You have to make them happen. Reading opens up a whole new world of possibilities. It gives you a better vision for your children and yourself. Let's stamp out illiteracy today by learning to read," he said.

Boy, he sounded good. I said, "I can do that." For those few minutes people were so excited, and then the sugar rush was over. Most of them returned to their state of low mentality. Until people want to change for the better, and want to do their part to make it happen, things will remain the same. I thought about the banker's words. The people were excited indeed, but they were looking for something for nothing. I shook my head and went on my way.

I was about a mile and a half away from home when I passed by the Mount Zion Baptist Church and saw a man sitting on the steps. He spoke to me first and asked me how I was doing. I told him fine. He was a very nice man and asked me to sit with him for a minute. He told me he was Rev.

Isaac Young, the pastor of the church. I told him they called me Tehh, and he asked me for my real name. I said Thomas Edison Hamilton Hancock. He said, "Wow, that's some name you got there, son." I told him that my mama wanted me to have a name that wouldn't kill me. He just smiled and said, "I think she succeeded." He had an extra soda with him and offered it to me. He said he often sat on those steps and shared the love of Jesus Christ with anyone who would listen. I sat down and talked with him for a while. He told me he was the new pastor of the church and had been there about a year and a half. He had moved his family there from Indiana. He expressed his concern for the young people of Box City. I could see that he was hurting on the inside by the expression on his face. He said he had never seen anything like the people in Box City. Most of his young people had lost hope. The evil forces of the world were pulling them farther away from the church. They were dropping out of school. Girls were having babies and not wanting to get married. Boys didn't want to own up to their responsibilities. He groaned for the young boys who were dying from drugs, drinking, gangs, fighting, and in prison. He said he buried three boys the week before who had been killed in a car wreck. It was the hardest thing he ever had to do. Then he said he just didn't know how to reach his young people. It seemed as if his prayers weren't working. It was as if God had turned His back on him, but he was going to stay in the race. With tears in his eyes, he told me he wasn't ready to give up yet. He looked at me as if he was asking me for help. For some strange reason

I asked him, "What do you preached about on Sundays?"

He said, "I tell them they are going to hell if they don't change their ways."

I thought to myself, *They probably think they are there already just living here in Box City.*

Well, I asked him if he had ever thought about taking a different approach. He asked, "What do you mean by that?"

I said, "Have you ever tried preaching to the people you want them to become?"

Then he asked me again, "What do you mean, son?"

I said, "Like let there be light and there was light." I began telling him that in the midst of all that darkness God called for light, not more darkness, and then light appeared. God asked for what He wanted. That darkness had to move out of the way and let the light appear because that's what God needed most at the time. Rev. Young looked at me kind of puzzled. I said, "If your people are in spiritual darkness, they can't see. They need some spiritual light. If they are spiritually dead, maybe you need to preach life into them, not more death. They may need to be spiritually resuscitated."

He looked at me, smiled, and said, "Keep on talking, son." I said, "Rev. Young, while traveling these streets, I have learned that our colored people have been in a state of hopelessness for a very long time. It has been passed down from one generation to the next. When you have the time, go to the library and check out the history of Box City between 1940 and 1960." He looked at me, nodding his head as I talked. "Our people haven't been taught to see a better way or even dream of a better day. They just wake up each morning, doing what they did the day before religiously. It never entered into their minds to do something different because there was no vision in them. God gave them great minds, and He wants them to use them. But they don't know how. He wants us to live a better life. I think the Bible says an abundant life, but they don't know how."

He kept saying, "I see, son."

I said, "They want to be happy, but they don't know how. You have to teach them as if they were little children how to live right because they just don't know how. They are not ready for the meat of the Word yet. You have to give them the milk of it a little at a time."

He smiled and said, "Amen, son. I see what you are talking about now."

I said, "Like little children, you have to paint a better image of Jesus on the canvas of their minds like an artist so they can see it and treasure it in their hearts. That's why God sent you to show them the way to Him because they are spiritually lost. God gave us the power to get wealth. Teach them how to get it God's way, not from drugs, gambling, robbing, and stuff. God wants us to love one another. Teach them how. Tell them God loves them because they need to know that."

Tears began to run down my face and his. I said, "I know God loves me, Rev. Young, and that has nothing to do with me pushing my wagon. Don't feel sorry for me. Pushing my wagon is a constant reminder of how blessed I really am. I push it because I choose to. I thank God for *me* every day, no matter what people say or think about me. You see what I'm saying?"

Rev. Young smiled with tears in his eyes and said he understood exactly what I was saying. I said, "These are your precious people, and God gave you the power to reprogram them in the way they should go, like Romans 12:2 in the Bible. It will take some time, but it will be worth it when you see their lives changing, and like the prodigal son, they come back home to you and the Lord."

Then he said, "I never thought about it like that. You sure have helped me today, son. It's like a burden has been lifted off of me." Then he asked me how old I was. I told him that I was sixteen. He told me that I was an amazing young man and wiser than my years. Then he asked me if I was a preacher.

Man, I jumped up and said, "Oh no, sir, Pastor Young." I said good-bye and went on my way, thanking him for the soda. I told him I would probably visit him again one Sunday. I pretty much knew the Bible. The strange thing was sometimes I didn't know where the stuff I said came from, but it worked. I felt like it wasn't me that was talking at all.

I started back toward home, checking junk piles as I went along the way and humming a little tune. A lady driving by asked me if I collected junk because she had some stuff in her car. I said yes. She gave me several bags and a box of stuff, and I put it all in my wagon. She told me that I saved her a trip to the junkyard and gave me twenty dollars for my help. I went along my way, thinking about the preacher, our trip on Saturday, and starting my GED class. I decided to call it a day and went home. I put up my wagon and went in the house.

Shortly after that, I smelled smoke and went outside to see where it was coming from. It was coming from one of the apartments across the street. I went in the house and called the fire department. I closed the door and went to see if anyone needed help. I called to see if anyone was in the apartment. The neighbors heard me yelling and came out of their apartments, running to see what was going on. They told me that a man lived in the apartment and that he was in a wheelchair. I went banging on the man's door, but he never answered. I forgot at that moment that I was a dummy and incapable of making a decision as to what to do. I took a chair and tried to break the window. The apartment was filled with smoke, but the man was in there. I could see him on the floor. I tried to kick the window in so I could get inside. I called for someone to help me get the man out. The fire was at the back of the apartment at that time. He was near the front door. I crawled in and picked up the man and handed him to someone outside the window, and then I crawled out. We took the man to a safe place away from the apartment, and I tried to revive him. I asked people to knock on doors and tell people to get out of the other apartments in case the fire spread. The fire department and ambulance arrived. They checked the man and rushed him to the hospital, and the firemen put out the fire. It had started spreading at the back of the apartments on the right and left sides of him. The people in those apartments managed to get out safely thanks to our quick thinking.

For the first time I saw people come together to help someone. Everybody was knocking on doors and calling out to people, trying to get their attention.

As I was going back home, one of the neighbors said, "Tehh, how did you know what to do? Everybody knows you can't read or reason. How did you do it? I watched you, man. You didn't act like you didn't know what you were doing. You are smarter than folks think around here. Now I know you got some sense in that head of yours. You gave that man mouth-to-mouth necessitation." I smiled at that one because he had a speech problem. I told him that in life-threatening situations even dumb people can do some amazing things.

He said, "You see there, you don't even talk like a dummy." He thanked me for what I did and went on his way. "I'm proud of you, little man," I heard him say again. I was so glad I came straight home, or Mr. Gibson and a few others would probably be dead by now.

After all the excitement I went home and started dinner. Mama had four Cornish hens in the refrigerator. I checked the recipe book on how to prepare them and what would go with them. I decided to make a cranberry stuffing for them with steamed cabbage and Tehh's baked cheesy potatoes. One thing I learned is that if you can read and follow instructions, you can do just about anything. For dessert I was making peach cobbler with ice cream. Everything smelled so good. All of a sudden there was a knock at the back door. I knew it was Miss Emma. I turned up the music like I didn't hear her. She just continued to knock, and I continued to act like I didn't hear her. Then there was a knock at the front door. I went to see who it was. It was Miss Emma. I should have known. "How you doing, Miss Emma?" I said.

She said, "Tehh, turn that loud music down, boy. I have been knocking for the longest, and you didn't hear me. I know your mama ain't home. Is that you doing the cooking?"

I said, "Yes, ma'am."

"It sure smells good. Well, tell your mama I'll be over for dinner, okay?"

I said, "Yes, ma'am," as she walked away. *That's one strange woman,* I thought. A man almost died. His house was on fire right across from us. Smoke was everywhere. The firemen came with the truck blasting, and she couldn't hear or smell that. But she could hear my music and smell food cooking in our kitchen. I just didn't get it.

Everybody came home tired and hungry, including Miss Emma, and we enjoyed dinner. Later that evening after Miss Emma left, we talked about our trip to the other side of town. I asked Mama if we could spend the night at a hotel. We had never done that before. We were all so excited and went to bed. Since Mama had a car, we could get up early and eat breakfast in a restaurant on that side of town. We had never done that either.

CHAPTER 14

It was Saturday morning, and we were so excited you would have thought it was Christmas. We all got ready and got in the car to go to the other side of town. I told everybody to take a good look at Box City and see how things were going to change when we got on the other side of town. Diamond and Benjamin sat in the backseat looking from one side of the highway to the other. Suddenly, Diamond said, "Look, Mama. It's so clean over here, ain't it?"

Then Benjamin said, "Look, y'all. Ain't nobody's drawers hanging up on clotheslines either." I just enjoyed them seeing life from a different point of view. Mama stopped at a nice restaurant, and we got out and went in. The hostess took us over to a table by the window and gave us a menu. That was a first for us too. I told everybody to look at the menu and pick out what they liked for breakfast. The waitress would be over and ask us what we wanted. That's the way they did it on television. The waitress came over and brought us water and a plate of hot biscuits with butter and jam, and we didn't even ask for them. That was so nice of her. Then Diamond asked Mama if that was all we were going to get to eat because she was hungry. The waitress smiled and said, "No, sugar, they are for you to enjoy while we fix your breakfast." Then she asked us for our order, starting with Mama. We slowly looked around to see how the other folks conducted themselves, and we tried to do the same.

Occasionally I noticed people watching us. There were very few colored people in the place, mainly because it was so expensive. We all ate biscuits and talked until they brought out our breakfast. It really looked and smelled so good. In fact, it looked like the breakfast we cooked at home. We laughed and talked about how we could live like this all the time. Mama would look at me and smile because she knew that we could. Benjamin leaned over and asked me if I thought they would bring us some more biscuits and ham to take with us. I told him to ask when the waitress came back. I wanted him to learn how to conduct himself in public when we went out. The waitress came back to see if she could help us with anything else, and Benjamin said, "May we have some more biscuits to go please ... with ham," and he blew my mind. I was so proud of him.

The waitress smiled and said, "You sure can," and she brought us more biscuits and ham. Mama paid the bill and left a twenty-dollar tip for the waitress because she was so nice.

We left there after having a very pleasant first time eating-out experience. We got in the car and drove off, enjoying the view. Mama saw a nice hotel with a swimming pool and asked us if we wanted to spend the night there. We all told her yes. We had never stayed in a hotel before, especially one this nice. All we were used to seeing in our area were those roach motels. She pulled into the parking lot, and we all got out and went inside. Mama was so happy that she could afford to stay in a nice hotel. She went up to the desk and made the reservation. Mama asked the clerk if they had a room with two bedrooms, and the clerk told her they did. We were so excited. Mama said that she would take it and asked if we could go on in. The clerk smiled and said the room was ready. Mama paid the lady, and she gave her the key. It was a ground-floor unit near the pool, restaurant, exercise room, and a lot of other stuff. It was really nice. The room was magnificent. It had a living room with a television, a small kitchen and a dining table and another television. Man, we were in heaven. For the very first time in my life I saw how the white folks lived, and I was glad to be rich, even if it was a secret rich.

Mama was truly where she belonged. This was like heaven to her. She and Diamond just fell backward on the big queen-size bed with some of the softest pillows I had ever seen. Mama just laid there, soaking up the comfort. We watched television for a while and later asked Mama if we could go swimming. Diamond said, "But Mama, we don't have no swimming suits." Mama smiled and gave us money to buy swimsuits at the store in the hotel. We came back to the room, put on our swimsuits, and went out to the pool to have a good time. There were quite a few white people already having fun there. We weren't noisy, disrespectful, or anything. We were having so much fun that we didn't notice that we were the only ones left in the pool. All I could say was that their loss was our gain. Diamond said that she wanted to do like the people on television and sit in the lounge chair and read a book with her shades on. Then she asked, "How do I look?"

I smiled and said, "Just like the people on television. You are a natural born star, Diamond." She just sat there, smiling. We finished and went back to our room, showered, and got ready to hit the road again.

Mama gave all of us one hundred dollars to spend. She told us that when our money was gone, that was it. Diamond asked Mama if she had given herself a hundred dollars because it wouldn't be fair if she didn't have any money to spend. Mama told her that she had given herself a hundred dollars to spend as well. Diamond was very compassionate when it came to Mama. That was mainly because I always told them that we had to always look out for Mama and treat her right because she made so many sacrifices for us. Mama saw a store with restaurant equipment in it, and we went in and looked around. She said that if she decided to open the restaurant, she had an idea of what she wanted in it. She wrote down all the items with their prices. Diamond and Benjamin even helped by suggesting things that children would love. Mama's total came to twenty-five thousand dollars for everything to start a restaurant.

Diamond said, "Wow, Mama, you are going to have to wait until I finish college and get a good job to get that restaurant because that's a lot of money."

Mama smiled and said, "The Lord will make a way, sugar." We left and went to several department stores and everybody bought something, watching their spending.

We were back in the car and on the road again when I saw a little antique shop from the road. It was very colorful and really caught my eye. That's what I wanted mine to do. I asked Mama if we could stop and go in. It was pretty much like what I had in mind. It was very spacious. It had everything, including furniture. As we looked around, I watched how the salespeople were conducting themselves. They were all very friendly and knowledgeable of the merchandise. There were a lot of people in the store, and no one complained about waiting in line. The prices were very reasonable. There was no dust or clutter. Everything was very clean and well organized. I even heard a customer ask if they could order certain items from the catalogs they had, and the clerk said they could. That was very good to know. I went and looked in the catalogs and made a mental note of them for my store. I thanked Mama for bringing me over, and we left. She told me it was a very good idea to come because I had in storage a lot of the stuff they had in their store. Now I had an idea of how to price my merchandise and stay competitive. All I had to do now was follow my plan.

We were back on the road, and Benjamin wanted to get a few items for his upcoming trip to Washington, DC. He picked out some nice things with his seventy dollars. By now we were all hungry, and Mama stopped at another nice restaurant for lunch. Diamond said she wanted shrimp and couldn't pronounce it. Benjamin wanted lobster but was afraid to pick it out and didn't want it killed. Mama said she always wanted a T-bone steak, and I just wanted some good old fried chicken and a strawberry soda. We all had a great time. The food was absolutely delicious, and Benjamin enjoyed his lobster. We left and went to the hotel and rested. We were too stuffed to do anything else for a while. Benjamin asked if we could go to the movies later, and we all agreed. This was the best family day out we had ever had.

We all went to our rooms and took a nap. We awoke up from our nap and were sitting around and talking when there was a knock at the door. We all looked at each other and said, "Not Miss Emma." Mama smiled, got up, and went to the door. It was the hotel clerk with a big basket of fruits and snacks. We all laughed, and Mama thanked the lady and sat everything on the table. She just stood there, looked at the basket, and said, "This is like a dream that I wish would never end."

We all got ready to go to the movies. Mama stopped by the front desk and asked the clerk, "Where is the nearest movie theater?" The clerk told her that it was three blocks down and to the right. We pulled up to one of the largest movie theaters I had ever seen in my life. It was like there were a million cars there already. Mama drove around that huge parking lot, trying to find a closer parking space. Suddenly someone pulled out, and Mama said, "Thank You, Jesus," and pulled in. We all got out and went up to the window. There were so many movies on the board we didn't know where to start. Then all of sudden we said, "That one!" It was our favorite superhero. Mama paid for our tickets, and we went in. We all went up to the concession counter and got hot dogs, popcorn, candy, and soft drinks, and then we went in to enjoy the movie. The screen was so big that it was like you were in the movie itself. Every now and then I would hear Mama say, "Oh, my goodness."

Mama decided we should leave a little early so we wouldn't have to spend the night in the parking lot because of all the cars. We knew what was going to happen at the end of the movie because we had seen it on television. Seeing it at the movies on the big screen was the best thing ever. That was a first for us too. We made it to the car and got out of there. We arrived at the hotel, went to our rooms, and went to sleep. There wasn't a sound to be heard other than Benjamin's snoring.

It was Sunday, the day of dread for us because we were going back home to Box City. Mama told us to cheer up because we had the whole day to enjoy. She still had a little money, and we could eat out and do a few other things. This was our vacation. We asked Mama to let us try a different restaurant this time for breakfast. We pulled up to "The Pig in a Blanket Restaurant." The sign outside read, "Grandma's good old home-style cooking with a smile." I really wanted to see what it was like. We stood and waited to be served for several minutes as people passed us by. When we did get a seat, it took the longest to get service. I guess the sign wasn't for colored folks. I asked Mama if we could go back where we had breakfast the day before, and we left. Then someone came rushing over to see if they could help us after we were leaving. We went to the other restaurant anyway. The people waited on us quickly, and we had the same waitress. She brought us a big plate of biscuits with jam and took our order. We ate biscuits and talked about how we enjoyed ourselves and asked Mama if we could come again. Mama said that she would think about it and see how much money she could save in a couple of months. Just maybe we would come back. Benjamin and Diamond were so excited about that. I looked at my mama, and she looked ten years younger. She was so beautiful. She had bought herself a beautiful orange and white dress and a pair of shoes with her hundred dollars, and she was looking good. The way she was looking she could turn any man's head.

As I sat there waiting for our food, I noticed that a man kept looking toward our table. He was well dressed and apparently had some money since he was eating in this place. He came over and introduced himself as Harold Crumpton. He said that it seemed like he had seen Mama somewhere before. Mama was reluctant and told him that we didn't live in the area. There was no way possible he could have known her. He smiled and said that he thought it may have been over in Box City at the bakery. She had on a uniform then, but the smile was still the same. Mama wiped the smut look off her face and smiled. She apologized and told him that she worked at Ricko's Bakery in Box City. He laughed and said, "That was it. I thought I recognized you when I saw you." He told Mama she probably never saw him because she was usually busy in the back. He said Ricko's had some of the best muffins he had ever eaten. He would drive all the way over there just to get them. The waitress brought our breakfast, and then Mr. Crumpton asked if he could join us since he was alone. Mama told him that he could.

I thought to myself, *This man is trying to hit on my mama in front of her children.* Then Diamond leaned over and whispered in my ear, "Tehh, Mama got a boyfriend."

I said, "No she don't. Be quiet."

It turned out that he was a real nice man. He was respectful not to just Mama but to me, Diamond, and Benjamin, which was a first. His wife died five years ago of breast cancer, and they had no children. He took the insurance money and decided to start his own business since that's what she always wanted him to do. He owned Crumpton's Big and Tall Men's Clothing Store about twenty-five miles from Box City. He said he wanted to open up another store and thought about Box City. He just wasn't sure if it was a safe investment because he didn't see any new business start-ups there.

"When I see some new businesses come to Box City, I'm going to join them," he said.

We all finished breakfast and said our good-byes. The waitress brought us a bag of biscuits, jam, and ham for the road. Mr. Crumpton told Mama that he would see her around at the bakery sometimes. It was really good to see a nice, professional man interested in my mama, and hear that someone was interested in opening a business in Box City one day. Mama was getting ready to pay for our breakfast when Mr. Crumpton asked her to let him pay for it, and she let him. Mama looked at me and smiled. He paid the bill and left a big tip too. Mama had never had anyone take all of us out and pay for it, not even at a burger joint. I knew she would be smiling all the way home.

We left there and hit the road. We stopped in various places and picked up a few things for the house. As we were headed toward home, I saw a sign that said, "New homes. Open house today." I asked Mama if we could look. We pulled into this beautiful gated community and got out and looked around. One house really caught Mama's eyes. She just stood there, looking at it like she was in a trance.

I asked, "What's wrong?"

She said, "The house is so pretty I'm afraid to go in it." We all grabbed her by the arms and pulled her into the house, and she was just amazed. She said she had never been in a house so beautiful before in her life. It had everything, three bedrooms, three bathrooms, walk-in closet in every room, huge kitchen, formal dining room, a two-car garage, large backyard with a patio and swimming pool. Mama was like a child in a candy store. I didn't realize people had houses like that. She whispered in my ear and said, "I really like this house. Can we afford it?"

I told her we could, but we should wait a while and let our money build up some more before we invested most of it on a house at that time. We left that house and looked at some more. Inside every house she would ask the same question, "Can we afford this one?" We left there feeling pretty good about what we wanted to see in a house when the time came to get one. Each of us talked about the house we liked the best and what room we wanted. Mama was so excited that she just wore herself out. She told us this was the best weekend of her life, and she owed it all to the Lord and me. We got home, said good night, and everyone went to bed without a struggle.

I got up early that Monday morning and fixed breakfast, thinking about our wonderful weekend. I must say it was great to have money. Otherwise it never would have happened. I just couldn't stop smiling as I thought about how happy my mama was and that a wealthy man took notice of her.

CHAPTER 15

It was my first day of school to get my GED, and I was so nervous. I had to be at the library at eight o'clock, and I didn't want to be a minute late. Everyone got up, ate breakfast and got ready to follow their daily routine. Diamond and Benjamin went to school, and Mama went to work. I asked her to give me a lift to the library so we could talk about our plans for another weekend with Diamond and Benjamin. Before I knew it, we were at the library. She dropped me off and I went in. I was the first one there, and I couldn't sit still. All I could think about was my future and how it depended on me getting an education. I thought about the guys getting their education and how I was going to inspire them to do it. I believe the worst thing people can do is be afraid to take a chance on themselves. I don't care how people try to squash your dreams. If *you* can believe it, you can achieve it—that is, if you are willing to work hard for it. People have put me down all of my life and said that I was nobody, but something on the inside of me wouldn't let me believe that. I trusted what was on the inside of me. I built myself a little wagon and collected junk here and there and discovered the underground city and found more than a half million dollars plus other stuff. I bought that city and more. *Now I am somebody, but don't nobody know it.* My mind was going ninety miles a minute, thinking about me and Box City. If things were going to change, it had to start with me first. I had to do it. Failure was not an option. If I was a genius, this was the time to prove it. I paced that floor so many times, thinking and looking at the clock until I got dizzy. Finally several teachers came in followed by students, and I was so relieved.

I went into a classroom and took my seat with the other students and teachers. There were about sixty students in the class and most of them were white. I didn't realize there were so many white folks who didn't have an education. There were Mexicans, Chinese, two people from Africa, and some other strange-looking people from around the world, but no real colored folks, except me. The one thing we all had in common was that we were there to get an education to better our lives. The teacher was very nice. Her name was Mrs. Mumford. She and the other teachers were going to work as hard as they could to help us. She explained that without an education it was hard to get a job, obtain a driver's license, or even find your way around town. The class was divided into groups of twenty and assigned to different teachers. I kept Mrs. Mumford, who had two other teachers with her. We were given several textbooks to start with. They were simple reading, writing, and arithmetic. It was like the sixth grade all over again for me. Mrs. Mumford said she wanted to start there to see where everyone was. Hopefully by the end of the year we should all be pretty much at the same level. That sounded so good to me. We spent most of the day spelling and writing sentences. It was sad to see that so many people had difficulty writing a simple sentence. I told myself that I was not going to be difficult or try to be a know-it-all. I was going to go through the whole process just like I didn't know so that I could teach everything to the guys. I asked the teacher if we could take our papers and books home. She told us we could. This way I would have something to show the guys to prove to them that I was in school. She encouraged us to keep up with our books because we would have to pay for them if we lost them. When class was over, she asked us to take a few minutes to get to know one another each day, and we did.

After I left school, I felt kind of strange going home without my wagon. I looked around and saw several trash piles. Some had some unusual stuff that I could use in my shop when it opened. Mama called the real estate office for me to have someone come out and start remodeling the building. I just couldn't wait to see it when it was finished. I stopped and got me something to eat and went home and got my wagon. I still had a couple of hours to kill, and then I would go home and start dinner.

While I was walking up the street, I saw those same bankers again sitting on the bench. I thought I would go over and hear what they were talking about. I pretended I was looking in the trash as they talked. One banker said, "Somebody got some money around here because they have been buying up a lot of these properties. Several buildings have been sold already, even our bank."

The other banker said, "What? You mean we didn't buy our own bank building? Now that's something. Somebody did some research to know that we hadn't bought the bank."

The other one said, "It had to be an investor. Ain't nobody around here got that kind of money! It's got to be one of those out-of-town tycoons coming in here. They're always looking for places to invest."

Then the other banker said, "The family must have advertised these buildings for sale everywhere, and those investors quickly hopped on the deal."

"That's probably right. Those investors will come in here and buy up everything and build a shopping mall or a sports complex in a minute." Then he smiled and said, "Man, that's good business for us and the bank." They finished talking and went back into the bank. That was some more good information for me to know. *So ain't nobody around here got that kind of money, huh?* If I had been a snake, I could have bitten them both.

I left there and went on over to the trash piles I saw. I began putting stuff in my wagon and noticed some strange little boxes. It was about twenty of them packed together. I opened one, and there was jewelry. I put it back quickly to open when I got home so that I wouldn't attract attention. Apparently the family was having this vacant building cleaned out to sell it. There were several antique pieces of furniture, boxes of linens, and a lot of stuff I would check later. I had to make several trips for this one. I had run out of space in our storage room, so I asked Miss Emma if I could put it in hers. She said I could and gave me the key. It was about time she paid for all of those free meals she had been getting. I decided to call it a day and went in and watched television for a while. I sat there, watching cartoons. They were so funny. Then I thought about how happy Diamond and Benjamin had been during our weekend trips. I wanted them to finish high school, go to college, and make something of themselves so badly. That's why I just had to get my GED so I could go to college and be an example for them and Box City.

It was now late May, and there was a nice breeze in the air. It was going to be barbeque ribs day at the Hancock's house. I was going to cook them outside myself, even though I had never done it before. I remembered seeing people cooking them on the other side of town on one of our weekends there and was very impressed. I got Mama's cookbook and thought I would try one of those recipes. I knew Miss Emma was going to come running, so I had to look stupid just for her. I fixed up a crazy contraption to barbeque on. I took an old, beat-up, rusty washtub, an old grill rack, which I washed thoroughly with bleach, some wood, and charcoal. I sat the tub on some bricks for height, put the wood and the charcoal inside, and started the fire. I got a chair and a table to sit all of my meat on. I had bought some ribs from the grocery store, but I took all the meat out of the refrigerator freezer to put on the grill. All the meat was seasoned and looking good. I put ribs, chicken, burgers, hot dogs, and anything else I could find on the fire. I knew I needed to have some water on hand just in case the fire blazed up. Man, I was so proud of myself. I sat there listening to the smooth sound of the music, and dying of smoke inhalation as the wind would blow the smoke my way. They didn't mention that would happen in the cookbook at all. Everything smelled so good. Before I knew it, there she was, Miss Emma. "Boy, what you doing out here?" she asked.

"Cooking barbeque, Miss Emma," I said.

"You sure you know what you doing, Tehh?"

Then I got a visual of Miss Emma roasting on a barbecue rack with an apple in her mouth. "Yes, ma'am, Miss Emma," I said.

"You sure got it set up pretty sturdy and it smells so good to, Tehh."

"Thank you, Miss Emma," I said. I thought I would test her. "You want a hot dog, Miss Emma? That's all that's ready right now." She took a couple of hot dogs so quick you would have thought she was a thief.

She smiled and told me to be careful and not to burn up the meat because she wanted some of that. Then came those famous last words before every meal. "Tell your mama I will be over for dinner, okay?" Then she left.

Before she could get in the house, all the neighbors were coming to see what was happening on the back of the apartment. They thought something was on fire because of all the smoke. They checked out my grill and asked me a few questions, and before I knew it, the whole neighborhood was barbequing. They made all kinds of barbeque contraptions. The man next door made one with a wheelbarrow. If Box City didn't look good right then, it sure smelled good. I cooked all my meat, went in the house, and made the potato salad, bake beans, and chocolate cake. I sometimes wondered why I loved to cook so much. I guess when I taught my mama how to bake, it did something to me. It started my own creative juices flowing. I discovered that I enjoyed cooking and watching people enjoy eating what I cooked even more. Not only that, but we were a family, and we all had to pull our weight. I got home first. Mama shouldn't have to do it all. We all enjoyed sharing the responsibility so our house runs smoothly. As the older child, I set the example, and Diamond and Benjamin followed. I try so hard to keep them positive in a negative society that it becomes exhausting sometimes.

Benjamin came home first and talked about how hungry he was. He was smelling barbecue everywhere, and it was just killing him. He said it smelled so good that he wished we had some. Then he said the smell was all over the house. He went in the kitchen to get a glass of water and came back and gave me a big hug. He said, "Thanks, man. You are the best brother in the world." I told him to get a hot dog till dinner.

Then Diamond came in saying she smelled barbeque everywhere. It made her so hungry she didn't know what to do. She went in the kitchen, came back, gave me a big hug, and said, "That's why I love you so much, Tehh. You really know how to please a girl." I told her to get a hot dog till dinner.

Then Mama came home all out of breath. "My goodness," she said, "the smell of barbeque is everywhere. Tehh, the next time we go to the grocery store, let's get a few ribs. That smell is killing me." She gave us all hugs and went in the kitchen to get some water and came back and gave me an even bigger hug. "I just don't know what I am going to do with you, Thomas Edison Hamilton Hancock. You never cease to amaze me." I asked her if she wanted a hot dog or if we were ready for dinner. She said, "Let's eat now, honey!" We all washed up for dinner and came back into the kitchen.

On the way home from school I had picked up some flowers for Diamond. I put them in the center of the table, and she just smiled. I saw a tear fall from her eye. She said they were so beautiful and they always made her feel so good. "Thanks, Tehh. I love you so much," she said. I asked Benjamin to bang on the wall for Miss Emma. Diamond counted her down. Fifteen seconds flat, and she was knocking at the back door. Mama let her in, and she joined us at the table. The ribs were truly a best seller. Everyone was enjoying them, including me. Miss Emma told us with a rib still in her mouth, "These are the best ribs I have ever had in my life. What did you do to them?"

One thing I learned is to never give away your trade secrets. "I told you, Meyel, you need to open up a restaurant. You should have seen what

Tehh was cooking this meat on, and it tastes like this. The boy is a genius no matter what they say. Child, I tell you, you are one blessed woman with children like these. You don't have to make them do nothing. They just do it! I never hear you fussing at these children." Mama smiled and thanked her. Then she asked Miss Emma if she was going to come and work for her when she opened up the restaurant. Miss Emma jumped up from the table and said, "Girl, yes! You really gonna do it? Meyel, I am telling you the truth. Whatever you want me to do. Child, I will do it. You are like a sister to me!"

Then Mama said, "Guess what, y'all?"

We all said, "What!"

She said, "We are going to open up a restaurant with a bakery in it. What do y'all think about that?" We were all so excited. We jumped up from the table and hugged her. Our trips really paid off. Mama had finally made up her mind. We had talked about a building we owned that would be perfect for a restaurant. All she had to do was have it renovated. My mind was beginning to take off. I had to make myself stop thinking so I could enjoy my ribs. Then Miss Emma asked me, "What did you put in the baked beans to make them taste so good?"

"Nothing really," I said, "but beans," and everybody laughed. Then I thought, *Wait until I put the cake on the table.* I decided to make it look like a cake from the bakery, but it was what was inside that made the difference. Everyone was so excited when they cut into the cake and saw the cream filling with walnuts, strawberries, and caramel running out. It was just delicious. Mama jumped up from the table and said, "This cake is coming to my restaurant."

Miss Emma was licking her fork and smacking, saying, "Lord, yes!"

CHAPTER 16

Nearly a year has passed, and things were progressing as planned in spite of a few setbacks. I got arrested for driving Mama's car. Here I was trying to get my life together, and something like that happened to me. One evening I driving home from a meeting. A policeman recognized me as the dummy pushing the wagon and pulled me over. I didn't usually drive without my beards and stuff. I just forgot to put it on. After I felt comfortable about going to school, I forgot that people still recognized me as the dummy who couldn't read, write or understand, especially the police. I had traded my wagon for a car too soon. I could just imagine what the poor man was thinking. *He is going to kill somebody in that car.* They actually thought I had stolen the car, and they took me straight to jail. Because I was so scared, I stuttered really bad. That didn't help the situation at all. I tried to explain while I was stuttering that I could read and write, and that I was in school, but they wouldn't believe me. If there was ever a time I appeared dumb for real. It was at that moment. I was absolutely a helpless mess because I was so scared. They put me in a cell and slammed the door behind me. All I could think about was what I had seen on television about how they treated young colored prisoners. All I could see in my mind was some big old guy name Juice trying to take advantage of me. They called my mama with my one phone call, and she came down all upset. They wouldn't believe her either when she tried to tell them that I was in school. They said they were sorry, but they had to have proof. That meant they had to speak to the school administrators. They were convinced that we were lying. I couldn't believe it when I saw my picture on the jailhouse wall, pushing my wagon. Under it read, "Mental person but harmless. Approach with caution." No wonder the police were always on my case and telling me to move on when they saw me.

Since it was a Friday evening and school was closed until Monday, I had to spend the weekend in jail. I thought about how this was going to ruin my record and how I had messed up my future. Something on the inside was telling me that everything was going to be okay and to calm down. I could have had Mama call our lawyer, but I decided to keep a low profile unless things got worse. I may be dumb to them, but I certainly knew my rights. I told Mama what to do just in case. Reading those law books really came in handy. She came to the jail each day to check on me and brought me a few goodies from the bakery. I had never been in jail, so I got to see it firsthand. It was definitely not a nice place to be. There were several cots and a toilet in the corner. I hated to think what would happen if several people had to use the toilet at the same time. Was I scared? You'd better believe I was. Here I was a seventeen-year-old secret millionaire, the only one in Box City thrown in jail with all kinds of criminals. There were actually bout nine at the time, but my mind was playing tricks on me.

I was relieved when I heard one of the policemen tell another one to keep an eye on me and make sure I was okay. Thank God there were no hardened criminals in there. He said I was a pretty good kid and that I probably didn't know what I was doing. I was probably playing around with the car, and it drove off. He was surprised that I knew how to stop it. He said they just wanted to teach me a lesson so I wouldn't steal cars anymore. After I listened to the policeman, I wondered if this was part of God's plan for me too. Jail definitely was never a part of my plan. Strangely enough, it allowed me to take a closer look at some of the men in Box City in a different light. Several of the guys in jail said they saw me all the time pushing my wagon around town and asked me what I did to wind up in there? I started stuttering all over again, and they just laughed. I finally got my nerves together and began talking to them like a normal person. It was a very interesting three days with the men wanting to talk to me about school and stuff.

Monday came, and Mama called the school. They verified that I was indeed a student there and one of their brightest. The policeman apologized, cleared my record, and let me go. One of them told Mama that they kept a watch out for me because inside he felt that I was a good kid. I thanked God for that man. Mama told him that I was the best kid in the world. She invited him to her restaurant for lunch when it opened in a few weeks. He asked, "What kind of school are you attending, son?" I told him I was getting my GED next month and starting college in the fall. He looked over at my picture on the wall, pulled it down and threw it in the trash. "Good for you, Mr. Hancock. Good for you," he said.

Looking back on my jailhouse experience and talking with some of the guys, I realized they had great potential but just didn't know it. They too, had been sucked into the hopeless mentality of Box City. They were just looking to get something for nothing, or a handout. It wasn't drugs or murder or anything like that they were there for. It was stealing and selling hot merchandise to get a quick buck. It had never entered their minds to get a job or an education to better themselves. They just kept saying there were no jobs and accepted it. They never realized that they could have created their own jobs. Some didn't want to be like me pushing a wagon and trying to give somebody advice. However, two of the guys were so impressive that I invited them to our meeting when they got out. They were very smart guys with a lot to offer Box City if they were given the chance. They just needed a push in the right direction.

CHAPTER 17

As I looked back over my life, thinking about what I've accomplished in a very short period of time. I had to pinch myself. We now at this point own four apartment buildings, and none of the tenants knew that we were the owners. The amazing thing is that we were getting ready to remodel our apartment building, but it made no sense to remodel it and have three eyesores in front of us. So we decided to buy them too. It was a great decision. We remodeled them and added an on-site laundromat in each unit to keep folks from hanging clothes outside. Shrubbery and grass was planted. Each apartment has its own privacy fence in the back and a barbeque grill for safety. Those homemade grills were getting dangerous and causing fires. There was now a beautiful playground and park area. Our section of the street looked really good.

Every three months there's a tenant's meeting with food and door prizes to keep them informed. If there was food, you could just about expect a full house. The cost of remodeling those apartment buildings and the small increase in rent was always discussed in the meeting. I tell you that investment cost us a pretty penny. The tenants were asked if they felt better living in a nicer apartment building, and they would always say, "Yes." They had to know that if they lived on the other side of town in the very same apartment, they would have had an increase of nearly two hundred dollars a month. Our apartments were much better. Just knowing that changed their attitudes. Everyone was told that the owners of the buildings would hate to go up that much on their rent. All they had to do was take care of their apartment building and the surroundings, and their rent would remain low. Was it working? You bet your bottom dollar it was.

I remembered what the banker said. "You would have to reprogram these people for that kind of change." That's what I did as a twenty-five-year-old Mr. Edison in one of my disguises. The tenants thought I drove down from Tennessee to let them know what the owners planned for them. The owners did consider a low-cost on-site daycare center that would help the working mothers. Those mothers who wanted to go back to school or get jobs would not have to worry about finding childcare. This opportunity would also create jobs for those in the complex. I told them about all the free educational opportunities available to them and the possibility of a training facility in the near future. I knew education would be the key to our success in Box City. Each tenant who tried to get their GED or went back to school would get twenty dollars off of their rent each month. If Box City was going to change, it was going to have to begin with each of them and spread to the rest of the city. It made me feel really good to walk out of my apartment door and see all the progress.

My antique store was up and running, and it was a big hit in the community. The store had already profited more than one hundred thousand dollars with four store clerks—one white, one colored, one from India, and one from Mexico. That profit was mainly because of several famous oil paintings that had been thrown away from that old antique shop. Each of my store clerks brought a certain flair to the interior design of how items were displayed in their area of the store. Each clerk was assigned an area to keep stocked and maintained. I encourage them to use their artistic abilities to make the store more appealing. They also helped in ordering items from their countries they thought customers would like. I had two experienced managers—a white manager and a colored assistant manager who worked well with me (Tehh) and the clerks. I got the idea of hiring the different races from the people in my class. The lady from India was a classmate, but she didn't know that I was actually her boss. That way the store catered to all the people in Box City, not just colored and white. The shop looked breathtaking from the street.

All the junk that I collected off the street was actually very valuable merchandise after I had it all appraised. It was cleaned up and sold to antique dealers and collectors or beautifully displayed in my store. I had so much stuff at home and in Miss Emma's storage room that I had to rent two trucks to move it from our home to the store. There was an overflow room for merchandise before it went out to the floor. That way when an item was sold, it was quickly replaced.

When I did the interviews to hire people for my antique shop, it was so funny. I put on one of the wigs and beards that I had ordered and changed my voice. I told the applicants that I was Mr. Hamilton from Atlanta, Georgia, handling the business for the new owner. It really worked. In fact, it worked so well that a woman came in and it seemed like she wanted to give me more than an interview. She had to be twenty-five or so. I was so nervous, but I tried not to show it at the time. She wanted to know all about me. She asked, "Where do you live in Georgia? Where are you staying in Box City? Are you married?" She crossed her legs and hiked her skirt way above her knees. Quickly I told her that I was happily, happily, happily married to one of the greatest women in the world and I wasn't looking for anyone else. She wiped the smile off of her face, got up, and left. I was so relieved. I didn't anticipate anything like that happening at all. I didn't know what else to do. I didn't even have a girlfriend at the time. I never saw anything happen like that on television. I may have looked and sounded like a man on the outside, but I was still a boy on the inside. The school of life was really teaching me how to become a man.

The clerks in my store knew that twice a week Tehh (me) worked there part-time. This way I got to see what was going on, and how they handled the customers, the merchandise, and my money. They all respected me as an employee and asked for my help when needed. For bringing in a good profit all of the employees were rewarded with a monetary gift each month, even Tehh. That was the part they loved best, and they gave more than a hundred percent to their jobs. My managers deposited all the money in the appropriate accounts. Mr. Hamilton (me) came to town once a month to check the books to make sure everything was running smoothly.

I also remodeled and leased several other office buildings, and the tenants are doing great and enjoying their new renovations. Right now I have a lot to be thankful for being seventeen years old and getting ready to start college in the fall. One thing I have learned from all of this is that success is possible when you are willing to work hard to achieve it, and keep an open mind. It's not about how old you are but your determination.

Mama opened her restaurant, and it was a whopping success. I tell you that Box City was hungry for all of my recipes. Miss Emma was definitely right. Mama had twenty-five full and part-time employees. Some worked in the restaurant and some in the bakery. Her working at Ricko's was great job experience. He never thought she was smart enough to own her own business. He nearly had a heart attack when she told him she was leaving. She learned everything about the baking business from him. The inspiration came from me and Miss Emma, but the reality of it all came from God. It was in her all the time. Mama took that leap of faith and took a chance on herself for the first time in her life. She was truly Ricko's competition, but she was fair. There were some bakery items that could only be bought at Ricko's. She told me that we were already millionaires and he was not. She named the restaurant Meyel's Family Restaurant, and that was truly what it was. Everyone was treated like family.

On the days I was not at my store or checking on the million other things I was doing, I was helping out at the restaurant, managing Mama's books. She even gave Toe Joe, Jason, Mad Dog, and Brock jobs to work after school. Yes, they were in school trying to get their GEDs. Nothing came easy with these guys. It was really hard convincing them, but they made up their minds and gave it a try. They felt that if a person like me who couldn't read, write, or understand could write a decent sentence the way I did. They could do it too. I was so proud of those guys that when they started the class, I added a thousand dollars to their savings account. That was just how serious I was about getting an education. I must say that I never told them what I did. Mad Dog finally learned the value of a dollar. The guys all have a better outlook on life now and feel good about themselves.

Through hard work, we added twenty other members to our Finang Gang of Box City, and they were getting ready to start their GEDs. Our gang was very exclusive. I personally checked them out before they joined. They had to really want something out of life. We didn't play around. We meant business. My investment was too great to waste. They had to want to get an education and commit to it and follow our rules and regulations. One of those requirements was to save their money. If they could complete college, they didn't have to worry about looking for jobs. I would automatically put them to work, but they didn't know that.

The guys sometimes forgot that we were around the same age, and they would accidently say to me, "Yes, sir." They said it was something about my voice at times that commanded respect because I spoke like a much older person. That being said, I didn't make it an issue of it. We all met in the office next door to Mama's bakery. On the days the gang meet, she loads us up with food and drinks. Mama became a member too. She wanted to get her GED so she could be a better example to her family and employees. She finally realized that she needed the knowledge to stay successful. The place was set up like an actual classroom, and I was the teacher. I taught them the exact way I was taught at school so that when they started, the transition would be easy for them. No one ever knew that I was rich. They just knew that I was Tehh. The boy who was once dumb but was now getting his GED and going to college in the fall. I think remaining humble has been the key to my success. Most kids my age would have gotten big heads and told the world they were rich and probably lost everything.

CHAPTER 18

One day I decided to pull my wagon out of retirement and hit the streets. While I was looking for junk, I noticed the city was looking a lot better. There wasn't a lot of paper lying around, and there were very few junk piles. It looked like people were trying to put me out of business for good. Business owners were putting flowers in front of their stores. A number of buildings had been painted or sandblasted. There was a different attitude in the people now. Maybe it was because of the huge signs I had put up throughout the city that said, "A bigger and more beautiful Box City on the rise. Join us in helping to make this the cleanest city in the USA." The sign had a beautiful picture of a new Box City that was breathtaking. This was all part of my reprogramming plan. Nearly everyone thought that some out-of-state investors had them put up. They wondered what they were going to bring to Box City to make it better. I went on down the road a piece, counting the vacant buildings that had been leased. I looked up and couldn't believe it. It was Crumpton's Big and Tall Clothing Store for Men. Mr. Crumpton kept his word, and was leasing one of my buildings. I parked my wagon and went in. He was hanging up some beautiful sweaters. "How you doing, Mr. Crumpton?" I said.

He jumped and said, "My Lord, how you doing there, Tehh? It's good to see you, son," and he gave me a hug. "It has been a while, hasn't it? How is Benjamin and Diamond?" he asked.

"They are fine, Mr. Crumpton," I said.

"And how is your mama?" I told him she was just fine. "I noticed that she wasn't at Ricko's bakery anymore. It kind of killed my appetite for muffins."

I told him that she opened up her own restaurant and bakery a few blocks over. "She makes tasty muffins there too."

"Say what?" he said with excitement. I think it was more about Mama than the muffins. "I knew there was something special about your mama, son. She was such a hard worker. Your mama is one beautiful woman there, Tehh. I hope you don't mind me saying that."

I told him that I felt the same way. "Just look for Meyel's Family Restaurant and Bakery when you're hungry, Mr. Crumpton. You can't miss it because it's always crowded."

He said, "That's great, son. I'm proud of her." I asked him if he ever got married again. He told me he just hadn't found the right woman. "Your shop really looks good, Mr. Crumpton. How is your business going?" I asked.

He told me that it was kind of slow, but he thought business would pick up soon. He had the windows so cluttered with signs and stuff that it was hard to see all of the beautiful merchandise he had inside. I thought about the stores on the other side of town. There was no clutter in their windows, and that made you want to go inside to see more. I asked him if I could make a suggestion, and he said I could. I told him that the people in Box City were led by their eyes and not with their minds because many of them couldn't read. He wasn't aware that the majority of the people in Box City were illiterate. I suggested that he place some of those beautiful colors in the window and leave space so people could look in and see all of the beautiful clothes inside. I guaranteed him that his business would pick up in no time. He thanked me and said that he would do just that.

"Son, you live in this area, and you should know the people." Then he said, "Tell your mama I said hello. I just might go over to Meyel's Family Restaurant and Bakery for dinner tonight."

We said good-bye, and I was on my way. "Lord, if my mama has to marry any man, please let him be the man for her," I asked.

While I was walking along and pushing my wagon, I thought about an area of Box City that was still a major problem. It was the area where the pimps, prostitutes, and drug dealers hung out the most. Don't tell me that the police couldn't see that. On the other side of town I knew there was crime because crime is everywhere. However, they managed to keep it down. It seemed that here in Box City even the police didn't care. There were several abandoned buildings where those people hung out. The area was an eyesore, and I considered buying a few of the buildings if I could get them at a good price. I still had a few charitable dollars I could put into another area in Box

City. I had Mama call the real estate office and check on the price and to buy the property if it was for sale and she did.

You see, I didn't put all my money in one basket. I read that you can actually go broke that way. You have to keep good records and keep track of your money. Most people didn't do that around here. I had my business money to manage my business, like payroll, benefits, inventory, and stuff like that. I had my personal money. That was my profit, and it just sat there in the bank, growing. I had my investment money. That was the money I used to buy property, fix up businesses, buy stock, etc. I had my charity money. That was the money I gave away to a good cause. Then I had my pocket change for things I liked to do for myself and my family. A lot of people may not do this, but it worked for me. I have been calculating money most of my life, and I can pretty much tell you where every penny goes.

I thought a brand-new jailhouse would be perfect there. If someone was willing to donate the land and half the money, would the mayor take the bait? If we could reduce the territory of those drug dealers, pimps, and prostitutes that would force them to find another place to go outside of Box City. My goal was to drive the ills of our society out of Box City if they didn't want to change for the good of the city.

Going home one evening, I thought, *Since Mama got the restaurant, we haven't been together at home like a family for a while.* Diamond and Benjamin usually went to the restaurant to be with her after school. I really missed our family time at home together. I called Mama and asked her not to bring dinner home because I was going to cook and told her to bring Miss Emma too. I hated to say it, but I kind of missed her getting on my nerves. I stopped by the store to pick up a few items for dinner. I forgot I was supposed to be dumb and went in and got a basket to do my shopping myself. The clerk that usually helped me rushed over and asked me if I had the grocery list and told me that she would take care of it. I always kept a grocery list for me and Mama because we tried hard to avoid impulse buying. I gave it to her, and she did my shopping for me. She usually picked out the best meats I had ever seen. She rang me up, and I paid for my groceries. I thanked her and told her that I was going to get her a Christmas gift because she was so nice. She smiled, thanked me and then told me that I was so sweet.

Just as I was getting ready to go out the door, I turned and looked the other way for just a split second and ran into a basket. *Clang, clang, bang, bang* was all I heard. I quickly turned to say I was sorry, and there was the most beautiful smile I had ever seen again. It was the girl from my class before I was expelled. I told her I was so sorry, and she said, "That's okay. We really need to stop meeting this way."

I got my nerves together this time and said, "Tell me your name? I forgot to ask you the last time."

She smiled and said, "Alicestene Edwards." I forgot we had the store door blocked with our grocery baskets when a couple of customers asked us to let them by. We moved out of the way and continued to talk. She asked, "How have you been doing, and what have you been up to?" I told her I was fine and that I was getting my GED next month and starting college in the fall. She looked at me amazed with those beautiful puppy dog eyes, and said, "What? We are nearly the same age. You are going to college, and I will still be in high school. That is truly not fair." She folded her arms and shifted her hips and asked, "How did you do that?" Then she said, "You are kidding me, right? I don't believe you." She never let me answer one question before she was asking another. For a second it was almost like I was hearing my mama.

I said nervously, "I'm telling you the truth. If you don't believe me, come and see me get my GED diploma. What you got to say about that?"

Then she said, "Well, I have to ask my mama. If she says I can come, I will be there."

I had to really reach deep down within myself to ask her this question because I was about to fall apart. I took a deep breath and said, "Alicestene, can I have your phone number so I can call you sometimes?" She went in her purse and wrote her number on a piece of paper and gave it to me. She said she only gave me her number just to see if I was going to call and remind her about my graduation, and that was all. She said she knew that I was just fooling her anyway. I told her thanks and that I would call her for real. Then I said devilishly, "By the way, I'm really a genius. That's why I'm going to college so early."

Then she said, "Yeah, right," and turned to do her shopping. She had a really sweet walk as she sashayed away.

I went out the door, feeling like I did the day I found all that money. I felt like a conquering king, but I was so nervous. I put the groceries in my wagon and headed home. Every time I thought about Alicestene, I would get nervous all over again. My legs got weak, and my stomach started to feel funny. There had to be something special about this girl because I had never felt like this before. If I was getting a stomach virus or something, I needed to hurry home quickly. I pushed my wagon as fast as I could. I was breaking out in a sweat as I thought about her. I would get cold and hot again. All of a sudden my chest started tightening up. I had to take a rest. Then I said, "This is not a good time for me to die right now. I've got to get my GED if nothing else." I had to calm myself down. I took several deep breaths and tried to relax. I got up and headed home. Then I thought, *Say we hit it off. How could I tell her I was rich? She wouldn't believe me anyway. If she can't believe I am going to college, she definitely won't believe I am rich.* Then I said, "Look at you, man. You are pushing a wagon. No one would believe you." My mind was driving me crazy again. I had to quickly pull myself together and focus. One thing I was definitely not going to do was let a girl kill me before I got my GED. If she couldn't accept me as I was, a person trying to do the best he could with his wagon, then she didn't need to know that I was rich. I need a levelheaded girl who wants to help me make things better, and not spend every penny I made pushing my wagon. I wanted her to want me for me. If we did hit it off, that means I would have to meet her again. Time would definitely tell. I had to think about something else to get her off of my mind. So I kept saying, "GED, GED, GED, GED," all the way home.

I finally made it home, put up my wagon, and went in the house. GED was still ringing loud in my head. I turned on the television to relax for a few minutes. They featured the program on illiteracy again. I just knew they were going to show the same old depressed pictures I saw before, so I got up to change the channel. Before I could touch the knob, there was a picture of my sign, "A bigger and more beautiful Box City on the rise." It was so beautiful. I became so emotional that tears ran down my face. That was free publicity for the new Box City. *Now people will want to shop and live here,* I thought. They showed our revitalized apartment complex. It looked so nice on television. They took better pictures of the people. The mothers were with their children at the playground, in the library, or at the park. There were no clothes hanging from buildings or boarded-up windows. The new Box City really looked good on television. The spokesperson was one of my classmates who talked about getting her GED and all the new changes in the city. They showed my shop with people going in and out, Mr. Crumpton's store, Mama's restaurant, Ricko's Bakery, and many other areas of the city.

The reporter said, "Something was happening in this little city that has caused the people to wake up out of a long, deep sleep. They are going back to school, getting their GEDs, and cleaning up their city. This new Box City is not like it was nearly two years ago." She said that was the kind of news worth reporting.

I felt so good at that point that I just wanted to shout! I was making a difference in Box City after all. I just didn't know how much. I thought about just how amazing the Lord is and how He works through people to accomplish His plan for our lives. I was so excited I thought about going over and checking out that preacher I had met a while back. I did tell him I would visit him one Sunday.

After I saw the positive side of Box City on television, I felt like cooking up a storm, and I did. I tried to fix something that Mama didn't serve in her restaurant. I had rack of lamb and grilled lamb chops with a delicious sweet and sour sauce, a scrumptious corn bread dressing, cheesy broccoli baked with mushrooms, corn pudding, sliced tomatoes, and rolls. For desert I had pineapple coconut cake with a delicious cherry pecan sauce on the side. I bought a beautiful center piece for Diamond that was a little bigger this time. The house smelled so good. I had ordered Mama some beautiful dinnerware and linen and set the table with it. It was simply elegant. The only thing missing was Miss Emma knocking at the back door and asking what I was cooking. All was done, so I decided to take a nap until everyone came home.

While I was asleep, I must have dreamed about the girl with the beautiful smile and big puppy dog eyes. Diamond said she tried to wake me up, and I said, "I love you, Alicestene." Man, what did I do that for? Diamond went calling Mama.

"Tehh got a girlfriend. Tehh got a girlfriend, and her name is Alicestene. He said he loved her, Mama."

Mama said, "Leave your brother alone." She came and gave me a big hug and said, "What have you done in here? This table is simply exquisite. Honey, I sure don't serve this kind of food in my restaurant."

Then I went back to teasing Diamond. "Hey, Benjamin, I'm not speaking to Diamond ever again."

Then Diamond started crying and said, "Mama, Tehh don't love me anymore because I said he had a girlfriend." She went and laid her head on Mama's shoulder and stuck her tongue out at me.

"Diamond," Mama said, smiling, "You know you brother loves you. Leave him alone. Now everyone, let's get ready for dinner. This is a feast fit for a queen." All of a sudden there was a knock at the back door, and everyone clapped and smiled. Mama didn't get up. She just said, "It's open, Miss Emma." She just came on in and took her seat at the table like she used to.

"What was all that clapping about I heard?" she asked. "Child, it has been a while since we sat around this table together." She looked at the table and the food and said, "Lord have mercy. Meyel, we sure don't serve nothing like this in our restaurant." She would never let you answer a question or get a word in because she talked so much.

Mama said, "And I don't plan to either. Some things we need to keep special for moments like this." Then Mama looked at me and said, "Thank you so much, honey, for doing this for us. I must admit I have missed our times together too."

Everyone started eating, and Diamond said, "Thank you so much for the flower, Tehh. It is the prettiest one I have ever seen, and it smells so good too. They really make me feel so good inside."

I smiled and said, "You are welcome." We all ate and talked.

There was another knock at the back door, and we all wondered who it could be. Mama asked me if I had invited anyone else, and I told her no. She opened the door, and it was the guys, Toe Joe, Mad Dog, Jason, and Brock all out of breath. "Man, we are so busy that we don't hang out like we use to," Toe Joe said.

Then Brock said, "We heard Miss Meyel telling Diamond not to eat much because you were cooking tonight."

And Jason said, "Man, we hurried up and got through with our work because we didn't want to miss this. We knew that whatever it was, it was going to be good. It is okay for us to come, isn't it?" they asked.

"Sure," I said, "y'all pull up a seat." They sat down so quickly you would have thought they hadn't seen food in a week. They all worked at Mama's restaurant.

Miss Emma said, "Meyel, I think he got you beat, girl. This lamb meat is so good."

Then Mad Dog said, "Lamb meat? Man, I ain't never had none of that. I just got to try it." He reached over and got him a piece. "I thought it was pork chops cooked another way." We were enjoying our dinner and talking about everything.

I thought, *Ain't nothing like family being together. Working together is fine, but being home together and sharing with one another makes all the difference in the world. It makes you feel so good on the inside.*

There was another knock, but it was at the front door. We couldn't figure out who it was since everyone we knew was at the table. Mama got up, went, opened the door, and said, "Oh, my goodness, it's you. I am so sorry. I just forgot." We all got up from the table and went to see who she was talking to. It was Mr. Crumpton. He was such a welcomed sight. He had gone to the restaurant looking for Mama, but she wasn't there. He apologized for asking for the address, but he said he just had to see her. Mama asked him if he wanted to come in and if he had eaten. He told her that he hadn't. She told him we were having dinner and asked him to join us. I went and found another chair, and he sat by Mama. Man, they looked so good together. He looked at the table and said, "My goodness, it looks like Christmas in here. I tell you right now that leg of lamb is my favorite piece of meat. My wife use to fix it for special occasions, but I must say that it didn't look or taste nothing like this."

Mama just smiled and said, "I tell you, Tehh knows his way around the kitchen."

Then Brock said, "Mad Dog thought it was pork chops cooked another way," and we all laughed.

The kitchen was so crowed, but no one complained. You could just feel all the love. That's something families don't seek after. You have to make time for your family, or you will lose them in the hustle and bustle of life. We all enjoyed listening to one another, and Mr. Crumpton gave us young men some manly advice. He talked to us about making something of ourselves, how to love a woman and make her feel special. I just watched Mama as she hung on to his every word. Then they started talking about the good old days and singing those old songs. It was something to hear. Mr. Crumpton told us that those songs were what love was all about back in the day. They did something to a man and a woman that our kind of music didn't do. He said one day he would tell us what that was. We finished dinner. Mama and Miss Emma said good night, and she went home. Mama and Mr. Crumpton went out and sat on the front porch and talked for hours.

Diamond turned to Benjamin saying the strangest thing. "Benjamin, Mama got a boyfriend, and Tehh got a girlfriend. What you got?"

He looked at her and said, "I got a girlfriend too. That's what I got." Then he started dancing and singing, "She makes me feel so good, real good," and he started laughing. We left Diamond and Benjamin to clean up the kitchen and put the food away.

The guys and I went on the back porch and had a great time just hanging out together like we use to. That day we promised to always make time to get together. We talked about how much money we were saving, getting our GEDs, going to college, getting married one day, and all kinds of stuff. I had introduced them to the savings account a while back and encouraged them to save their money and showed them how to use a checking account. What they didn't know was that I secretly put fifteen thousand dollars into each of their savings accounts later. One of the requirements of our gang was to save your money for the future and not check the account for one year and hold on to all of your banking receipts. That way they wouldn't be tempted to take the money out so soon and keep records. If there was an error, we could track it. So I pretty much knew they wouldn't be checking their savings account for a while, and they didn't think they had that much anyway.

The guys thanked me for helping them plan for their future by getting an education. We all talked about moving out of the apartments into real homes with nice yards one day. They all wanted something out of life now. Brock said, "You know, man, I don't know who put up those big signs, but I'm telling you it makes me feel good every time I see one." Then he smiled and said, "I'm picking up paper and stuff now and putting it in the trash. When people see me doing it, they do it too. I can see myself as a businessman now right here in Box City one day. I never thought that would ever happen to me."

Toe Joe said, "Man, me too. Box City ain't never looked this good before in my life. Pretty soon it's going to look better than the other side of town. I want to have a business here one day like Mr. Crumpton."

Then Mad Dog said, "Yeah, but somebody needs to do something with that place on East 57th Street. They need to paint it or something, man. You got that big, old, ugly building with the paint peeling off it with all those filthy windows. It makes all that hard work look bad. I'm telling y'all." He was very emotional. The reprogramming was really working. A year or so ago he never would have noticed it. I realized he was right. It was the next project on my list.

Jason said, "Man, things like that takes time. That's a big project. Somebody has been spending a lot of their money to make Box City look better for all us. All we are doing is nothing, nothing but complaining." He got up, started walking around, and said, "I am quite sure they, whoever they are, were going to do something with it. Man, I can just feel it. Whatever it is I want to be part of it. For now we need to start doing our part."

Then Toe Joe said, "Tehh, man, I done listen to you so much telling us that things don't just get better. We have to make them better. I hear you in my sleep. I really want to get involved to make things better around here too. One day we are going to have a family, and I want them to live in a safe and beautiful city like this. I want them to have a daddy they can be proud of."

Brock jumped up and said, "Me too, man. I want to do something now too, so I can tell my children one day that I helped build the new Box City." As I sat there listening to the guys. I realized they were no longer talking like boys. They were now talking like men, and I was so proud of them. They had finally become aware of the world around them and realized they, too, could make a difference in Box City. We all had to get up early and go to school, so everyone left and went home.

I went in the house, and Mama called me to come and sit down by her. She said, "Now tell me about this girl Diamond was talking about."

I said, "Well, Mama, her name is Alicestene Edwards. She is a girl who was in my class when I got put out of school. She seems like a real nice girl and reminds me so much of you. I saw her in the grocery store today and asked her for her phone number."

Mama smiled and said, "That's wonderful, Tehh, but remember, you are not an ordinary boy. You are a millionaire. You must be very careful about the people you take close to your heart. I know you are a very good judge of character, and I hope things work out. You deserve a wonderful girl, because you are such a wonderful young man and I love you so much." She gave me a big kiss and headed off to bed.

Then I said, "Not so fast, young lady. Come back here and tell me about the young man who had dinner with us tonight."

She turned around with a big smile on her face and said, "Well, he's been coming by the restaurant to see me, and I really like him a lot. We haven't gone out on a real date or anything yet, because we have both been so busy. I feel so comfortable with him, Tehh." I just smiled as she talked. "He came by the restaurant earlier today for lunch. He is a real nice man. I bet you already know that, don't you?" I just nodded my head. "Tehh, I was so excited about having dinner at home, I forgot he said he was coming by the restaurant to see me when he got off work. He told me that he had opened a store here in Box City not too far from the restaurant."

I said, "Mr. Crumpton?" Then I told her that I knew, and he was leasing one of our buildings.

"For real, Tehh?" she said.

"Yes, ma'am, and it really looks good."

Then she softly slapped me up beside my head and said, "Boy, why didn't you tell me that?" I told her that I didn't want her to get her hopes up. If it was God's will, I wanted him to find her if he was interested, and he did. "Mama, you are just that special to me. I didn't want you to get hurt."

She just smiled and said, "Can I go to bed now, Daddy?" I told her yes, and we both laughed and went to our rooms.

CHAPTER 19

The time had finally come, and it was the day of my graduation. I was so excited and nervous at the same time about receiving my GED. This was one piece of paper I wanted to embrace like a man embraces his bride. This was my day. The day I had prayed for and dreamed about. This was my giant step in the right direction. All of the family was there, even Miss Emma, Alicestene with that beautiful smile, the guys, Mr. Crumpton, and the members of the Finang gang. As gang members, they were all encouraged to support one another's success when possible. I had never attended a graduation before, so I didn't know what to expect. This was supposed to be a special ceremony. I saw all my classmates with their family and friends and several of the teachers talking together. Mrs. Mumford left them and came over and asked me if I would say something in the way of encouragement since I was their top student. She apologized for asking at the last minute. I told her that I would do it. She thanked me and returned to be with the other teachers. Speaking was not a problem for me since I did it most of the time anyway in disguise.

We followed the program as it was printed, and then it was my time to say something. I was introduced. I got up and stood before the podium, thanking God in my heart for bringing me to this point in my life. Benjamin had the camera, and was taking my picture. Humbly, I acknowledged all the key people listed on the program like they did on television. First I told them, "This is one of the happiest days of my life. They have not always been happy or easy." I told them about some of my struggles. How doctors had falsely diagnosed me with a severe learning disability. I said, "They said I had the attention span of a three-year-old, and that I would never learn to read, write, or understand, but you see, I did. I had a tumor that caused me to have some very bad headaches. One day at school it burst and sent me into a rage. I had to be restrained from hurting myself and others, and I passed out. For this I was put out of school at the age of thirteen years old and was told that I needed to be placed in an institution where I could get the help I needed. My wonderful mother, who is sitting over there, chose to keep me with her because she knew I could learn. She had faith in me when no one else did. I love you, Mama. I wasn't raised to be lazy, so I made me a wagon and started collecting junk on the streets to help my mama take care of us. I was cursed at, spit on, and talked about. In some cases I was treated worse than an animal. I was told I would be nothing but a burden on society. Something on the inside of me wouldn't let me believe that. I chose to trust what was on the inside. No matter how people treated me or called me dumb and stupid, I was determined to make something of myself. With every fiber of my being, I decided I was going to get my GED or die trying with the Lord's help. Today, I'm proud to say I did it! I challenge you today. Don't believe all the negative things people say about you. It's nothing but a trap of discouragement to keep you from moving forward. Trust your heart and take a chance on yourself. You will be amazed at what you can do if you believe and try. If I can do it. You can do it too! Thank you, and have a great life. God bless you all."

I sat down and took a deep breath after I had spoken. I looked up, and people were still standing and clapping. Some had tears in their eyes. It was a very emotional moment for me. The program went on, and I received my GED and several scholarships. I sat there, looking at my name on that piece of paper that now said I had potential—the potential to be whatever I wanted to be. I was no longer the dummy of Box City. *Thomas Edison Hamilton Hancock is a name I am proud to have*, I thought. I thanked Mama in my heart for my name, and her dream for me as tears ran down my face.

While I was going over to be with my family, the men I met at the library who felt I had cheated on my pretest came over and shook my hand. They told me they were very proud to have met me, and said that I was a young man who was going to go far and make a big difference in this world. They presented me with a special gift to help me in college. It was a check made out to me for five thousand dollars. They wanted to invest in my future, they said. I smiled and thanked them for their gift with tears in my eyes. I learned that people don't mind investing in you when they see that you are going somewhere in life. They saw something in me, and I was proud they did.

Mama came running up to me and gave me a big hug with tears in her eyes. She was so proud of me and said, "Now they know." Everyone gave me hugs with compliments. Then all of a sudden a man standing behind me said, "Excuse me, son. Let me shake your hand." It was Mr. Nelms, the teacher who held me down when my tumor burst, and who had said that I was a waste of their time. He had tears in his eyes and asked me to forgive him. He told me that he would never tell another child he or she was a waste of time as long as he lived. He wiped the tears from his eyes and invited me to come back to the school and talk to the children sometime because I was truly a walking miracle. He told me he was now the principal of the school, but today he felt like a student listening to a master teacher. I told him that I would be glad to come and talk to the students and thanked him for the invitation. He walked on with tears still in his eyes as he took his handkerchief and wiped them away.

Suddenly Alicestene came and grabbed me and gave me a great big kiss. At that moment things clicked, and I didn't want to let her go. I was in heaven. I had never been kissed by a girl before, not even in my dreams. Everybody just looked at us and smiled. Mr. Crumpton came over and shook my hand and said, "Proud of you, son. Just proud of you." I didn't think Alicestene meant to kiss me like that. I think she was just caught up in the moment. She still had that "I didn't mean to do that" look on her face. I thought to myself, *You can do that any time you want.* Then the lady who had done the television story on illiteracy came over and interviewed me. She said, "You are the young man who pushed the wagon." She wanted to do her next story on me. I was so grateful. For the first time in my life I actually felt like I was somebody in the public's eye. She said I would be featured in their next program, which would be on television in about two months. It was truly an exciting day. We all went to Mama's restaurant to celebrate. I said, "Tomorrow I am going to get my driver's license and buy me a nice used car." In my heart, I thought, *After that, I'm going to ask Alicestene for a date, and just maybe she will kiss me like that again.* She told me later that evening that she was sorry that she didn't believe me at first, but she was very proud of me.

CHAPTER 20

I finally got my car. It was an old Chevy, and it felt so good to drive from place to place. It was kind of funny thought. Even with a car, I missed pushing my wagon. Maybe it was because it was all I had for a very long time. I went to the post office to get the mail. I was shocked to receive a letter from the real estate office concerning the building on East 57th Street. It read, "Join us in helping to make this the cleanest city in the USA. There is a bigger and more beautiful Box City on the rise. The building currently located at #9 East 57th Street is a nuisance and must be cleaned up or torn down in ninety days, or you will be fined." I guess my signs were working better than I thought.

Well, since I was the owner, it seemed like now was the time to start cleaning it up. It was the largest piece of property in Box City and quite an eyesore. I mean it really looked bad. I was just trying to decide what I was going to do first, the inside or the outside. Now I didn't have a choice. I needed to clean up the outside first. I called the restaurant and left a message for Mama to call me. It took several hours before she was able to get in touch with me. Then I thought I would call the contractors myself and tell them that I wanted to get the building sandblasted and painted depending on the condition of the bricks. I also wanted a steel door placed on the back side of the building and I needed an estimate for the work. If things went well, I would possibly contract them for the inside as well. I had to disguise myself to meet the contractors and hopefully get the ball rolling.

Now that Mama had her own business, it was becoming more and more difficult to reach her because her responsibilities had increased. Since I was still underage, she had to handle a lot of my business as well as her own. I thought it was time she had a secretary and some part-time office help. The building right next to the restaurant would be a great place for her office. All I had to do was have a door and window cut into the restaurant. They would be close to her and handle all of her phone calls, take messages, and help her with the inventory, paperwork and stuff. I wanted to surprise Mama, so I had the construction crew working at night to make it happen. The office furniture was moved in, and I had already hired a good secretary and two office helpers. One was for the restaurant, and the other for the bakery. We blindfolded Mama and brought her in to see it. She took off the blindfold and just screamed. "Lord Jesus," she said over and over. She was so excited and kept saying, "I just can't believe it." Mama is enjoying her new office, her secretary, and her office helpers. The help allowed her time to breathe, take a break, and have lunch with Mr. Crumpton from time to time. Even though she had all this help, I still checked the books because I was her money man.

One day I was thinking about Mama's birthday, which was several months down the road, and how I wanted to give her something that she always wanted. Now that she had the restaurant and money was rolling in, I didn't think people would question her if she moved from the apartment into a new house. At least they wouldn't think that she was a millionaire. I noticed some beautiful land for sale just inside the city limits of Box City. It stretched as far as my eyes could see. To my surprise, the price was way below what I had expected. You could probably fit more than a hundred houses on that land. It wasn't too far from the restaurant, and the bus could still pick up Diamond and Benjamin for school. I remembered how Mama really loved the first house we saw at the open house we went to on the other side of town. I thought I would have one built with a few of its features and some special features she always dreamed of. I had to find out exactly what kind of furniture she wanted, even though she loved everything in the first open house. I had to put on one of my disguises and let my money do the talking to get that done.

I didn't want to owe anything on the house when it was finished. I read in one of those real estate magazines that was how people wound up losing everything when their money stopped coming in. Rick Asher, who wrote the article, said cash is always the best way to buy a house if you have it. Many people have the money to buy a home but chose to take out mortgages and pay three or four times what the property is worth in interest. I was glad I read that one. We needed to know how to possess the land according to the

Bible. He said that if you were paying on it, it wasn't really yours until you had paid in full. If I hadn't read or understood, I wouldn't have known that. Some people don't have the money to pay cash for a home. That is why teaching the gang to save their money was a big deal to me. You have to program yourself to save. I discovered by reading a book and applying what I read that putting aside a little each week or month and forgetting about it added up in a major way. If you can save when you don't have it to save. He said you were on your way to financial success.

CHAPTER 21

We all had a great summer, and I'm in college now. It wasn't as bad as I thought, but I really had to make some adjustments. I knew I would enjoy it after I learned my way around. It was hard for me to live with strange people in a dorm or any setting for a long period of time. I felt like I was losing my personal space, which made me uncomfortable. I decided to stay in an off-campus apartment all by myself so I could breathe. This would also make it easy for me to handle all of my business affairs without folks watching my every move. I chose to major in business management and finance to understand more about the banking and financial industry. Something told me that the stocks, bonds and other stuff could still be worth something. I just needed to learn firsthand about them and the process. If they belonged to someone, I wanted them or their descendants to have what was theirs, even though the items had been found on my property. Oh, but if legally they are mine, meaning transferrable. That money is going to start the First Hancock Bank of Box City. I really wanted to get that bank in the Underground City up and running first. This could be a third bank in Box City, and that spelled success. After that, I could lease out all the other spaces there, and hopefully those people would bank with Hancock.

When I moved from home to college, Mama was devastated. Even though I was close to home, she said she cried for days because her baby was gone. I wanted to tell her that I was almost a grown man. I just knew she would slap me up side my head. She said she felt safe, knowing that I was there. I told her that Benjamin was a big boy now, and he promised me that he would take care of her and Diamond. Mama kept telling me it wasn't the same and that I could still live at home and go to school. She knew she would have to let me go eventually, but she wasn't ready yet. She promised me she would try. That old Benjamin told me he was excited when I left because he could have his own room. Knowing how he felt hurt my feelings a little, but deep down inside I knew he didn't mean it. I sadly took the bunk beds down with all of their memories and sold them in my store and let him buy what he wanted. He finally started telling me how much he missed me. Diamond still has a way of making me cry with all the love she gives me. "Tehh, I miss you so much. It's not the same since you've been gone. I love you so much," she would say, and then she would cry. I try to go home a few nights a week and sleep on the couch. I got up and fixed breakfast just to let them know how much I loved and missed them.

Alicestene and I are getting a little closer too. I told her that she had the prettiest smile I had ever seen in my life. She would just blush all over. Her parents were very strict, and we haven't been able to date like I wanted to. They do let me come over some evenings and stay until ten o'clock. Her father always look at me like he didn't trust me with her. I soon got over that. Oh, but Alicestene was still having trouble with me going to college because she was still in high school. She keeps telling me that it wasn't fair because we should be graduating around the same time. One day I had to tell her, "Don't blame me. Blame the school. If they hadn't kicked me out. I wouldn't have tried to get my GED. I would probably still be there, trying to catch up with you." I told her that I was a genius. She would laugh and say, "Yeah, right!" I love that girl because she accepted me for who I am, wagon and all.

She invited me to go to church with her one Sunday, and I did. I was so surprised to discover that her pastor was Rev. Young. The preacher I had talked with a few years back. His church was packed, and he had a lot of young people there. They were just jumping up and down, praising God with all they had. It was such a joy to see. I had never seen anything like that. There was a nice, warm, loving spirit there that I had never felt before in a church, and tears fell from my eyes. This was the same church where the pastor told me the young people were dying, dropping out of school, and having babies. He couldn't reach them, and his prayers were not being answered. Somebody was doing something because it was a great service. It was so uplifting, and his church was packed. He painted such a beautiful picture of Jesus Christ with words from the Bible that it was like my mind became his canvas. I could see and understand everything he was saying with love. The last thing I remember him saying was, "Your life should be worth living because you were worth dying for. Jesus died on the cross and rose from the grave so you could have the abundant life because He loves you so much. God has given all of you the power to get wealth and become successful in life, but you have to have a vision for yourself." Then he told us to close our eyes, and he asked us if we could see it! Then he said, "If you can see it, grab it and hold on to it! The Devil wants to steal it from you. Tell the Devil he can't have it." Everyone repeated those words, and they rang throughout the building. He said, "You don't have to be poor anymore. Live, children! Live! Get your education and go and get what God has promised you. Get in a hurry and go get it now! Amen." He made me want to take off running to find whatever it was I didn't have. I was still on a spiritual high when it ended.

We were leaving, and the pastor was at the door. He remembered me. He shook my hand and thanked me for coming and asked me to come again. He told me that Alicestene was a wonderful young lady. He was proud of her and told me to treat her right. He asked me if I enjoyed his message. I told him that I really did. Then I asked, "What did you do to get the young people back in church?"

He said, "I prayed and took your advice, son. I preach love, life, and learning into them. I preach to the people I want them to become in Jesus' name, and it was working. Praise God. They did all the work of bringing others to hear me." Then he asked, "You sure you are not a preacher, son?"

I said, "No, sir, God gave me another calling," and we left.

It was taking longer than I thought for them to finish the building on East 57th Street, but it was coming along greatly. The outside really looked good. It didn't need painting after all. I put on my disguise as Mr. Thomas, who was handling the business for a New York client, and I could go in and out as often as I pleased. I also had IDs made to go with the names just in case I was asked for identification. Most contractors and business people were used to dealing with white folks around here. A colored man had to always be able prove himself. Every now and then the contractor would try to get over on me. I had to be a man and let the contractor know that when things were not done right, I had to answer to my bosses in New York. He was being paid good money to do the job right. If he came down and saw that things were not right, both of us would be out of a job. Since that time I have had no more trouble with the contractor. I even gave him the contract to start on the inside of the building, and boy was he happy.

The Underground City was a huge place that housed twenty-five or more businesses years ago from the old layout of the building. Most of it was designed for night life. I wanted to use it for both day and night. Luckily the place didn't need many major repairs inside. It was just removing a lot of the dust, furnishings, minor wiring and replacing bricks. A lot of the furnishings were moved to a storage facility to be reused. With everything out of the building, it looked awesome. The windows were being cleaned or replaced, and the light poured into the building. I took pictures of every area so that I could decide what would go where in my planning stages. Once painted and everything, I would advertise on a local and national scale for people to lease the spaces. I already had an idea in mind for Benjamin and Diamond. Since the place was so large, I was thinking of having at least six to eight different kinds of restaurants throughout the place. I would love to have an events area for parties and weddings that people could rent. Clubs for night life would find homes at the other end of the building, which opened from the outside as well. This was really going to be a tough job with me in college and all. I had to tell myself that failure was not an option. Box City was depending on me, even if they didn't know it.

One day I was driving through the side of town where the prostitutes, pimps, and drug dealers hung out, and I jumped for joy in my car. Someone was tearing down the old buildings. I decided to check with the real estate office to see who the interested buyers were. This would be a huge cash deal. It turned out that an out-of-town investor wanted to put up a four-star hotel in Box City. I said, "That's wonderful." I didn't want to do it all, but that was my property. The free television publicity really paid off. This company was going to bring about twenty-five or more jobs into our area. The police were beginning to do their jobs now. They were actually putting people in jail with high bail. Some of them were still awaiting trial. No one had the money to bail them out. We still have a long ways to go, but Box City has come far in a little more than three years.

I decided to drive down the road and see how Mama's house was coming along. Wagon Trace Subdivision was what I thought I would call the place one day. I wanted a nice wagon logo on the sign. The wagon logo would be in memory of my wagon, which made it all possible. It would be a nice gated community like the people have on the other side of town. There was enough land for a hundred or more homes, but Mama's house would be the first one. Today I was Tehh, Mama's son, looking at the house, and it was looking good. I knew Mama would love it.

I decided to see if I could get Alicestene to drive by with me to look at it. I just wanted to see where her mind was and how she was going to react. This was the girl I wanted to marry one day. Her reaction would make a big difference to me. If she said she didn't need all of that in a house to be happy, or she wished we could have a house like that one day, she was going to be my wife when she finished college—if I could wait that long. Now if she tells me she wants a bigger house, bigger pool, and all that stuff. She was going to be on slippery ground with me. I just want a simple, caring girl that I can give the world.

Her folks were beginning to trust me a little now, but they clocked us down to the second for her curfew. Sometimes we had to get a doggy bag because we didn't finished our food by her time limit. One day she took her food home, and her daddy asked her where was his as he looked at me. I let her take them something home every now and then. It looked like they were going to be my Miss Emma.

Speaking of Miss Emma, she made a ninety degree turn. She has a special man in her life now. His name was Dwight Hornsby, and he's a businessman. Since Mama had met Mr. Crumpton, she decided she would find someone too. He's a real nice man, and he cares a lot about her. I thought Miss Emma was a really old woman, but she wasn't. She just carried herself that way. That woman came out of the closet, and she really looks good these days, perhaps fifteen years younger. Having the right person in her life brought out the beauty in her.

I must have brought out the beauty in Alicestene because she was really looking good to me. I couldn't afford to buy her much yet (as Tehh) in college. What I loved about her is that she appreciates whatever I give her. My gifts were always followed by a big kiss and a thank you. Every now and then she would stop by my antique shop, where I worked part-time. She really liked the place, especially the jewelry. Sometimes she wanted something that she couldn't afford. I would secretly have the clerks discount it so she could buy it. She tells everyone that she finds the best deals at my shop. Yes, it was a good deal for her, but not for me, according to my sales clerks and managers. They told me I didn't make that much money to do that because I made up the difference when she left. My clerks said they wished they had men like me. Alicestene just don't know how much this man loves her, they'd say. Some weeks I didn't even get a paycheck because of her. I thank God every day for making me a wealthy man.

I realized that one day when Alicestene and I get married, she was going to faint and then probably kill me for all the things I never told her. Not knowing that I was a millionaire all the time we were dating would be the biggest one. Every now and then I would slip up and order something on a restaurant menu, and she would tell me that I couldn't afford that and ask me if I was crazy. I really appreciated her even more for doing that. I knew she was looking out for me. I spent most of my life looking out for everyone else.

CHAPTER 22

I was at my apartment one evening, getting ready for an exam when there was a knock on the door. I looked through the peephole, and saw that it was several of my classmates. I opened the door to see what they wanted. They were looking for a place to party, and I didn't do that. It was five of them. It was as if they were trying to push their way inside. I was praying I wouldn't have to fight with them. I stopped them at the door and told them I had to study for the exam tomorrow. Then I asked them why they weren't studying. One said they wanted to party. I said boldly, "I didn't come to this school to party. I have a family that is depending on me to be successful." I got all emotional, saying, "I don't drink and I don't party! I want to be somebody one day. That's all I care about. There is a business in Box City with my name on it, and I want it! I have been watching our people live this hopeless existence all my life, and I am sick of it. That's why I'm studying to make a better life for myself and my family one day. All you want to do is party? I tell you, one day you will wind up in the gutter with the world throwing their filth in your face, and you will lay there and ask for more. If that's what you want, fine, but if you don't mind, I would like to continue with my studying."

One of them said, "Man, we are sorry. We didn't know you were so serious about this stuff."

I said, "Stuff? Man, you are talking about my life! The only way out of this poverty is to get an education."

Then one of the girls said, "I really need to study, y'all. Can I study with you?"

Then another one said, "No, man, can we all study with you?"

I pulled myself together and said, "Only if you leave your alcohol and stuff in your car and you have your books. I have some sodas and snacks in the refrigerator. Otherwise I don't have the time." They went and put whatever they had with them in their cars and got their books. I took a deep breath because I was so scared. I thanked God in my heart for turning things around. We all studied together and got to know one another. Some of them had had pretty rough lives, and some were still living on another planet. They asked me questions about financing, and I tried to answer them. All of a sudden they made me the teacher. I thought, *Here I go again.* We had a really nice time without the booze and stuff.

One of the girls said, "This was the best time I have had in a long time and remembered what happened."

It was late, and everyone left. I heard that voice again say, "One person at a time." I learned not to compromise who you are. Stand your ground if you can. If you don't stand, you will fall in life for anything. It was scary, but I stood. I did it, and I won!

The next day we were all in class. Hopefully we were prepared to take the test. It was an hour and fifteen minutes long. I looked it over, and in thirty minutes I was through. I got up and gave the teacher my paper and walked out. As I looked back, everyone was looking at me like they were wondering what was wrong with me. *I'm a genius. It was an easy test to me,* I thought. My time was valuable. I had to get over to Mama's restaurant so I could do her books and then go by the Underground City.

I arrived at Mama's restaurant only to discover she had a new employee. Alicestene was working there. That beautiful smile just made my day. She came over and gave me a hug and told me my mama was in her office. I went in, and there she was sitting at her desk just as pretty as she could be. I gave her a big hug and went over and sat at the big desk in the corner. She brought me the books, and Alicestene brought me my lunch. Mama told me that Alicestene asked her if she could work there. She wanted to start saving up some money for college, and Mama hired her. She asked me if that was okay with me and told me that Alicestene was a very good employee. I told Mama that was fine because she was a good judge of character. I was glad to know that Alicestene was a good employee. That was another star in her beautiful crown. Mama knows how much I loved fried chicken, and I had my way at it. My lunch was so good. I washed it down with a cold strawberry soda.

After that, I was ready to take on the books. I sat at the table and went through one book after another to make sure everything was okay, but then I ran into a problem. I had the books for the restaurant and the bakery, and both books were in error. I had trouble balancing them. It was off by a thousand dollars, and I couldn't find the problem. Checks had been written to two companies, but there was no record of those companies receiving the checks. I had searched for more than an hour, and I was tired. I always double-checked myself by keeping another set of books in case someone altered something, and I made notes of certain vender transactions. These I kept in a locked file cabinet that only I had the key to. I looked through the books to see where the error may have occurred. It was in the area of the restaurant's inventory, and Connie was responsible for that. Two check totaling one thousand had been written, but posted in the wrong book. Mama asked her staff if anyone remembered what happened that day. It turned out that Connie remembered receiving the checks and gave one to Adger's Refrigeration and another to Watkin's Wholesale Company. She had a stomach virus that day that kept her in and out of the restroom. She accidently picked up and posted in the wrong book, but there were no record of the receipts. I sat back and let Mama handle her business. She explained that a business could not afford those kinds of mistakes.

She said, "A thousand dollars is a lot of money in this kind of business. I would hate to not pay you because of someone's miscalculation."

It was going to be a while before that problem happened again. Mama did tell Connie to double-check herself even if she had to paste it on the restroom wall. I knew if I had made that mistake, she would have slapped me right upside my head. Connie did eventually find the receipts that she had accidently placed in books that were meant for storage. With that done, I asked Mama for some more fried chicken and a piece of cake with my strawberry soda. I waved bye to Alicestene, and she gave me that beautiful smile again. *Man, I love that girl.* I headed on over to the Underground City.

Driving up East 57th Street was never a beautiful sight. It was the ugliest place in Box City. However, this time there was this huge, beautiful building that welcomed you with all of her splendor and grace. I couldn't believe my eyes. I pulled my car over to the side of the road and stopped to look at it as tears ran down my face. She was truly magnificent—a glorious piece of architecture. The windows were beautiful, and it looked like rainbows were bouncing off them everywhere. It was simply breathtaking. *Wait until Mama sees this*, I thought. I knew I couldn't go in as Tehh, so I just drove around to the side of the building and parked. I looked around calculating all kinds of stuff in my mind. It had tons of parking space and plenty of lights around the place. I tried to imagine all kinds of plants and trees around with a nice statue out front at the entrance. My mind was lost in the Underground City. I could see things happening as if they were real.

I was just sitting there in my car daydreaming when a policeman pulled up and asked me what I was doing there. I was startled for a second and thought about what Mama said about the children who had been killed there years ago. I didn't stutter this time. I said, "I was looking at the place because it's so beautiful. I never thought it could look like this."

He said, "It sure is beautiful. It has been an eyesore around here for years. I guess some out-of-state company bought it too. They are buying up everything."

He took off his shades and cleaned them with his handkerchief and said, "That's good for Box City's economy. For the first time in years money was flowing through the veins of Box City."

This place had been down for so long that even he thought the city would never change. He told me that he noticed a new subdivision coming up on the outskirts of town and that was a beautiful house someone was having built. He was interested in having one built there too, but he didn't see a sign. He hoped they would put one up soon because his wife was throwing a fit about it. She wanted him to buy a house there no matter what it cost.

"It seemed like somebody from out of state has been buying up everything," he said.

We finished talking, and he asked me to move along. He told me he was doing his job of patrolling the place to keep crime down. The city was looking good, and they had been told to keep it that way. I went on and drove off since he was protecting my building. It was good to talk with him though. Once again I had been asked to move away from my own property. I wondered if it was because I was colored, and then I smiled. Well, I need to make some signs saying, "Homes for sale in Wagon Trace Subdivision." I bought the land cheap. Now I can put some money in the First Hancock Bank of Box City and give that contractor another job.

Being in my position as a young colored man had its pros and cons since I chose to remain anonymous. I was now the only millionaire in Box City and no one knew it. I owned most of Box City, and no one knew it. I owned the Underground City, and no one knew it. I was building a subdivision, and no one knew it. I helped to change the image of Box City, and no one knew it. People thought it was someone from out of town. The banker was right again. "Low-class people will never have a high-class mentality." These people couldn't see anyone from Box City trying to make things better because they couldn't see themselves getting involved. They were only depending on someone else to do it for them. Things will only change for the good around here when people wake up and get involved. I got involved. I help people get an education, and no one knew it. The funny thing about my life is that if I stood in front of my own building, the police knew, and even if I parked in my own parking lot on the side of my building, they knew that too and would ask me to move. Sometimes I just wanted to shout to the world that I was Thomas Edison Hamilton Hancock, a millionaire genius. I wanted someone to know that it was me doing all of these things and not someone from out of town. The voice on the inside of me would tell me that time will come, and to be patient.

CHAPTER 23

It was a cold November day, and Mama's birthday celebration had arrived. I asked Alicestene to take a drive with me. I was going to show her the house to see what she thought about it. As we were driving, she noticed the house ahead and told me that it was so beautiful. Her dad had been telling them about a new subdivision being built in Box City, and she wanted to see it. She said he never thought something like that could ever happen here. She even told me that he said he hoped that one day she would find a man who was able to buy her a nice house like that, but he doubted it.

Then she said, "Tehh, you would have to own an antique shop like the one you work in to live in a place like that. I know that when you finish school and get a good job, you will be okay wherever you live."

I pulled her close to me and said, "Alicestene, will you marry me?"

She was shocked and started crying and shaking her hands. I thought she was having a fit. She said, "Yes, but I've got to get my education first. I don't want to put nothing before my education. That's all you talk about to have a better life."

Once again I had put my own foot in my mouth. *Why do people listen to me?* She had two and a half years to go in college, and I had one and a half. This was really going to kill me. The Bible said it was better to marry than to burn. *Lord, what do I do now?* This woman counts how long we kiss so we won't move to the next level. She counts to ten and stop. Then she would say, "That's enough, no more." After that, we would talk to cool down. I have to love this girl to put up with that. She finally got herself together and gave me a big hug and told me she was sorry for crying all over my shirt. I told her that was okay and drove on down the road and picked up a few items for Mama's party. She was shocked again when I told her that the party was going to be at that house, and it was a surprise for Mama.

She said, "No kidding. Get out of here! I can't believe this. I will get to see the inside of the house. My daddy will be shocked."

Then I told her that I had invited her parents, and she said, "Get out of here. You are such an amazing man, Tehh. I love you so much."

We went back to the house to greet everybody before Mama arrived. Alicestene couldn't believe her eyes. The house was absolutely stunning. We took a brief tour of the house and then went to the enclosed patio where all the festivities were set up. The caterers were preparing the food, and there was soft music playing in the background. Diamond and Benjamin quickly came and got me. They took me to another side of the house because they wanted to ask me something privately. They were concerned about Mama.

They both said, "Tehh, don't this house look a little like the one we saw that time at the open house on the other side of town?"

I said, "Just a little bit. I'm glad you told me that."

Benjamin said, "Man, I wish we could live in a house like this. This place is awesome."

Then Diamond said, "You know how Mama was that time at the open house, Tehh. I'm telling you, we may not be able to get her out of here tonight."

I smiled and said, "Well, I guess we will all be spending the night then." They looked at me, smiled, and told me that I was so crazy. We went back to the patio to wait for Mama and Mr. Crumpton. I invited the guys and their girlfriends and the thirty-five members of my secret Finang Gang of Box City because Mama was a member. The patio was filled with people of all colors and races. It was truly a beautiful sight. These were the people who would change the future of Box City in the areas of banking and finance, education, health care, management, and politics. These were the jewels society had thrown away.

Mr. Crumpton was bringing Mama to the party after he thought everyone had arrived. He was going to tell her that he was stopping by one of his friend's house for a few minutes and that this friend had bought the house in the new subdivision.

Suddenly Diamond came rushing in, saying, "They're here. Everybody hide. They're here."

Mr. Crumpton came in through the front door so Mama could see the house and give us enough time to hide. I watched as she turned around looking at everything, saying, "This house is so beautiful. Oh, my goodness. It's just like the house of my dreams."

She had tears in her eyes. I was getting emotional just watching her.

Mr. Crumpton asked, "What's wrong, Meyel?"

"Nothing, I'm ok," she told him.

I got Mr. Crumpton's attention to bring mama to the patio. When they came out the door, everyone said, "Surprise," and began to sing "Happy Birthday" to her. My mama was shocked out of her senses. I was so afraid and didn't want her to have a heart attack. She had never had a party before. Her legs got weak under her, and she was going down like a sunken ship. Mr. Crumpton quickly caught her. We rushed over to see if she was okay.

She just cried and said, "Oh, my God. I never thought something like this could ever happen to me. Thank y'all so much." Then she asked Miss Emma, "Did you know about this?"

Miss Emma just smiled and said, "Girl, you just don't know how hard it was keeping this secret since we talk about everything."

Then she turned to Mr. Crumpton and asked, "Were you in on this too?" Then she looked at Diamond and Benjamin and said, "Don't stand there looking all innocent. I will get you both later." Then she looked at the gang and asked, "All of you knew?"

Everyone nodded and said, "Yes."

Mama had to sit down a minute to catch her breath. She was scaring me a little. Then she smiled and said, "You all are so wonderful, and I love you so much. Thank you! Thank you." Then she looked at me and said, "Tehh, how in the world did you manage to get this place? It is simply exquisite. This is the best birthday of my life."

She got up and said, "Come on everybody. Let's sit down and enjoy my birthday party."

Everyone sat down at the tables, waiting to be served. Everything was so elegant. The waiters served everybody as they talked with one another. It was like the dinner parties you see on television. There was a comedian who kept everyone laughing and live music. It was a wonderful time. Then the band began playing all of Mama's favorite songs. All of a sudden Mama began to groove to the music in her seat. I looked at my mama who was so happy, and thanked God for answering my prayer. Then I noticed how she looked at Mr. Crumpton. I knew this relationship was going to lead to more. Benjamin and Diamond looked at me. We all looked at Mama and smiled because we knew she was so happy.

Everyone was experiencing something new in the atmosphere at Mama's party. It was a sense of love and family. For the first time I saw the guys acting like gentlemen and the girls acting like ladies. There was no fussing or arguing, just sheer enjoyment and a pleasure to be in the company of others. I remembered what the banker said. "Low-class people will never have a high-class mentality." Then I thought, *They can if they are trained and given the opportunity to prove it.* Everyone ate, danced, and enjoyed themselves. I asked Mr. Crumpton if I could steal Mama away from him for a few minutes. We walked slowly through the house enjoying the splendor of it. She said the kitchen was made for a chef, and she just loved it. She wanted the kitchen in her house to look like that. I took her to see the upstairs and then to the master bedroom.

She said, "Oh, my goodness. Lord Jesus, this room is so beautiful." She put her hands over her mouth and said, "Oh, my goodness! This bed is just like the one I told you I wanted." She became so excited and said, "Tehh, honey, I just love this house. I just got to have it! Can I have one built now since the restaurant is doing so well?"

My mama was actually begging me like a child for this house or a house like it. I had to be strong and hold back my tears because I really wanted to surprise her.

I said, "No, Mama, I don't want you to have a house built right now. Please don't ask me again."

She looked at me like I was some kind of fool, frowned, and said, "Boy, do you know who you are talking to? Now you tell me why not, Thomas Edison Hamilton Hancock?"

I knew I had struck a major nerve and a slap upside my head wasn't too far away.

"You are about to ruin my birthday, boy," she said.

I asked her to sit down for a minute in the chair that I had found on the junk pile a few years back and had restored.

She said, "Tehh, this chair looks just like the one you found that time. It is gorgeous."

I kneeled down in front of her with a smile on my face.

She said, "Tehh, what are you doing?"

I smiled and asked her to give me her hand.

She said, "Boy, it's against the law to ask for your mama's hand in marriage," and smiled.

I said, "No, it ain't nothing like that, Mama," and I smiled. She gave me her hand, and I reached in my pocket and pulled out a jewelry box and gave it to her. I told her I didn't want to give it to her in front of everyone because of the cost.

She said, "Oh, my goodness, you didn't, Tehh."

She just knew it was a big diamond ring. *No,* I thought, *that's going to be for Alicestene.* I wanted to give Mr. Crumpton that opportunity first.

She opened it and saw a key and asked, "What is this for?"

I said, "Happy birthday, Mama. This is the key to this house. Your dream home all paid for. You don't owe one cent for anything."

She started to scream, and I had to put my hand over her mouth again. She told me I had to stop doing that. I said, "Don't scream then, Mama. One thing you have to do for me again is pretend that you bought this house later, okay?"

Mama grabbed me by the neck and almost choked me to death as she tried to hug me. I pleaded with her to let me go. She told me that she was so sorry, and released me.

She said, "This is another one of the happiest days of my life. Tehh, honey, you got me my dream home! It's more beautiful than I could have ever imagined. Thank you, honey."

I told her to take her time and enjoy the room for a few minutes. I would let our guests know that she would be down shortly. I told her we could all spend the night if she wanted to get a feel of the house. I left her with tears in her eyes. While I was leaving the room, she whispered, "I love you so much, Tehh."

I said, "I love you too, Mama."

As I closed the door, I heard her say, "Thank You, Jesus. Thank You, Jesus, for my wonderful son, and my new home."

I went on back to be with our guests and Alicestene.

She asked, "Is your mama okay?"

I told her she was just a little overexcited and needed to rest a minute.

She said, "This place is so beautiful. My mama and daddy just love it so much. They're glad you invited them."

Mr. Crumpton came over and asked, "Is your mama okay, son?

I told him she just got a little overexcited. "She should be down in a few minutes."

Mama fixed her face and came back to the party just glowing. The waiters rolled out her birthday cake and everyone began clapping. All I ever wanted was to see my mama happy.

Diamond said, "Blow out the candles, Mama, and make a wish."

Mama blew out the candles and thought for a second with her eyes closed. She was simply divine. Benjamin took her picture at that exact moment. Then Diamond asked her, "What did you wish for, Mama?"

Mama said, "I wished for this house and everything that's in it. And, if it is for sale, I am going to get it!"

Diamond got so excited and said, "Didn't I tell you, Tehh. Mama was going to want this house? I told them, Mama."

Mama smiled and said, "If I can get it, all of you are invited back to the housewarming party."

Mr. Crumpton came over and gave Mama a big hug and told her she deserved that house and a whole lot more. Then he said, "I want y'all to know I really love this woman."

Everybody shouted, "We love you too, Miss Meyel."

We all laughed and went over and gave her a big group hug. The cake was cut and given to everybody. It was simply delicious, and melted in your mouth. We had so much food that our guests were given plates to take home.

Everyone left except the guys and their girlfriends, Miss Emma and her friend, and Mr. Crumpton, who were all asked to be our overnight guests. Alicestene's parents couldn't stay, but they did allow her to. Her daddy was hesitant and told me that he was watching me. Now, no one slept together. All the girls were going to be in a room. All the guys were going to be in a room. Mr. Crumpton was definitely going to be with me. Diamond and Benjamin actually slept in their own rooms. We all decided to take a dip in the pool. There were swimsuits in the pool house for our guests. Mama had never been in a swimming pool before. I asked her to get in the shallow end. She was afraid, but she was willing to try. Mr. Crumpton came over and told her that he was an excellent swimmer and asked her to trust him, and she did.

Alicestene and I sat in the hot pool, talked, and watched everyone enjoying themselves. We talked about how beautiful everything was. She told me she was so proud of me and knew I had saved for a long time to give my mama a party like that. She said she had never met anyone who cared for his mother and family the way I did. Alicestene was so beautiful at that moment that I just pulled her close to me and asked her to marry me again when I finished college. I told her that she would still be able to finish school. She looked at me with those puppy dog eyes and beautiful smile and said, "Okay."

I felt like a man who had won a marathon at that moment. I gave her the biggest kiss. I was like butter in her arms when Mr. Crumpton called us and said, "What's going on over there?"

I told him, "She said yes! I asked Alicestene to marry me, and she said yes!"

Everyone clapped and said, "Congratulations."

A little later on it turned out that Mr. Crumpton asked Mama to marry him. The guys asked their ladies to marry them. Even Miss Emma was asked for her hand in marriage. Mama's birthday was an amazing event. It was the night that everybody said yes to getting married—that is, everybody except Diamond and Benjamin. It was also a night that made me take a good look at my influence on those around me. I had no earthly idea anything like that would happen. There was a mixture of happiness and sadness. I thought, *What if I had not done what God wanted me to do and chose the wrong path? Things may have turned out much differently.*

Everyone showered and got ready for bed. All we could hear was the chattering and laughter of the women. It was like they had found designer clothes in a bargain basement.

Mr. Crumpton asked, "What you think about me marrying your mama, son?" He told me how much he loved her and how she had changed his life. He wanted to become a part of our lives with my permission. I told him she couldn't have found a better man and welcomed him to the family.

I woke up early, thinking about all the excitement. I decided to try out the kitchen that was made for a chef. I made sure it had everything. There was also a wall-to-wall freezer in a closet filled with all kinds of meats and frozen goods. While I was pulling out what I was going to fix for breakfast, Mr. Crumpton came in and asked if he could help. Then the guys came down, talking about Mama's birthday party. They wanted to help too. The kitchen was big enough for everyone to work and have their own space. I allowed Mr. Crumpton the pleasure of assigning the duties. Mad Dog cooked the omelets and eggs. Jason cooked the bacon, ham, and sausage. Toe Joe cooked the rice and cheese grits. Mr. Crumpton made the pancakes and waffles. Brock and I made the coffee cakes, toast, juices, and coffee. We were all working like a well-oiled machine.

To look at us, you would have never thought we were society's rejects and lived in the projects. These guys were so transformed they could walk into any company and get a job. Mr. Crumpton started singing a song, and we all joined in. We had some good harmony going on. Then Toe Joe broke out with a song. We joined in holding big spoons to our mouths for mics. We were having a good time fixing breakfast. The house smelled so good. We were so caught up in what we were doing we didn't even see the ladies standing behind us. When we looked up, the ladies burst out laughing at us.

Everybody said, "Good morning," and joined in the fun. The ladies broke out with a song, and we joined them. We really sounded good.

Mama said, "We need to take this thing on the road. We really sound great!"

Benjamin came in and asked, "Is everybody dying this time since all of you are cooking?" Everybody wondered what he was talking about. Mama kindly explained it to them. Benjamin and Diamond's friends arrived, and it was time to eat. All the food was set up on the patio, and it was a feast for a king.

I asked Mr. Crumpton to bless the food, and he did. We all fixed our plates and enjoyed ourselves. It was Sunday, and no one had to rush.

Someone said, "The omelets are the best I have ever tasted."

Mad Dog jumped up, took a bow, and said, "Thank you, thank you."

Mr. Crumpton's pancakes were out of this world. He told us that he was a cook in the army and could make pancakes in his sleep.

Then Jason said, "Tehh, if it had not been for you, we never would have had the opportunity to experience a weekend like this, man. I tell you God made you special. Here I am in college, man. I couldn't see nothing like this in my life until I met you. I don't even sound like I used to. It scares me, man. I sound intelligent now. All I ever heard was that I was no good for nothing or that I would end up dead somewhere." Tears were rolling down all of our faces because his words were genuine. He told us that I saved his life. Each one began to talk about how our coming together had changed their lives.

Even Mr. Crumpton told us about the day in the restaurant on the other side of town when we first met.

He said, "The day you saw me in the restaurant was the anniversary of my wife's death, and I was so down in spirit. When I saw your mama, a familiar face, and had the opportunity to dine with you, everything changed. You gave me hope to live on."

He told us how he brought his store to Box City, and it wasn't doing as well as he wanted it to. Then one day I walked into his store and gave him some advice, and his business went through the roof.

He said, "All I did was take the signs down and let the people peep through the windows, and it worked." He wanted to thank me too, and he called me son. There was something magical about me, he said. I wondered what that something was.

CHAPTER 24

A year has gone by, and it has been a very busy time for me with graduation and all. My antique store was doing very well since I took out one of those ads in the newspaper and an antique book. The profits more than doubled. I was in training with the guys to manage some of the stores. Some of the apartments advertised still hadn't sold. I wanted to talk to the guys about buying their own apartment building to secure their future. It was truly a hard sell. They couldn't imagine themselves owning an apartment building, just a house one day. They feared the maintenance expense, and all the other responsibilities would be more than they could handle—or so they thought. I told them I wouldn't ask them to do anything that I wouldn't do. Even thought I knew firsthand, I told them I had been getting some information about the apartments. I found out that the real estate company would handle the rent and keep their identities a secret. Nobody had to know they owned the building, not even their parents. The tenants would tell the real estate company when there was a problem. All they needed to do was put aside money in the bank each month for maintenance expense and insurance when they got their check for the rent. I told them I had saved some money and was thinking about buying one myself. Even thought we would make money when we finished school, it would be nice to have money coming in now. I asked each of them to calculate how much money Mr. Zorbinski made on their apartment building a year and divide it by twelve to see how much money they would earn legally each month. They all agreed and totaled up how much money the units they lived in would bring in monthly, and they jumped for joy. Sometimes if you can just do the math, you will see things differently. They were shocked, knowing they didn't have that kind of money to buy their building. I knew what they had. I asked them to check their savings accounts at the bank to see how much they had actually saved. It had been more than two years. They were all stunned to see how much money they had saved, and bought their own apartment building.

They had that money because they were faithful to the gang. They were not to check their accounts. Even when they could have, they didn't. Since I talked them into it, I had to buy another apartment building. I owned five twelve-unit apartment buildings now. This was my way of introducing them to the world of real estate and becoming businessmen. Colored folks could never own anything in Box City before because they didn't have any money until now. The banker was right. They had to be reprogrammed for change. I wanted to teach them the power of being an investor early in life and remaining humble at the same time so they could hold on to what they had. I learned over the years the dangers of greed and ignorance. I advised them to keep their business matters to themselves so they could enjoy their lives. The less people knew about you and your money, the better off you were.

I was leasing the spaces in the Underground City faster than you could say, "Jack rabbit." It looked fantastic. The bank was coming along very well. Most of the equipment had to be replaced because of new technology. It wasn't a waste though. It turned out that I was able to sell it to a man collecting antique banking equipment for some sort of a museum. I got a part-time job at the bank near Mr. Crumpton's shop. This would give me the banking experience I would need to teach others in the gang who would work in the Hancock Bank and other areas. The bank would be a great convenience for the tenants in the building. There would be clothing stores, bookstores, shoe stores, toy stores, a piano company, a bridal shop, furniture stores, several restaurants, coffee shops, and so much more according to those who had already leased spaces. Wagon Trace Subdivision was 60 percent complete. The houses sold for more than I thought because so many people wanted to live there. People were leaving the other side of town, and nearby cities to live in the new Box City. That forced the property's price to rise, so only the highest bidders could afford it. Now I was starting another subdivision for those who wanted a home in Box City with low to moderate incomes. I was still holding my quarterly tenants' meetings, and they have made a hundred and eighty degree change. I am so tired, but I am determined. Failure is not an option for me.

While I was driving home one evening totally exhausted. I fell asleep at the wheel and almost killed myself. I drove off the road and went down a hill. For some strange reason I heard Mama's voice calling me, but she wasn't in the car. I woke up just in time. I was headed straight for a large tree. There was no way I would have survived if I had hit that tree. I managed to prevent the car from hitting the tree, but I went into a ditch and hit my head on the steering wheel really hard. I was in pain and suffered some other cuts and bruises. I was shaking like a leaf on a tree. I was scared to death. No one had to tell me. I knew it was the Lord that had spared my life again. I got out of the car and looked how far I had come off the road while I was sleeping. I realized at that moment I had too much on my plate. In just six months I would be graduating college and getting married. I thought about how I could have lost it all. I leaned on the car with tears in my eyes. I thanked God for His amazing grace. My car was stuck and damaged. I had to make my way up the long hill to the main road. I was sore, out of breath, bleeding, and my chest was hurting so bad. I took my time, stopping along the way, trying to breathe and climb up the hill.

As I topped the hill, a driver stopped and said, "Hey, man, you need some help?" They must have seen my head bleeding. I asked them to take me to the hospital. I had a car accident and was having chest pains. I asked the Lord, "Please don't let me die." I couldn't believe He would let the car stop before hitting that tree to let me die of a heart attack. The people kindly took me to the hospital, and I was admitted. I thanked them and asked them to leave their names and phone number with the nurse. I wanted to send them a *thank you* gift later. Someone kept telling me to stay awake. I felt very weak. One of the nurses said, "He's going into shock," and I passed out. The hospital called Mama as they took me to be examined. Mama must have called Alicestene, and she called everyone else.

The doctor talked to me after they had gotten all the results from the tests. He said my head was fine on the inside, but I had a few stitches on the outside. He asked me to calm down. Then he told me there was a slight problem with my heart. I was under a tremendous amount of stress for a young man my age. He said I needed to get some rest! He told me he was going to keep me in the hospital for two to three weeks to get it. I tried to tell him about all the things I had to do.

He said, "Nothing is more important than your life. You would be no good to anyone dead. You are slowly heading to the graveyard, son." That really got to me. I had been looking out for everyone except myself.

Before I knew it, everyone was coming in the room to see me. My head was wrapped in bandages. I looked pretty bad, not counting the fact that I was sore all over. The doctor told the nurse to tell everyone that I was okay but just needed rest for now, and no visitors. Only the immediate family could see me for a few minutes. Everyone left, and Mama, Mr. Crumpton, Alicestene, Benjamin, and Diamond were left in the room. Everyone was crying. I felt like I was actually dying. I told them I was okay, and that I had fallen asleep at the wheel and ran off the road down a hill. I told Mama that I had heard her voice calling me and woke up in time before I hit a tree. Tears were running down my face when I told them that the Lord had stopped that car, and I was grateful to be alive. I told them what the doctor said about my heart, and they all began to cry. I hugged everybody and told them that I loved them and I was going to be okay. I just had to get some rest, that was all. The nurse came in and gave me a shot. That was the last thing I remembered.

Since Mama owned Meyel's Restaurant, they gave me a private room because they knew she could afford pay. Normally I would have been sent back home to rest or die. I must admit, I have not had any time to just rest in a long, long time. Thinking back, I can't remember ever being sick after the tumor went away, other than when I fell out of the bed. I have been going since I was thirteen years old. I didn't know what it was like to just do nothing. I would toss and turn in the bed or go from the bed to the chair and look out the window.

The funny thing was that one day I was just lying there, trying to make myself fall asleep. One of the housekeepers rushed into my room with her cart and parked it over in the corner. She sat down and quietly took out her GED book and began to read like I wasn't there. I guess she thought I was heavily sedated or something. She began reading without looking up, and that caught my attention. She was heavily invested in her studies, talking to herself and everything. She would take a bite of her sandwich as she turned the pages of her book. I sat up in my bed and just watched her for about fifteen or twenty minutes. She bit off her sandwich and pulled out her notebook and began writing, never looking up. I could have turned over and went to sleep and let her finish what she was doing. No, I decided to clear my throat to see what would happen. She almost jumped out of her skin. The book flew across the room and part of her sandwich flew into my bed. It took everything I had to keep from laughing. That was so funny. She was so scared and made all kinds of apologies with tears in her eyes. She feared she would lose her job. I asked her to calm down and told her that I wouldn't report her. She thanked me and told me she wanted to get her GED but had to pass the pretest first. She really wanted a better job and didn't want to be a housekeeper for the rest of her life.

I asked her if she was on the clock, and she said she was on her lunch hour. Then I asked her why she had chosen my room.

She said, "It was empty for a long time. Each day I would come in here to study, not thinking that someone was in here. It was the only place I could study in peace."

Even though she was wrong I admired her courage and desire to better herself. I asked, "What problems were you having?" She brought me the book and showed me. I said, "Oh, I can see how you would have trouble with that," and I showed her what to do.

She was so surprised and said, "You know about the GED?"

I said, "Yes, I was kicked out of school at age thirteen. A few years later I decided to get my GED, and now I'm in college, getting ready to graduate in a few months." She looked at me with amazement. She told me it was nothing but the Lord who allowed her to meet me. I asked, "Why did you decide to get your GED?"

She said, "I dropped out of school after having twins but never had the time to go back. Lately, I have met quite a few colored people who were trying to get their GEDs, and they inspired me. Everybody in Box City is talking about getting an education for a better life. It must be working because there are so many new opportunities coming to Box City, especially on East 57th Street. That place is so beautiful."

I encouraged her to keep up the good work and go for it. I asked, "What do you wanted to do when you get your GED?" She told me her cousin worked in a bank, and she was thinking about something like that.

Then she said, "I want to go to college too."

I asked her to call me when I got out of the hospital because I wanted help her if I could. She was a great candidate for my Finang gang. I thought, *If she gets her GED, I will gladly help her with college.* She thanked me for helping her. I told her to come by and see me if she had another problem. She gathered her cart and left the room full of excitement. All I could think about was how determined this girl was. She could have almost lost her job because of it. The nurse came in, and I asked her for something to help me sleep. She went out, came back and gave me a shot of something, and that was all I remembered.

After two weeks and three days of rest, I was released from the hospital. I felt like a brand-new man. My whole body felt light. I decided to reorganize my day planner so I wouldn't be so stressed. My accident was really an eye-opener. The one who had blessed me with all of these great opportunities was the one I had put on the back burner, even though I talked to Him every day. I wasn't going to church to worship Him. I called Alicestene and told her that I wanted to go church with her that Sunday. She was so happy. I put that in my planner and circled it in red. I wanted to do something great for the church, but I didn't want anyone to know it was me.

CHAPTER 25

Sunday morning came, and I drove over to pick up Alicestene so we could go to church. We had to get there early in order to get a good seat. I noticed a box that read, "Special offering for expansion fund." I quickly put the money in it before she or anyone noticed. The service began, and the choir was getting their praise on. All the songs were about thanking God or praising God for His goodness toward us. When I thought about how close I came to dying. I couldn't help but thank Him. All the young people and old were praising Him like never before. No one was concerned about who was standing next to them or what they were wearing. They just gave themselves to God. I just let the tears run down my face, and I praised Him like everyone else. I felt such a great release deep down inside. I felt like I was on air. I knew then that I was in the place where God wanted me to be.

The preacher recognized all the visitors and thanked us for coming. Then he made his announcements with an appeal. He asked us to look around the church. It was packed from wall to wall with people. He told us we had outgrown the building and needed a bigger one. He asked everyone to dig a little deeper into their purses and pockets to help with the expansion. He said a special collection would be taken up each Sunday for just that purpose, starting today. There was a special box up front if anyone had to leave early. I had gotten an envelope earlier and put my money in that box with no name on it—all twenty-five thousand dollars of it. When they passed the offering tray, I put a dollar in. Alicestene frowned at me to put in more. I gave ten dollars and smiled at her.

She looked at me with those beautiful puppy dog eyes and said, "Now tell me. Don't you feel better?"

I just smiled at her. The preacher preached a heartwarming message about the prodigal son, who went back home to his father. I felt like he was talking to me. When he extended the invitation to join the church, I got up filled with joy and went down with the others. Alicestene got up, grabbed my hand, and went down with me. It was a very emotional moment with her by my side. I had been so busy trying to build Box City that I had forgotten about my own soul. God had used that accident to get my attention.

The pastor prayed for us and welcomed us into the church. He said, "You are all now new creatures in Christ Jesus. Old things are passed away. Your chains are loosed from sin, and you are free—free to fly high and be everything God wants you to be. Satan has no more power over you."

Man, I felt so good. I couldn't imagine that after all God had done for me already, there was a higher height I could fly. If it was there, I was certainly willing to try to find it.

As the pastor was going back to the pulpit, several of the church officers came over to him all excited and told him something. He went up to the pulpit and told us that he had a special announcement. He was so excited he was about to burst. He said, "The Lord works in mysterious ways, children. Someone put twenty-five thousand dollars in an envelope in the special offering box for the expansion with no name on it." Everybody jumped up, clapping and praised God.

"Will you please stand so I can thank you?" he asked.

No one stood. Then he said, "The Lord knows who you are, and I want to say thank you and may He continue to bless you. Our offering for today is twenty-seven thousand dollars," and he asked us to give the Lord a big hand clap of praise again. It was a wonderful time. Spiritually I needed it.

Alicestene said that it was just great that someone would do that for the church and wondered who it was. I just said, "Baby, I don't know." She said no one had ever given the church that kind of money before and hoped that one day we would be able to give like that.

On our way out the pastor was at the door. He paused and asked me to wait for him a minute. He finished saying good-bye to members of the congregation and came over to talk to Alicestene and me.

He said, "I heard there is going to be a wedding after you graduate college, Brother Hancock. I want you to know that I am proud of both of you. I think you and Alicestene will make a fine couple."

He was even prouder that I had joined his church. He wanted to find a special place for me to work in it. He told me I could have gone to another church. He was grateful to God for sending me there. He asked Alicestene if he could speak to me alone for just a few minutes. We left her and walked down the hall toward his office.

He said, "I want to thank you for your gift today, son."

I said, "Sir, the ten dollars."

He said, "No, the Lord showed me that it was you that gave the large sum of money."

I said, "Pastor, how can you be so sure it was me when no one stood up?" He told me that whenever I came to his church, something wonderful always happened. He just put two and two together. He knew the giving patterns of his people and subtracted them from the equation, and that left me.

I asked, "Why do you think I have that kind of money?"

He said, "I don't know, but there is something amazing about you."

I smiled, thanked him, and said, "I am going to leave that with you and the Lord."

Then he asked, "How would you like to help me with the expansion project?" I told him to let me think about it and get back with him since I just got out of the hospital. I really wasn't ready to start working in the church so soon with all the other things on my plate. I rejoined Alicestene, and we left.

CHAPTER 26

A few months later while I was having dinner with Mama at her restaurant one evening, something shocking happened. A strange, heavyset man with a beard came in. He went through the line, got his food, went over to a table and sat down. As he ate, I noticed that he just kept staring at Mama and me. It was really making me nervous. I asked Mama if she knew the man. She said she didn't, at least not that she knew of. He continued to stare at us, and we were beginning to worry. I hoped this wasn't someone planning to rob us later. Mama and I got up and went into her office. Mama had a window where you could see out but you couldn't see in. We watched him as he would turn from time to time and watch her office. He finally finished his meal and walked out the door. We were so relieved. I told Mama I would wait and go out with her to make sure she was safe when she got off since Mr. Crumpton was out of town on a buying trip. All of a sudden, the man came back into the restaurant. He went through the line and got a cup of coffee and sat down again. This was really beginning to bother me. He started staring at us again while he drank his coffee. I told Mama that was enough. I was going to see what this man wanted. I asked her to call the police quickly if there was trouble. I went over to his table and said, "How are you doing, sir?" I told him that I noticed he had been watching us for a while and asked him if he knew us.

He said, "I just want to speak to Miss Meyel if it was okay."

I asked him why he wanted to speak with her and if something was wrong with his coffee.

He said, "No, I just want to speak with her. We used to be good friends a long time ago."

I went and told Mama what the man said. She came over to see him. He looked up at Mama and said, "How you doing Meyel?" Mama took a good look at the man and told him that she was fine, but she didn't seem to remember him as a friend.

He said, "Meyel, it's me, Jimmy. We were once married, remember?"

Man, I could have fainted. He told her that he had just put on some weight over the years and grew a beard. That was why she didn't recognize him. Mama was shocked and backed away from the table. It was like she had seen a ghost. I was shocked because if they were married, this was my daddy in the flesh. This was the man who had left us to starve to death. It became a very scary moment.

Through all of Mama's pain, hurts, and disappointments, somehow she had managed to erase this man completely from her memory until now. She didn't even recognize him the tiniest bit. Oh, but when she thought for a few minutes. It was like she came out of some kind of coma. She became furious, and I had to quiet her. You would have thought this man was the Devil himself to her. She had a permit to carry a gun. You'd better believe she was ready to use it. I stayed close to her to make sure she didn't. At that moment everything Mama had worked so hard to accomplish in her life was on the line. He told her he had heard that she had a restaurant in Box City. He was in the area and thought he would stop by to see it.

He said, "Meyel, the restaurant is very nice, and the food is very good." Mama never responded. He didn't even realize that I was his son. It was like I was invisible to him too. I guess he thought I was the help.

Then Mama said, "Tehh, this is your no good daddy, the one who took the money and left us to starve to death years ago." He looked up at me with shame on his face, never saying a word. I believe if Mama had a match and some gasoline, he would have gone up in flames that very moment. She was madder than I had ever seen her in my life.

He must have forgotten that he had three children by her because he said, "So this is little Tehh?" In his mind I never grew up. I was still a little boy.

I said, "No, sir, I had to grow up quick when you left us. I am six-foot-four and still growing." I told him boldly, "I am a grown man now, Daddy, and taking good care of my mama." Mama asked him to leave the restaurant and never come back before she called the police. I realize he had done nothing wrong but show his face after all those years. Then he asked her how Benjamin and Diamond were doing. What did he do that for?

Mama just went off like fireworks. She said, "If you wanted to know how they were doing, you should have been here so you would know." I knew Mama's blood pressure was rising. I had to calm her down because there were still customers in the restaurant.

We went outside to finish the conversation. She had come too far to turn back now to that old state of mind. Mama asked him, "Why are you so concerned about us now after all of these years, Jimmy? Where were you when I was working four or five different jobs a week trying to keep a roof over my children's heads? Why now, Jimmy? Are you looking for a handout or something?"

I asked her to calm down. He said, "I don't need no handout, Meyel. I'm just fine. I got married again and have three more children."

All of the color went right out of Mama's face when he said that.

He said, "I heard people talking about Meyel's Restaurant in Box City, and I wanted see if it was you—that's all."

I said, "Lord, please help us."

Then Mama said with that evil voice, "Three children, Jimmy? You mean you left me with three children to go and have three more by somebody else? Well, take a good look. Now you see me, Jimmy. Now go and crawl back into the hole you came out of. I hope you love those three children because you sure didn't love mine. I don't ever want to see you again as long as I live." Mama was so angry that she had sweat on her nose and tears were running down her face.

It was a sad thing to see my mama and daddy in this way after all those years. Facing the reality of what he had done, my daddy walked away like a dog with his tail tucked between his legs. He got in his car and drove off without even saying, "Good-bye, son." He had been a fool twice in his life to me. The first time he left me as a little boy with a dream. This time he left me as a man whose dream came true.

As the tears rolled down my face, I said, "Daddy, I'm a millionaire, and you don't even know it." I soon got over the hurt because I had cried away my pain in the early years.

Sometimes it hurt me so bad when I hear mothers tell their children they didn't have fathers or they didn't need them. The mothers were so hurt by their past experiences that they never considered the pain that those children held within—the desire to know their fathers. In my case my father didn't realize how much he had hurt me. I pulled myself together and tried to console Mama, and we went back into the restaurant and sat down. Mama was truly hurt. Her inner world had been turned upside down. I realized as the tears ran down her face that all of Mama's pain from the past was not dead and buried as I had thought, but was lightly dusted with sweet success.

At that moment she forgot about all the Lord had done to give us a better life in spite of what my daddy had done. She almost lost it all because she had never forgiven him. That moment taught me that unforgiveness was a dangerous thing. She was ready to kill my daddy and probably would have if I had not been there. Even in his absence he still had power over her, and she didn't know it. You have to be able to let go of some people, some places, and some pain in order to move forward and enjoy the blessings of God. Otherwise they will destroy all of your hopes and dreams.

While I was talking with Mama about the past and the future, she realized that she had been very wrong in how she had treated Daddy and asked me to forgive her. She said she didn't realize that she had been holding all that hatred in all of those years. I asked her to please forgive Daddy and thank God for him leaving. I just believed deep down in my heart that if Daddy had been there with us, our lives would have turned out for the worse. God knew exactly what He was doing. Mama looked at me and said, "Boy, you sure you are not some kind of preacher?"

I smiled and said, "No, Mama." She gave me a big hug and told me that if she ever saw Daddy again, she would apologize so she could close the book on that chapter of her life. I looked at her and said, "Now that's my mama." It wasn't a total loss because Daddy had given us some good information that we had never considered. The Lord worked in a mysterious way again. Daddy had remarried but had never legally divorced Mama. Mama and Mr. Crumpton would be getting married in a few months. I asked her to have her lawyer track him down and serve him with divorce papers. She shouldn't have any trouble getting it. I knew it would cost him more than he would be willing to pay. For a moment I thought that if my daddy had recognized me as his son and apologized for what he had done to us, I would have been glad to call him my father and develop a new relationship with him. I would have invited him to my wedding and one day let my children sit on his knee and call him Grand-daddy. At that moment I was so glad my mama didn't name me Junior, but I was grateful for the Hancock in my name.

CHAPTER 27

Time rolled around, and it was the week of Mama and Mr. Crumpton's wedding. Daddy had signed the divorce papers the very same day he had received them and personally took them to the lawyer's office. He must not have wanted any trouble after all. Everybody, even members of the gang, had some part in the wedding. The ladies tried on their dresses, and the guys tried on their tuxes at Mr. Crumpton's store. The wedding coordinators and caterers handled all the details of the wedding. I had finally come to my senses and learned to let go and let people do the jobs they were paid to do. Mama's bakery did her wedding cake, and Ricko's Bakery did the groom's cake and other deserts. Mama's wedding was the first in the Underground City's Weddings and Events Center. The decorations were simply amazing. The coordinator did a fantastic job. Several people wanted to see the other areas of the Underground City, but I told them they couldn't. They would have to check with the owners another time. The entertainment area was closed off from the shopping area until the place actually opened the first of the year. We all met there for the rehearsal dinner, which I prepared with a little help from Benjamin and Diamond. Benjamin was the best man, and he and Mr. Crumpton had begun to bond during that time. Later he told me that Benjamin and I would be his sons and that he was proud of us. Diamond was his little lady, and she was growing so fast. He was going to have to keep a shotgun at the door to scare off some of the boys. We went through the rehearsal dinner, and afterward we left and went home to get ready for the wedding.

The next day we all arrived at the Underground City around the same time that evening. It was truly a spectacular place to see. This was a huge wedding, and people arrived early so they could look around the place and mingle. Mama sent a message to me and said she wanted to see me. I hurried to the dressing room to see her. I opened the door, and there she was. My mama was simply breathtaking. Oh, what a beautiful bride she was. She took my hand and asked me to sit down. She told me how proud she was of me and thanked me for all I had done to make our lives better. I said, "It wasn't me. It was the Lord." She said it was hard for her to let me go, even though she loved Mr. Crumpton. She depended on me for everything and didn't know what to do now. She was so scared. I told her she didn't have to let me go. I was going to always be her son and be there whenever she needed me. It was hard, but I had to let Mr. Crumpton take care of her now. Either way I was definitely going to be watching closely. She smiled, and I told her that he was going to be a great husband and father. Her confidence came back and she just smiled even more. I told her that I wouldn't be too far away because I was having a house built in Wagon Trace too, only six blocks away. I wanted to surprise Alicestene when we came back from our honeymoon. She gave me a big hug and said she loved me. I told her that I was proud of her for believing in me and trusting me when it didn't even make sense. I took a napkin and dabbed the tears away, brushed her hair back, gave her a big hug, and asked her to not keep Mr. Crumpton waiting.

As we were coming out the door, Diamond and Benjamin were there waiting to get a glimpse of her. They took one look at Mama, and tears fell from their eyes. They said she was so beautiful, and she gave them both a big hug. We all walked Mama down the hall to marry Mr. Crumpton and took our places. Rev. Isaac Young performed the ceremony. Standing there beside my mama made me realize that I would be in this place again a few months from now.

All of a sudden two of the most beautiful bridesmaids I had ever seen emerged from a room. First there was Diamond, my baby sister, who was so beautiful and growing up before my eyes. Then there was Alicestene, my queen, my future wife. Time stood still for me for just a minute because she was just breathtaking. In my heart I felt like I was one lucky man to have these three beautiful women in my life. It was time for Mama to go in, and I was so nervous. The wedding march played. Everyone stood, and she gracefully made the long walk down the aisle with me by her side. I glanced at her and saw the tears slowly running down her face. Then tears ran down my face, and I couldn't stop them. "I'm a guy," I said to myself. "Guys don't cry." But I couldn't help it. This was my mama. The first love of my life that I was going to give to another man for the rest of her life. Someone handed me a napkin as I passed by them to wipe my tears away. We finally made it up to the front, and she took her place by Mr. Crumpton. When the preacher asked, "Who gives this woman in marriage?" Diamond, Benjamin, and I proudly said, "We do," and everyone laughed. I took my seat with tears still in my eyes. It was indeed a beautiful wedding that was made in heaven.

All the pictures were taken, and we all prepared for the reception. There was food everywhere, and everyone could serve themselves. There was a huge fountain that overflowed with three flavors of delicious punch. There were huge hanging baskets of finger sandwiches and desserts to fill the void. Platters of beef, pork, and chicken with all the trimming filled one area. Everything was just beautiful, and the smell was out of this world. I heard people saying they had never seen a wedding so beautiful, and never in a place like this before. Some wondered how much a wedding like that cost. Others said Mr. Crumpton had to be a rich man. Whatever the case, that made me feel really good. Everyone seemed to be having a great time. Finally Mama and Mr. Crumpton got up and went to the dance floor as the music played. He looked into her eyes, took her in his arms, and held her close. I knew then I wasn't going to get her back. God had given her a soul mate at last, and I was so grateful. All I ever asked God for was to make my mama happy, and this was another one of the happiest days of her life. It seemed as if time stopped for a few minutes as we watched them dance. After that, a fast song played, and the party was on. Everyone, old and young, took to the dance floor and danced to early morning.

Mama and Mr. Crumpton were going to spend their honeymoon in beautiful Hawaii for two weeks, and I didn't have anything to do with it at all. Mama asked me earlier to let him take care of that part of the wedding. He asked me if I would run the store for him while he was away, and said he would pay me when he got back. I told him that was okay and not to worry about paying me. He smiled and said, "Boy, you are getting married soon. You are going to need every penny you can get. Trust me."

I just said, "Yes, sir," and smiled. I asked Benjamin and Diamond to help me in order to give them some job training. My plate was already full.

I was going to need all the help I could get. I didn't want to wind up in the hospital again.

While Mama and Mr. Crumpton were in Hawaii, we ran the store. Business for the week was good. Diamond and Benjamin took turns operating the cash register. It was Friday, and Mama and Mr. Crumpton would be home on Tuesday. I couldn't wait for them to hurry home. That was the first time in my life that I couldn't see my mama when I wanted to. We were unpacking sweaters and decided to try a few of them on because they looked so good. Even Diamond tried on one. She changed the whole look of the sweater. The girl really looked good. We saw a bus pass by but thought nothing of it. Diamond went outside to get something out of my car and came back in. The next thing we knew the store was filled with cheerleaders asking for one of the sweaters Diamond had on. They said it really looked cool. Then the guys on the bus came in and checked out the sweaters and other stuff. The store was filled with customers. All of them bought a sweater. Some bought several, and some purchased other stuff. We sold nearly two thousand dollars' worth of merchandise in just a few hours. They nearly cleaned us out. It was unbelievable. Women never thought they could find something at a big and tall men's store, and neither did we. Many of them said they would come back to the store again. That really sounded good to my ears. I had suggested to Mr. Crumpton earlier that he should stock some items for the average person even though he was a big and tall store, and it worked. Diamond was the star of the day and got a hundred-dollar bonus for selling the most merchandise and going outside with that sweater on at the right time. Benjamin did a great job too and got seventy-five dollars. I know Mr. Crumpton is going to be very happy when I tell him what we did. He averages a little more than $2,500.00 a week. We straightened up the store, and I went in the back and got some more items to restock the shelves. I took all the money we made and locked it up in the safe in his office. I must be a pretty good guy for him to trust me like that. I told Benjamin and Diamond not to keep more than three hundred dollars in the drawer at a time. If they had more, one of them was to take it to his office and hide it until I came back.

I had to run over to Mama's restaurant to make sure everything was going okay over there. Miss Emma said she had everything covered on her end. She said business was very good and wondered what was going on. Several buses had stopped by and nearly cleaned out the bakery and the restaurant, but they had restocked again. I left the restaurant and went over to my antique shop as Tehh, and everything was going great there. The shop was full of people. One of the clerks asked me to get something from the back, and I did. One lady asked me to help her put something in her car, and I did. Then one lady came over and asked me for my autograph, and I wondered why.

She said, "It's you. You are the young man I saw on television with the severe learning disability. They said you couldn't read or write, and you were pushing a wagon. They said you wanted to get an education because you wanted to be somebody one day. You got your GED, and you are now in college. That was an amazing story."

I said, "Yes, ma'am, that was me. Thank you."

Then she showed me a picture of her grandson and said, "You were a blessing to my grandson. He dropped out of school. He saw you on television and told me that if you could do it, he could do it too. He went back to school and is doing well, thanks to you." She gave me a big hug and asked the Lord to bless me. She told me the autograph was for her grandson and went on her way. I couldn't believe I missed that program, but I was glad it inspired someone to go back to school. It was my off day, but I finished helping them with whatever they wanted me to do and went to check on the subdivisions.

Box City was now a town full of life. All of the free publicity really helped us. It was like a shot in the arm. Diamond Ridge Subdivision, name after Diamond, was a beautiful place, and most of the houses were up. Sixty percent of them had been sold. Once the streets were in and the drainage problems corrected, people would be moving in. I was so glad we had a hard rain that caused the streets to flood before everyone moved in. I thanked God that there was no damage to the homes or other property. That gave the contractors and construction crews the opportunity to fix the problem before the people moved in. In the center of Diamond Ridge is a park with a beautiful lake. The ducks have already made their home there. It is truly a beautiful place. I left there and went over to see Wagon Trace and looked at the house I was having built for myself and Alicestene. The whole community was beautiful with stately mansions. There is a huge lake stocked with all kinds of fish and a gorgeous park for family picnics. That policeman I met at the Underground City finally got his house built. He is going to be shocked when he learns that I live in the area as well. Everything was going fine. A beautiful Box City was truly on the rise and was looking better than the other side of town. I had proved the bankers wrong. Low-class people can have a high-class mentality. It just takes a whole lot of work.

I stopped by the burger shop and picked up something to eat for Benjamin and Diamond and got myself two strawberry sodas—one for the road and one for later. I quickly drove on back to Mr. Crumpton's store. I got out of the car and looked through the window. Benjamin and Diamond were busy working. Benjamin was at the register ringing up a customer, and Diamond was assisting another customer. I was so proud of them. I went in and took the food to the back and came out to help them. They told me everything was okay. I just stood back and watched. I thought they were going to do well with their own businesses one day. Then I thought to myself, *I don't know why God made me the way that I am, but they wanted to be just like me and do whatever I did. What would their lives have been like if I had chosen the wrong path?* I hated to think about it.

All the customers were gone, and I told them to eat. I said I would take care of the front. I started hanging up sweaters when all of a sudden Mama and Mr. Crumpton came through the door. I was so glad to see them. I really missed my mama. Diamond and Benjamin flew from the back, and we all gave them one big family hug. I asked, "Why did you come back so early?"

Mr. Crumpton said, "I didn't like the sound of that volcano over there, and I really missed y'all."

Then with her big mouth, Diamond said, "Mr. Crumpton, we made a lot of money for you today. We sold nearly two thousand dollars' worth of clothes and stuff in a few hours."

Mr. Crumpton said, "What! I just barely do that much in a week. You see, Meyel, I told you that every time Tehh comes to my shop, something good happens."

Diamond said, "I got a hundred-dollar bonus for selling the most, and Benjamin got seventy-five dollars. Tehh didn't get anything." Everybody laughed, and Mama and Mr. Crumpton told us how proud they were of us. Mr. Crumpton even said he just might keep us on working for him after school if Mama didn't mind. Little did he know that I didn't need another job. My plate was already running over. I told him that he needed to order some more size-small merchandise because the ladies bought him out. They loved all the sweaters. He just couldn't believe it. He checked everything and closed the store. I thanked God that was over and went home with them. We sat around and listened to them talk about their trip, looked at pictures, and finally went to sleep.

Mama and Mr. Crumpton were really enjoying life now, and we were enjoying having a real father. I try to stop by often because I enjoyed being with family. They were acting like teenagers, running through the house, laughing, and picking at each other. My mama was finally happy, and it showed. Mr. Crumpton was like a new man, and he enjoy every minute of his new life. He told me he missed out on doing a lot of things with his first wife, but he didn't intend to do that with Mama. Mama thanked me for my advice and told me she had forgiven my daddy so she could get on with her life, and it felt good. She told me she thought she could never love again or have someone in her life who really appreciated her other than me. The funny thing about Mr. Crumpton is that he is always concerned about me having money in my pockets and doing the right things. "Take Alicestene out for dinner or a movie on me," he would say. He was truly a real dad looking out for my best interests, and I really appreciated that. If one day he found out that I was a millionaire all the time he and Mama had been dating, he just might ask for all of his money back with interest.

CHAPTER 28

It was the last week of November, and Mama wanted to decorate her home for Christmas. She was so excited about decorating the house that she ordered more decorations than she needed. Ten live Christmas trees arrived. They were all extra tall and sitting on the back patio with all the decorations. Mr. Crumpton just laughed and asked her if she was giving trees as gifts for Christmas. Mama said, "I thought they were the little trees. I wanted to put one in the window of each room." Diamond asked if she could have a big tree in her room, and so did Benjamin. She decided to give the rest to families who didn't have trees along with decorations and gifts.

Everybody was decorating, and Box City was lit up. It looked pretty amazing. I even had them put lights in the Underground City. It was truly a spectacular sight. People were coming from everywhere to see our little city for hope and inspiration.

One evening while I was driving down Rush Avenue, I noticed a pregnant woman with four or five children. They were going into a rundown house. I had never noticed the house before. The voice on the inside of me said they were in need and to help them any way I could. They appeared to be very poor, and there were definitely no Christmas decorations up. I slowly pulled into her yard and pretended to ask for directions so I could talk to her. It was cold, and the children were half dressed. Some had no shoes on, and begging her for food. She didn't have much to give them and began to cry, telling them to hush up.

I asked her if everything was okay, and she said, "No, everything is not okay for me right now."

She told me her husband had been killed a while back and it was hard. She was doing the best she could to make it, being pregnant and all. She leaned on my car and told me how tired she was trying to keep her head above the water. She was getting a little check each month, but it wasn't enough to take care of everything. She didn't have any family in Box City to help her and didn't know what she and the children were going to do. She said the house needed so much work, and it was so cold. She didn't have the money to pay her bills because she had to take one of the children to the doctor and buy medicine. I tried to consoler her. I told her who I was and asked if I could come in and look around. I just had to do something to help her after I had heard her story. It was cold. The temperature was dropping, and there was no power or heat in the house. I noticed a couple of cans of beans on the table, which was hardly enough to feed all of them. It made me remember when Mama had days like that. Days when she would try to take care of us, and tears would fall from my eyes. I asked her to let me go and call for help, and I would be right back. She took the children and wrapped them up in blankets. She sat them on the couch and told them not to move.

I went and called Mama and explained the situation. She told me that our old apartment was still vacant and said they could live there. It was fully furnished, and all the power was still on. She would meet me there. She told me later that she left it that way just in case someone needed help because God had been so good to us. I went back to her house, and the lady was so glad to see me this time. I asked her name, and she said she was Queen Collins. When I told her about the apartment, she lit up like a Christmas tree.

She was so happy and said, "You have to be an angel sent from God. You just don't know how hard I prayed for Him to help us. I was about to give up. I just couldn't hold out any longer, and then you came along."

I asked her to pack what she could. I would take them over to the apartment. She could get the rest of her things later. She got their belongings and got in my car. All of them were shivering. She told me the car was so warm and it felt so good. The children were still shivering from the cold and said the car felt so warm they didn't want to get out. I noticed one of the little girls had a cough, and they all had runny noses. Her name was Jordan, and she gave me a great big smile. I stopped by the store and picked up some children's cold medicine so they could all feel better.

We quickly made it over to the apartment and got out. I opened the door, and the heat kissed our faces as we all went in. Mama, Mr. Crumpton, Diamond, and Benjamin were already there with food, groceries, bedding, and everything. Mama had even set the table so the children could go on and eat. Mrs. Collins was so happy and thanked Mama for everything. We stayed and joined them for dinner to make sure she was okay and tried to help them feel comfortable about their new home. I watched the children's eyes sparkle as they ate. I smiled when they asked for more. I remembered a few times when we didn't have that much to eat either and a few good neighbors helped us.

Mama showed her around the apartment and explained everything and gave her the key. She said, "You can stay here as long as you need to, and don't you worry about anything."

I asked her if she owned her house, and she said, "Yes, what's left of it. My daddy left me the house when he died."

Mama told her that she would come back tomorrow and find out what she and the children needed. We all left and went back to the house. As I drove home, I never thought I could feel so good. I felt that God was pleased with what I had done. I was in His perfect timing to see Mrs. Collins with her children at that time. Her house was really rundown and in much need of repair, but it was her home. It was all she had in this world other than her children. The voice on the inside of me kept telling me, "Have it fixed up for her for Christmas." That voice had never led me wrong. The next day I called the contractor. I explained the situation, and he began working on her house to have it ready by Christmas.

The Sunday before Christmas we all got up early and went to church. The children were having their Christmas program. They were all dressed in red, green, and white. The choirs beautifully sang one Christmas song after another. They portrayed the Christmas story with Mary riding a donkey on wheels as Joseph pulled her across the stage. Alicestene told me she had a surprise for me, but didn't tell me exactly what it was. She just told me I would see at church. When Joseph took Mary off the donkey and she began to sing, I realized it was Alicestene. She sang a beautiful Christmas song and sent chills up and down my spine. I was so proud of her. I didn't even know she could sing like that. Wow, that certainly was another star in her crown from me. Pastor Young came with the Christmas message, "The child born to save the world." He preached that Jesus was born to save the world and us from sin. He made Jesus sound like a superhero destroying all the evil in man and releasing His righteousness in Christ.

He said, "No one in this world could have done for us what Jesus did for us on Calvary when He died for our sins. Not only was Jesus the gift to us when He was born, but He was also our gift when He rose from the dead. He had to come out of that grave for you and for me so we could have the victory. Then He went back home to His father and sent us back a third gift. Did you receive yours?" He asked. "It was the gift of the Holy Spirit." Then he asked us again, "Did you receive Him?" Something happened and the whole church began shouting and praising God. It was the most powerful service I had ever seen for a Christmas program. Then the pastor ended by telling the church we had raised the money for the expansion program and should be breaking ground early next year. We all praised God for all of His marvelous blessing and headed out.

As we were leaving, Pastor Young asked me to wait a minute. He came back and asked me to come into his office. He was excited to show me the new expansion building designs and asked what I thought about them. I looked them over and asked him if it was okay for us to go back and take a good look at the church and consider all the needs and wants before we approved what he had. It seemed like something was missing to me. I didn't see a recreation area for all of our young people. We needed to provide them with something to keep them busy and out of trouble. We agreed to meet that Tuesday evening. Then he said, "Son, I don't know how you did it or what you did, but I know you had something to do with the blessing that came to Mount Zion." I just continued to act like I didn't know what in the world he was talking about.

It was three days before Christmas and the contractor called to let me know that Mrs. Collins's house was ready and all furnished. I asked Mama and Mr. Crumpton to meet me over there. I drove down Rush Avenue and couldn't believe my eyes. The house was so beautiful and unrecognizable. I pulled up in the yard with tears in my eyes and got out to meet Mama and Mr. Crumpton. They couldn't believe their eyes either. The contractor told me the keys were under the mat on the back porch. We went around, opened the door, and went inside. I couldn't believe what I saw. The house was completely transformed. It was absolutely beautiful. They added two extra bedrooms so most of the children would have their own rooms. The decorator even put up a Christmas tree in the living room with gifts for all the children under it. The living room was beautiful, and Mama just loved it. They expanded the kitchen and added a huge pantry. There was a huge table in the kitchen to accommodate six growing children. The cabinets were stocked with food, and meat was in the huge upright freezer. Clothes were in all the closets. We really felt good about this house and this very special family. There was even a playground area out back for the children. The surprise was the furnished room for the new baby. I looked at Mama. She looked at me and gave me a big hug with tears in her eyes. Mr. Crumpton said he was proud of me too.

He said, "This is what Christmas is all about, helping others."

He really thought Mama had all the work done. He gave her a big hug and said, "This makes me feel really good. I want to pay up all Mrs. Collins's housing expenses for the next two years if it that's okay with your mama."

Mama smiled, looked at him, and said, "Honey, that's ok with me." He wanted to help her get on her feet and save a little money. Mama looked at him and gave him another big hug with tears in her eyes.

We drove over to the apartment to check on Mrs. Collins and the kids. She was so glad to see us. I felt good because the apartment was so clean with five children and she didn't expect us. Mama had explained the policies of the apartment to stay there rent-free. One was keeping it clean at all times. We asked if we could take her and the children out to get some ice cream, and she agreed. They were well-behaved children, which said a lot about the kind of mother she was. We stopped and got ice cream, and then I drove down Rush Avenue with Mama and Mr. Crumpton trailing me. It was now time for the surprise. Mrs. Collins recognized her street and then began looking around for her house. She was so confused and kept asking me, "Where is my house? It should be over there, but that is not my house. I am not crazy." I drove around the block and came back, and she said the same thing. "Thomas, where is my house?" She was getting a little upset. I pulled up to that place where her house should have been and asked her to get out. I told her that we needed to see what was going on. We all went around to the back of the house. She stopped, pointed, and said, "Now that's my tree, but this is certainly not my house. Please tell me what's going on here?" I slowly opened the door and asked her and the children to come in. Mama and Mr.

Crumpton were right behind them. She looked around and said, "Oh, my goodness. This house is so warm and beautiful." Then she asked me who the house belonged to because they had her tree in their yard. She told the children not to move so they wouldn't accidently break something. I took her by the hand and asked her to sit down at the table. Then her children got up and came over and sat down beside her on the floor. I knew she was wondering what was going on.

I looked her in the eyes and said, "Ms. Queen, this is your new home," and she almost fainted. That woman nearly scared me to death. I wasn't ready to deliver a baby that day.

Mama went over to her and said, "He's telling you the truth, honey. This is truly your house, Queen. We wanted to do something special for you and the children. So we had it remodeled for you and the children for Christmas. We hope you don't mind."

She jumped up, crying, and said, "I don't mind. I just can't believe it. You don't even know me. I just can't believe this. Thank you." She gave me a big hug as her stomach pressed deep into my side. I could feel the baby inside of her jumping for joy and saying, "Thank you," in his own special way. I really felt good.

We show her and all the children around their new home. Every time she went into a room, opened a closet, and saw the children's clothes and shoes, she would just scream, and more tears would fall. Her bedroom was special because she told Mama she always dreamed of a queen-size bed, and there it was. She just couldn't believe it. She went into the baby's room off of her room, and she just cried some more. "I have never had anything this nice in my life," she cried. All of the excitement made her a little weak, and she had trouble standing. She grabbed her stomach. I hoped she wasn't going into labor before her time. I couldn't take any more excitement from this woman. She was getting the best of me. I sat her down so she could rest a little while. Then she struggled to get up again. She went in the kitchen, looked in the cabinets, and saw all the food. Then she looked in the restaurant-size freezer and saw enough meat to last for several months. She was one happy woman, thanking the Lord with tears in her eyes. Even the children were acting like their mother, saying, "Thank You, Jesus." The children were so happy to see all the gifts under the Christmas tree. They just didn't know what to do.

Mama told them that they had to wait until Christmas to open them because Santa Claus would be very upset if they opened them early.

Mrs. Collins just kept saying, "I just can't believe it. Thank you. I just don't know how I'm going to be able repay you." We all told her that we didn't expect her to. It was our gift to her. Then Mr. Crumpton had the greatest pleasure of telling her that all of her utilities were paid up for the next two years, and she started jumping up and screaming again. It was like she had won the lottery, and she had in a sense. I asked her to make a list of all the bills she owed because we were going to pay them off too. I would come over and show her how to use a checking and savings account later. She started jumping up and down again. I couldn't take any more because I was becoming a nervous wreck.

I said, "Please don't jump up and down again," and everybody laughed. Mama asked her to just continue to take care of herself, the children, and the baby when it comes. I told her that we would be her new family from now on.

There was still more excitement to come for Mrs. Collins. We gave her the keys to the house, and she noticed an extra key on the chain and asked, "What's this one for?" We told her it was for the car on the other side of the house. She screamed, cried, jumped, and shouted! We wanted to make sure she had everything she needed to properly take care of her family. I felt like she had suffered enough. She said, "I didn't think God would ever answer my prayers, especially like this," and she cried some more. She told Mama that she would go over to the apartment and get her things. She would leave everything the way she found it and bring the keys to the restaurant. She promised to return the favor by helping someone in need whenever she could.

She gave me a big hug and whispered in my ear, "If it's a boy, I'm going to name him Thomas Edison, after you." My heart hit the floor, and I just didn't know what to do. I had never in my life been extended such an honor. I pulled myself together and thanked her. All the children gave us hugs and kisses and said, "Bye, bye." We left feeling better than Santa Claus. Mama told Mrs. Collins to let us know when the baby came so we could all be there for her. The Lord allowed me again to make a difference in someone's life with the help of Mama and Mr. Crumpton.

CHAPTER 29

Mama was having her first Christmas party and wanted me to spend the night with the family. Everyone was there, including the gang, Mrs. Collins, and the children. Mama had a huge tree in the family room filled with gifts for the guests. Then all of a sudden something caught my eye that I had never seen before. There was a boy sitting too close to Diamond. They were talking and laughing like they had known each other for a while. I wanted to get up and move him away from her, but I didn't. My little sister was now growing up. Then I looked at Benjamin, and there was a very cute girl with him. How did I miss all of that? I must have really been busy. For a moment I hated that I had ever left home for school. I looked over at Alicestene sitting with her parents. She was so beautiful. I said a prayer because I didn't want to miss anything about our lives together. We were all having a good time enjoying one another.

After we finished eating, we all gathered in the family room around the tree and sang Christmas carols. It was just wonderful. It was almost like church again.

Mama got everybody's attention and said, "I want all of you to know that this is the best Christmas I have ever had, and I have gifts for everyone. You are all part of my special family, and I love you so much." This was her way of thanking God for all He had done for her. She asked Benjamin, Diamond, and their friends to help pass out the gifts. Then she said, "Now everybody, please don't open your gifts until you get home, okay?" There were big boxes and small boxes until most were gone except the ones that were for her.

Miss Emma forgot just that quickly and opened her gift. She looked, screamed, and then fainted. Everyone wanted to know what was going on and what she had gotten. Her husband quickly revived her, and she said, "Lord have mercy. Meyel, thank you so much."

Mama had given her a check for a thousand dollars. I would have fainted too. Then everyone opened their gifts to see what they had. No one wanted to wait after that. Paper was flying everywhere. Mama just stood there smiling. There were screams, and people saying, "Oh, my goodness." Everyone thanked Mama and gave her hugs with tears in their eyes. She wanted to make sure everyone close to her had a very Merry Christmas, especially those in our gang. She came to realize that some of them were still struggling. She even gave some gift certificates to Mr. Crumpton's store, which he loved. I was so proud of my mama and Mr. Crumpton. He supported Mama in what she wanted to do. He never questioned her about how much money she was spending, and I liked that. Mama and Mr. Crumpton were the Santa Clauses of Box City that night. Everyone left filled with joy and gladness. Mrs. Collins and the children were the last to leave because she just wanted to thank us again. All the children gave us hugs and kisses, they said, "I love you," and, "Bye, bye." They all hopped in the car and waved good-bye to us. That was truly a great feeling. After that, we were all tuckered out and went to bed.

I got up early Christmas morning and began fixing breakfast in that kitchen that was made for a chef. Mama had some dough in the refrigerator, so I made some cinnamon rolls. The bacon, ham, and sausages were cooking to perfection. Then Benjamin came down and began to help me. He started the pancakes and waffles. Then Diamond came down with smiles and joined us by making the eggs, grits, and rice. I wondered why they were cooking so much. The house really smelled delicious and reminded me of the good old days at the apartment. I looked around, and to my surprise there was Alicestene and her parents, Mad Dog, Toe Joe, Brock, and Jason.

I said, "Man, when did y'all get here?"

They said, "Man, we never left." Mama had pulled one over on me this time.

Mama and Mr. Crumpton came down, smiled, and said, "Merry Christmas, Tehh."

She said, "Christmas would be nothing without family, and we are all family. We knew this is what you would want more than anything." Then there was a knock at the back door. "*In Wagon Trace,* I thought. Only one person was missing. Mama opened the door, and it was Miss Emma and her husband. Now the whole family was all here. I thanked Mama and Mr. Crumpton for what they did. It was like old times. I went over and gave Alicestene a big, big hug. I was so glad to see her and her mother. Her father still had a problem with me for some strange reason and told me that he had his eyes on me.

We all ate breakfast and went in the living room to get our gifts. The tree was packed with gifts for the family this time. Mr. Crumpton gave Mama a big diamond ring, and it was gorgeous. Mama gave him hers followed by a big kiss and asked him to open it later. We were all wondering, *What is it?* Then I gave Mama a gift, and she gave me mine. Everyone exchanged gifts.

Toe Joe, Brock, Mad Dog, and Jason stood up and said, "Tehh, man, we want to thank you for everything you did to make our lives better. Before we meet you, we were traveling down the wrong road, headed for trouble. You helped us get on the right path. We have money that we never thought we would ever have now legally. We don't have to be looking over our shoulders like other guys."

Mad Dog said, "Man, we can afford stuff we never imagined now because of you. You introduced us to a better quality of life and made us rich. We can't pay you enough for what you did, but we want to give you something that would show how much we love you, man."

I sat there, wondering what they were up to. Toe Joe gave me a key, and I asked, "What is this for?" I thought about Mama and Ms. Collins when I gave them a key.

He said, "Your brand-new car, man. It's parked outside." I was speechless. He grabbed me by hand and pulled me outside to see it, and everyone followed us.

"Wow! It's the Jeep I always talked about."

Tears were running down my face. "Man, this is nice," I told them. "Guys, you didn't have to do this for me."

I was so excited I just didn't know what else to say. "Thank y'all so much. Wow! I didn't expect anything like this."

All of a sudden the tears started running down my face again, and my voice began to crack. Then everybody else started crying too. I said, "I am a guy. Guys don't cry like this." Mama and Alicestene came over and held me because I was all messed up. True, I was guy, but I was crying like a baby.

These guys really cared enough about me to buy me a brand-new car. I just couldn't believe it. They were still driving their used cars.

Then Brock said, "Get in, man, and see how it feels." I got behind the wheel, and it felt great! I asked everyone to get in even if they had to take turns. They were hopping in and out of the car like children having fun. I thank God for these guys He had placed in my life. This was indeed a Merry Christmas for me.

We all went back in the house. I had gifts to give as well. I gave Benjamin three hundred dollars, and he was so happy. Then I said, "Benjamin, since I have a new car, you can have my old one." He jumped up and gave me a man hug that caused us both to fall down to the floor. He was so happy. Diamond was my little princess, even though she was growing up. I gave her, her first diamond ring and necklace. I put on the necklace and then the ring on her finger. She jumped into my arms, gave me a big hug, and thanked me.

As Tehh, I couldn't afford very expensive gifts for everyone, but I couldn't go cheap on Alicestene. She is the only one I spent a lot of money on, but it didn't look like it. I noticed she had been looking at a necklace in my shop that was about hundred dollars or so. I knew she wanted it but couldn't afford it. I bought it and replaced the stones with real diamonds and gave it to her. She was so excited and just screamed. She said, "Oh, my goodness, wow! I had been trying to save up enough money so I could buy it, but somebody bought it. That really broke my heart. Oh, thank you so much, Tehh." She was so happy that I had gotten it for her. She gave me a big kiss and thanked me some more. One day I am going to have to tell her some crazy story to get her to have it appraised. That necklace was now valued at five thousand dollars. For the guys I bought us each two 250 shares of stock in some new computer software company that was supposed to change America and the world one day. I gave a trip to Las Vegas to Mama and Mr. Crumpton. I hoped there were no volcanos there. I gave Miss Emma a gift certificate to her favorite store. Everyone was so happy. I even gave something to Alicestene's parents. Her father wondered how I could do so much to help the guys become successful and couldn't help myself. That thing was really getting the best of him. One day he will learn the truth, and it will undoubtedly shock him.

Later Alicestene came and told me how proud she was of me. She thought I had spent all of my money on gifts and was concerned about me being broke. I told her that I had been saving the money from my job at the bank, but I still had money from my job at the antique shop. She so sweetly told me that she had a little saved if I needed anything later. That girl just made me love her that much more. That was another star in her crown from me. My baby deserved the very best, and I was going to give it to her one day.

Mama was so excited about spending Christmas with her new husband and her family. She said that the restaurant was closed and that we were going to cook dinner ourselves.

She said, "Tehh, you've been cooking most of your life. Now hop to it."

She told all of us to take our places in the kitchen, even Mr. Crumpton. There was a meat crew, a dessert and bread crew, and a vegetable crew. Benjamin told her he wanted to be with the mac and cheese crew. Everybody was cooking away when Mr. Crumpton grabbed Mama and started singing one of those old love songs to her and got us all turned on. Mad Dog started singing to the turkey as he got it ready for the oven, and we all started laughing. He said he missed his fiancé and the turkey's breast reminded him of her. Mama told him to go and call that girl and tell her he was coming to get her because he had gone stone crazy. Then Brock started singing the blues to the ribs, "I want my baby back here. Right here by my side," as he was getting them ready for the grill. He asked Mama if he could bring his fiancé too. Then Diamond and Benjamin started singing about their loves, and that did it. Mama stood in the middle of the floor and said, "Listen here, colored people, all of y'all. Go right now and call your friends and fiancés and invited them to dinner. I don't want nobody in here to be alone this Christmas because I know how it feels." Then she went over and gave Mr. Crumpton a big hug.

We all sat around, laughing, talking, and having so much fun while all of the food was cooking. Then to pass the time, Mama and Mr. Crumpton decided they wanted to play the game where they had to cross over each other. What a funny sight they were. Mr. Crumpton crossed Mama this way and that way. It wasn't long before he was saying that his arthritis was trying to get in the game. Mama said they were trying to do the same thing to her. They were just huffing and puffing as they tried to reach the colors. Finally they just fell on the floor and started laughing, all out of breath. They were so happy and really enjoying each other.

Mr. Crumpton told us that married couples need to have fun with each other and touch more, not just sexually. Holding hands, gentle caresses, massage of the shoulders, and kissing the hands did wonders.

He smiled and said, "You will discover some other things too, because there is a powerful magnetism in the touch." Then he said we needed to learn to appreciate each other's laughter. It would tell us a lot about our ladies and how to enter into their worlds. That was something to really think about. He reached out and took Mama's hand and kissed it, and she just lit up before our eyes. At that moment I realized my daddy had walked out on the greatest woman in the world. The truth is, Mr. Crumpton really needed someone to love, and God had given him my mama.

The timers went off on the ovens, and we all jumped up and scrambled to get to our dishes. Everything was just about ready. The patio was already decorated, and we set up there to accommodate everybody. Everyone arrived, and Mama asked them to wash up and help finish dinner. There was so much laughter and happiness as everyone worked. Mama was frosting the cakes when Mr. Crumpton went over to give her a kiss. She decided to frost him and lick it off his nose. It was so funny because he had icing all over his face.

He laughed and said, "Baby, now I'm going to be your dessert for the rest of your life," and we all smiled.

Everything was done, and we all gathered at the table to enjoy our Christmas dinner. Mama thanked God for Mr. Crumpton and gave him the honor of blessing the food. Not only did he bless the food, but he thanked God for Mama, me, Diamond, Benjamin, and his new family of friends as well.

He said, "I never thought I would ever find happiness again in my life after my wife died until I found you, Meyel, Tehh, Benjamin, and Diamond. I want you to know that I love you so much and I thank God for you. God couldn't have given me a better gift."

We wiped away our tears, and each person stood and said what they were thankful for. After that we all fixed our plates and started eating. Everything was absolutely delicious. This was the best Christmas I had ever known, and the first one spent with a real father. The Lord had finally filled my need for a father at last.

CHAPTER 30

Christmas was over, and my dream had finally come true after nearly two years. It was the day after New Year, and the grand opening of the beautiful Underground City Shopping and Entertainment Center. I was excited and nervous at the same time. People came from everywhere. Some came from nearby states. They had seen our grand opening on television. I had never seen so many people in Box City in my entire life. It was like Box City had been resurrected from the dead at last. There were radio, television, and newspaper reporters as well as magazine writers wanting to document the events. Police and security guards were everywhere. The mayor and city officials were there for the ribbon cutting. The mayor spoke and welcomed everyone to the Underground City. All eight of the restaurants were very busy, and the people said they enjoyed the food. I had four businesses there—the First Hancock Bank of Box City, the Weddings and Events Center, the customer service center, and the business office.

The Underground City created jobs for more than 250 people. To my surprise, my bank, which I called, "My baby," was filled with people opening up new accounts. My heart was so full, seeing how God made my dream a reality before my very eyes. People were making their reservations at the Weddings and Events Center, and the customer service area was busy too. Things went even better than I thought, and no one knew that I owned the building. All of the businesses were very pleased with their turnout. The adult entertainment area, which included clubs, bars, and a small casino, were doing great business. Since alcohol was served in those places, it was sectioned off from the shopping area to keep underage kids from entering. I went over and took a look. It was so busy, especially the casino. *Where did all of these people come from?* I hoped it would always be like this. I asked Mama to give Alicestene a raise so she wouldn't want to look for a job here in the Underground City since we needed her at the restaurant.

I got a strawberry soda and went outside to look around. Cars were parked as far as you could see. I went and sat down just to thank God for all he had done for me. I thought about Ray James, the drug dealer who said a dummy like me would never see the kind of money he had in my life, and yet I had more money than he would ever see in two lifetimes. I thought about all the people who said I would be nothing but a burden on society, and yet I had eased their burden by creating jobs and business opportunities. I thought about all the people who wanted to put me in an institution, and yet I had created an institution that brought financial freedom to many. I thought about all the people who said I was crazy because they thought I couldn't read, write, or reason, and yet I am glad I was crazy enough to take a chance on me because I could read, write, and understand. I thought about the school that said I was a waste of their time, and yet I had taken the time to educate many of those they had discarded. Then I thought about the little boy with a dream for his mama and Box City, and how it all became a reality. Finally, I thought about the voice I had heard inside of me most of my life. The voice that kept me encouraged and wouldn't let me believe all the bad things I heard. I came to realize that God, who was present within me, proved that He was greater than all of my circumstances and pushed me and Box City to rise above them all. I achieved all of this not because of what I did, but because of what God did through me.

While I enjoyed managing the Underground City, I thought seriously about promoting some of my managers to run the place while I ventured into something else. My dream had come true, but my true love was the Hancock Bank. That was the part of my dream that intrigued me the most. It was becoming a very successful bank, and I wanted to stay hands-on in it. I could always create a new position for myself. Since I still had a few more months before graduation, I needed to start planning. I have a great assistant manager, a member of the Finang gang who took charge when I was not there. She would make an excellent manager for the customer service center.

Thirty members of the Finang gang were now employed in key positions in the Underground City and in the Hancock Bank. Others were employed in city government, running for political office, or working in education, health care, and other financial institutions. These were people who had given up on life until they joined the Finang gang. How did I do it? I did it one person at a time. These fifty people, including Mama, went out and spread the word about getting an education for a better life. It caught on, and people started believing and changed Box City. The young people are proud to go to school now because they can see firsthand what education has done for their families and the new Box City. This was a city on the poverty list and at the top of the illiteracy chart. The power of prayer and education caused all of that to change.

Brock, Jason, and Mad Dog were all married now and living in Diamond Ridge. They loved their new homes and told me how wonderful it was living in a house not surrounded by so many other people. They even have their own patios like Mama. They were all assistant managers working part-time in the Underground City and had no trouble getting a loan from the Hancock Bank. We all meet at one of our houses and have fun like we did at Mama's house. Their weddings were held at the Weddings and Events Center in the Underground City, and they were beautiful.

Toe Joe decided that he would have a June wedding like me and Alicestene. He is having his house built in Wagon Trace too. He is indeed a great guy. He asked me what I thought about Wagon Trace and offered to help me with the down payment if I wanted to buy a house there. He told me that I deserved the best, and he wanted to help me get it. I must say he really looks out for me, and I appreciate that. However, he's going to be a little disappointed when he discover that's my big house on the hill that's being built, and I didn't need his down payment. He was really doing great for himself. He moved his mama out of the apartment and into a home in Diamond Ridge. After he bought one apartment building, he saved up enough money to buy another one.

I am so proud of these guys, especially because the world had thrown them away and said they had no value. Like much of the junk I use to find on the streets, they had great value; however, no one saw it but me. I would love to hear what those two bankers were saying about Box City now. They would mourn how they had missed out on one of the greatest opportunities in Box City's history. They saw junk, and I saw a treasure worth pursuing. They later moved from their old communities and bought new homes in Wagon Trace that were financed by the Hancock Bank. Now that was music to my ears.

CHAPTER 31

It was finally the day of my graduation and the end of four of the most wonderful years of my life. Since there was an increase in college enrollment, the graduating class was larger than it had ever been in the history of Box City. The only place to accommodate it was the football stadium. Box City became an attractive place for out-of-state students and teachers. We were at home, and were scrambling as we tried to get to the stadium on time. There was so much traffic going to the stadium that police had to direct it. There was a sign telling all graduates to go left, and we did. I was so excited. I was like a kid in a candy store. I had finally earned the prized class ring, cap, gown, and everything. I was so proud of myself, and I thanked God for my journey. I looked at Mama as she looked at me with tears in her eyes.

She gave me a big hug and whispered, "I am so proud of you, honey. I love you so much." Then she said, "I told you. You were going to make a big difference in this world, Tehh. Now everybody is going to know it today. My baby is truly a genius."

I will treasure those words from my mama for the rest of my life. She saw greatness in me when everyone else saw the worst. Mr. Crumpton had tears in his eyes and gave me a big hug like a father and told me how proud he was of me. He just didn't know how he made me feel at that moment. I finally had a dad that was proud to share in my success. He told me God knew just what he needed, a son like me. I washed the tears from my eyes and went looking for Alicestene. I really needed that beautiful smile and a big hug at that time. All of a sudden I heard her voice and turned to see her making her way through the crowd. She ran and jumped into my arms and gave me the biggest kiss. She told me how proud she was of me. She was wearing that five-thousand-dollar necklace, the one she thought was costume jewelry. She was more precious to me than the necklace she was wearing, and I thanked God for her. Of all the hugs I received that day, there was none like Alicestene's. It was like we just became one in each other's arms, and I didn't want to let go. At that moment I had to let go and asked her to go and join Mama and the others as I went to join the class. I heard her say, "I love you so much, Tehh." *Oh, I love that girl.*

The stadium was packed, and it wasn't a football game. It seemed like everybody was there—the mayor, college officials, some celebrities, and a few other people I didn't know. The band played. People sang, and the mayor spoke. The president of the college spoke. The dean spoke, and some more people spoke. Then somebody song, and the band played again and again. I wanted to remember everything about that day. A special presentation was to be made to the student who had overcome incredible odds and had graduated with high honors. It was the Marie Abigail McBride Award, which came with a ten-thousand-dollar check. I thought that was certainly a great gesture on someone's part because I saw a number of deserving students. I was so nervous just to be graduating that I wasn't paying attention when they mentioned the recipient of the award. I was looking around to see who I thought it could have been and never heard my name.

The guy sitting next to me said, "Hancock, hey, man, they called your name." I could have fallen out of my chair.

They really caught me off guard. No one ever told me that was going to happen. I wasn't prepared. I believe in preparation. I was becoming a nervous wreck and felt the stuttering coming on. I had to calm myself down quickly. The voice inside me calmly said, "Stand up like a man. This is not the time to be dumb. You are somebody now. Act like it."

The man said, "Come on up, son." I pulled myself together and went up and stood by him. I was so nervous I was about to wet my pants. I was praying hard because I didn't need to fall apart on my graduation day. Cameras were flashing from every direction. I noticed the television station was filming the event. I tried to stay composed and asked the Lord to help me through it and say the right words. The man said, "In the history of this school we have never had a student ace every test he has ever taken. That means this young man has had a perfect score for every year he has attended this college, and that is worthy of recognition. Not only that, but he also has an extraordinary life story. He had to overcome some incredible odds to make it this far. He was diagnosed with a very severe learning disability and was told that he would never read, write or comprehend. He was put out of school at age thirteen because of it. They wanted to lock him away in an institution, but his mother fought for him. In his heart he said he was determined to be somebody one day. Today, I am proud to tell you that you are somebody! Let me present to you the Marie Abigail McBride Award and a check for ten thousand dollars." The whole stadium stood and applauded me and the graduating class cheered me on. I was so excited because that was more than what I had asked the Lord for. All I wanted was a college degree. Then the man asked me if I had anything to say to my fellow graduates.

I took a deep breath and quickly glanced at the program and noticed that his name was Mr. Callen. I thanked him and the school for the award. Then I stood tall and said, "What I would like to say to the graduating class is I am so proud of all of us. I know this journey was not an easy one. We had to work for it, and we had to work hard. There were many distractions along the way, but we were determined to succeed. We had obstacles to overcome, and we overcame them because we didn't give up. Life is just that way sometimes, but we must stay encouraged. Today we will embark upon a new journey that will take us in many different directions. Dream big and strive to make your dreams a reality because I did. Believe in yourself when no one else does. Don't be afraid to take a chance on you. You don't have to be like everyone else. God made us all different for a reason. It's that difference that makes us so unique. We are the first to graduate in the new Box City—a city that now stands tall and is filled with great opportunities where we can all have a better quality of life. We can now have homes, careers, families, and adventures that were never available to us before. New opportunities are popping up every day. Life is what you make it! So let's go and make it a good one. Thank God for our success here today, and thank God for the new Box City. Box City, here we come! Thank you." Everyone applauded, and I took my seat.

I sat there, hoping I said the right things when the guy next to me said, "Man, I liked what you said. That was so cool."

Then they started calling out names and giving us our degrees. I sat there, just shaking my leg, waiting for them to call my name. Every time they called a name, the crowd would cheer them on. Then I heard my name.

It was like all of heaven opened and the sun began to shine, casting a bright light directly on me. Thomas Edison Hamilton Hancock was called, and the crowd cheered me on as I went up to receive my degree. It was as if God had pulled back the curtains of heaven so He could see me that day. I thanked Him in my heart with tears in my eyes for what He had done for me and walked off with the other graduates. All of a sudden the clouds rolled over and blocked the sun. At that moment I believed God was letting me know that He was proud of me too.

While I was walking over to Mama and the family, one of the guys from the class said to me, "Man, did you see that? It was so strange. The minute they called your name and you got up, the sun shined a light directly on you and no one else. It was weird. Did you see that?" I told him I wasn't paying attention.

He said, "Man, you sure you are not some kind of preacher? Cause I know what I saw. By the way I enjoyed your speech."

I thanked him and wished him well. I went over and joined the family and every one gave me a big family hug. All the guys were there and excited to see what they were going to go through a year or so from now. Toe Joe asked me what I did to get a perfect score because ten thousand dollars was a nice graduation gift.

Alicestene joined me and told me how proud she was of me and asked, "What are you going to do with the ten thousand dollars?"

I told her it would help pay for some of the wedding expenses. She smiled and gave me a big hug. She told me she heard some people talking about giving me a job with six figures. I couldn't believe that. As good as that sounded, the last thing I needed was another job. She was so excited about that.

We all went to celebrate at Mama's restaurant. I praised God in my heart because I was now a college graduate. To the people of Box City I had done the impossible. I had a good job at the Underground City to keep me busy, and I was getting married the next month. Things couldn't get any better than that. While we were celebrating and having a good time, Mama became very sick and had to be rushed to the hospital. We were all so afraid for her. Mr. Crumpton was a nervous wreck. We all sat outside in the waiting room, praying that everything would be okay.

Diamond was saying "She was okay this morning. What could have happened to her?"

Benjamin said, "Mama had been sick and throwing up at work. I tried to get her to go home, but she wouldn't."

I hated that I wasn't there to help her when she needed me the most. The nurse came out and told us she was going to be okay. What a relief. We were so happy. I thanked God that she was treated and released.

Mama came into the waiting room, smiling, and then she made the big announcement with Mr. Crumpton, who looked like a deer caught in headlights.

She said nervously, "Tehh, Benjamin, Diamond, and everybody, we are having a baby. I am pregnant."

It was like an earthquake shook us. Everybody looked at Mama in shock and said, "What?" I almost passed out. I couldn't believe that.

Diamond was so upset and said, "Mama, you are too old to have a baby. Are they sure that's what it is? I'm sixteen years old, and I'm supposed to be your baby."

Benjamin wasn't too pleased with the announcement either and said, "I am not changing no baby's diapers and getting that stuff all over my hands. Mama, it's just not fair for you to be having a baby."

Mr. Crumpton stood there and said, "Now children, I never thought anything like this could ever happen to me. I'm going to be a father. A father—me?"

Mama smiled, looked at all us, and said, "I can't believe y'all. How do you think I feel? You'd better come over here and give me a hug." We all went over to her and gave her a big hug and told her that we stilled loved her, Mr. Crumpton, and the baby anyway. That was really something for all of us. Because of the timing, I knew I would love the little critter. He had waited until after my graduation to make himself known.

Mama was in her late thirties and having a baby, and Mr. Crumpton was so happy. It was like his heartfelt prayer had been answered. He asked us to take Mama home so she could get some rest. We went back to the restaurant and brought all the food to the house, and we continued to celebrate my graduation and the new baby to come. I never thought Mama would have another baby. Nobody did. To me that was truly a miracle. Mr. Crumpton was going to be a father at the age of forty-five.

Alicestene was so excited about Mama and the baby that she started acting crazy. She asked me if I wanted to wait to have children or start right away when we got married. *What is wrong with this woman?* I said to myself. I was so confused. I was still in shock from Mama's news, and now she's talking about babies. I wasn't ready for all of that. I thought, *Now I have a wedding, a wife, and a new brother or sister to think about. One day my children will be playing in the same sandbox with their aunt or uncle.*

We all sat around the table, talking about how old Mama and Mr. Crumpton would be when the baby got to be sixteen or how old we would be. We were just laughing and having so much fun when Mr. Crumpton brought Mama out to join us. She told us she was feeling much better and apologized for getting sick and ruining the party. We told her that we were glad she was okay.

Mr. Crumpton said, "Starting next week, we are going to find Meyel a maid. Miss Emma, it looks like you are going to have to run the bakery and restaurant for a while. What you say about that?"

Miss Emma was so excited. Mama was glad that she had someone like Miss Emma she could trust to take over. Miss Emma gave Mama a big hug and told her not to worry and just take care of herself and the baby. She could always stop by the restaurant and have lunch on the house, and we all laughed. Mama was almost back to her normal self, and the conversation changed.

Mr. Crumpton asked, "What are you going to do now that you have graduated, son?

I said, "I was offered a great job to manage the whole Underground City, including the bank."

He said, "Say what? That's a great job for a colored man in Box City. That's a wonderful accomplishment. You see how big that place is? Somebody recognized that you are some kind of young man, son. I'm just so proud of you."

Alicestene jumped up and said, "Tehh that is so wonderful. They are really going to miss you at the antique shop."

I said, "No, I will still be able to work there a couple of days a week for a few hours."

She looked at me and said, "Okay, mighty man. Oh, by the way, you didn't answer my question about the children." All of a sudden I just got sick to my stomach and had to go outside for some air.

CHAPTER 32

It was several weeks before my wedding. Alicestene and I had to meet with Pastor Young for counseling before we got married. We got there on time, and he was waiting for us. He took us into his counseling room where we could sit at a table and face each other. That way we could look into each other's eyes as we talked, he told us. I knew I had a lot of things I hadn't told Alicestene. Frankly, I just wasn't ready. I didn't feel it was time for me to expose everything about myself, and we were not married. Only Mama knew the whole truth about me. Pastor Young congratulated us and told us how proud he was of us and how he thought we would make a great couple. Then he told us that when there was a breakdown in marriage, couples usually couldn't look each other in the eyes. He said sometimes they stopped talking to each other altogether. I knew he was leading up to something, so I braced myself for what he was going to say.

He said, "Marriage should be based on love true enough, but it should also be on trust, truth, and commitment."

He asked if we had been totally honest with each other since we had been together. Then he asked me if Alicestene could honestly trust me with her life without worry. The voice inside of me said, "Go on and tell the truth about everything. They won't believe you anyway."

Alicestene smiled, looked me in the eyes, and quickly said, "Yes, and I have always been honest with Tehh, and I know he has always been honest me, Pastor Young."

Pastor Young said, "Not so fast, Alicestene. That's something that only Tehh can answer."

I cleared my throat and said, "Pastor Young, I haven't always been honest with her. I have been hiding a big secret."

Alicestene looked at me and said, "What? You are not funny, are you?"

I said, "No, girl! You know me better than that."

Pastor Young said, "Alicestene, please! Go on and tell her your secret, son."

I looked Alicestene in the eyes and said nervously, "Honey, I am so sorry for not telling you that I'm a millionaire and own most of Box City. Wow! That felt good." I took a deep breath and said, "Now I've gotten that off my chest."

Alicestene looked at me like I was one of the biggest fools she had ever seen in her life and said, "Tehh, why don't you stop acting crazy? This is serious business now. You are not a millionaire. You just got that job to manage the Underground City, and now you think you are rich. Have you gone and bumped your head somewhere? That is just so crazy." She just kept on talking. "Pastor, tell him what the Bible says about lying."

Pastor Young looked at me like he felt sorry for me. He said, "Thomas, there is nothing wrong with dreaming or wishing you were rich, but son, you have to be realistic. If you were a white man, I could see the possibility because they leave land and money to their children. That's not the case with you, son."

Well, I thought that if anyone should have almost believed me, it would have been him.

He said, "We live in the real world, and you have to accept that. You just can't go around telling people that you are a millionaire and own most of Box City when they know you don't. Your mama hadn't been out of the projects but a little while. Box City was here before you were born. It's just not right, son."

Well, it did feel good to tell the truth anyway. The voice inside of me was right. They didn't believe me. Pastor Young continued to tell us about marriage and what God expected of us.

"Honesty now, son. Remember that's what God wants."

He told us that it was good to have a sense of humor in marriage but that we shouldn't let it go so far where you can't see the truth. We thanked Pastor Young and left.

Alicestene pushed me on the shoulder on the way out and told me that I needed to stop playing with people so much. I wanted to tell her, "Baby,

I wasn't playing. I was telling nothing but the truth." We went on out to dinner and talked about the wedding. Everything was in place and paid for. All we had to do was dress and show up. Alicestene told me that she put our wedding announcement in the newspaper because she had seen others in there. I really didn't want that, but I told her that was okay. More people were reading now in Box City. Newspaper advertising had increased a hundred and fifty percent because of all the new businesses. The wedding was going to be held at the church and the reception at the Weddings and Events Center. The wedding coordinators had taken care of everything, and Mama's bakery was doing the cakes. Everybody was excited about our wedding, including the newspaper. I was quite sure a lot of unexpected people would show up.

Alicestene went to the restroom while we were waiting for our dinner to arrive. I sat there thinking about our meeting with Pastor Young. I was glad to get some things off my chest even though they didn't believe me. All of my life people refused to see me for who I really was. In many of their minds, I of all people could never rise to the top of life no matter what I did. To many of them I was just a bottom-feeder like a fish in a pond, always in search of something but never finding it, always trying to help others but never helping myself. What did I have to gain by lying? Most people refused to accept the truth about me because of my history. *Why is it so impossible to believe that I am who I said I am? Is it because I am a colored man? Even to my own people? Or is it my age that says it's impossible for a young colored man to be rich in Box City? It certainly was not my intellect because I was at the top of my graduating class.* It was staring them right in the face, but they refused to see it for whatever reason. *Was it because I didn't flaunt my wealth and just chose to act like the average person?* How did Pastor Young think he got the new church building built so quickly? I had secretly donated more than $250,000.00 over time. Where did he think the money came from? It was from a colored man. Even though I didn't admit that I gave it, he said I did and that he just didn't know how. I was getting a headache as I thought about it. I know God always use people to bless us—sometimes in ways we least expect. That money didn't fall out of the sky, and God didn't just reach down and put the money in the offering box. Yes, it was a miracle we got the church building built, but the miracle came from the money the Lord allowed someone to leave in that hole in the bank of the Underground City, and it changed our lives.

My poor baby Alicestene has accepted me in her little sweet mind as the struggling, pitiful Tehh, only rising as high as she thought I could go. She wants me to be successful, but thinks it's a long way off. The funny thing is I wanted to take her to Paris, France, the city of love, for our honeymoon. I wanted her to sit in my arms in one of those little boats going down the river, listening to the man sing love songs to us. I have never been to Paris, but it looked beautiful in the movies on television. I wanted to see the Eiffel Tower in person. I didn't have to wait because I could afford it the moment I asked her. She just didn't know it. No, she wants us to go to one of the hotels on the other side of town for our honeymoon. She said we couldn't afford anything better. I never said that at all. Assumption can cause you to miss out on some great things in life. I learned to never let people live your life for you, but rather let them share it with you. One day we will go to Paris and do all of those things I thought about. Since she didn't believe me with Pastor Young, perhaps she will think twice when I take her to our new home in Wagon Trace after the honeymoon. I just don't believe she will fight to go back home to her mama and daddy then. You don't have to try to prove some things. They will simply prove themselves.

While I was waiting for Alicestene to come back from the restroom, I watched a guy frantically counting his money to pay his bill. His lady was in the restroom too. He came over and asked me if I had five dollars I could give him because he was short. I politely gave it to him. What would have happened if I didn't have it? He would have become a bottom-feeder going to the next person, looking for a handout or something. This is one of the reasons why I try to teach young men and women in our gang the value of a dollar. It wasn't how much money you didn't have but what you did with the money you had. You can enjoy life without humiliation by planning ahead and saving. You can save your way into a better future with a little discipline and planning.

That is how I got my start before I found all the money. I would put ten dollars or more away in a jar every week until that jar was full. Then I just happened to read a book on banking and finance that told me what to do with that money. I tried it. I opened that jar and counted the money, and I was shocked! I had saved three hundred dollars. I took that money and opened up a savings account for Mama and went from there. I looked up, and behold, my angel was on her way back to the table. I just looked at her and thanked God for this beautiful and loving woman He had put in my life. I hope it don't kill her when she realizes that, though she has been a very concerned about her future husband not having enough money, he is indeed a millionaire. She already has a million dollars in the Hancock Bank as a wedding gift. All of those stars in her crown really added up. She sat down at the table, looked at me with those beautiful puppy dog eyes, and asked, "What are you smiling about?"

I just said, "You, baby, because you are so beautiful and I love you so much." She leaned over and gave me a kiss. We enjoyed our dinner and left.

I dropped Alicestene off at home and decided to drive over to our new home in Wagon Trace just to look around and check everything out. The contractor and decorator told me everything was all finished and I could move in when we were ready. I had called Mama and told her that I would be over to her house a little later on. I was so proud to have the opportunity to pull up into my own yard and drive into my garage and watch it close. The house was all paid for. I thought, *"Alicestene is really going to love this."* I walked into the huge kitchen, which was made for a chef like me. Across from it was the huge family room with a television and two convenient powder rooms around the corner. On the other side of the kitchen was the huge formal dining room. Down the hall there was the massive living room with a beautiful brick fireplace and floor-to-ceiling windows with beautiful drapes. Off the living room was a beautiful staircase leading up to five beautiful bedrooms with baths in each one, and walk-in closets. We were going to need them for all the children Alicestene wanted to have. I went into our bedroom, the master of them all. There was a private patio with windows that we could open to let the outside in, and I gazed at the beautiful water fountain. The decorators had laid it out for our comfort. There was a walk-in closet that opened to reveal a small stove, refrigerator, counter with sink and cabinets, coffeepot, beverage dispenser, and a small snack machine. The contractor told me he had a surprise for me in the bedroom, but I didn't think it would be like this. Alicestene would probably never want us to leave it. We were looking through magazines, and she saw the bedroom suite she loved to have one day when I really started making money. I didn't have to wait that long. I went on and got it for her. The room was simply breathtaking. I went in the walk-in closet, which was a room in itself. The master bath was out of this world. The tub was big enough for two people. Mirrors were everywhere, and there was another walk-in closet filled with bath towels and toiletries. I pulled myself from that room and went back downstairs.

Off the family room I went down a few more stairs, and there were our offices and an open entertainment area. It had a television, pool table, nice leather sofas, and another walk-in closet that had everything in it—a refrigerator, sink, cabinets, small stove, coffee and beverage dispenser, you name it. It even had a snack machine too. There was even a playroom for our future children and two other rooms. I went and turned on the television, sat in the soft recliner, and drank my strawberry soda. The next thing I knew I had slept through the whole night. Peace must have finally come to me as well.

I got up and washed my face and went out on the back patio. I looked at the swimming pool, heated pool, and all the beautiful furnishings. I walked down a small hill and went through the gate to the lake and sat there for a while connecting with nature. It looked just like a park. I got up from the bench and laid on the green grass. I looked up at the clouds in the sky. It was just breathtaking watching the clouds form shapes that looked like people, birds, and other animals. I had never done that before. I had always lived in an apartment surrounded by depressed people and found little reason to look up. I never knew a place like this existed until now. It was so peaceful and quiet you could hear the fish jumping in the water. I got up and did something I saw the boys do on television. I picked up a few rocks and threw them into the lake. The rock skidded across the water like a speedboat, and I was so amazed. I had never done that before, and it felt good.

I looked around and thought about how all of this was locked away, hidden in my mind until I put it all on paper and made it a reality. I looked at how beautiful the other houses were and thanked God for all of His blessings and for all of those children Alicestene wanted to have. I looked around and thought, *We will need them to share all of this with.* The way I was feeling at that very moment, she could start having babies on our honeymoon if she wanted to. She didn't have to do anything but love me and be my wife. She didn't even have to work if she didn't want to, but I would leave that up to her. I walked on back up to the house, locked up, and drove over to Mama's house. Everyone was still asleep when I got there. I went and laid down on the couch and fell asleep. It was a Saturday, and I was off from the antique shop; however, I decided I would stop by later to see how things were going.

CHAPTER 33

June finally rolled around, and it was the day of my wedding. I was a nervous wreck. I was so bad off I didn't think I could get married. I was sick at the stomach and throwing up. I sent for Mama, and she came back to be with me. She gave me a big hug and told me that she loved me. She asked me to calm down and tell her what was wrong. I said, "Mama, I'm sick and falling apart. I don't think I can go through with the wedding."

She said, "Now you know how I felt when I married Mr. Crumpton."

I said, "Mama, you felt like this!"

She smiled and said, "Yes, and you came in and calmed me down and walked down the aisle with me. I couldn't have made it without you. The Lord didn't bring you to this point in your life for you to give up now. Honey, I have seen you do some amazing things. This is what you have been waiting for. This is your time now, Tehh. I know you can do this. Alicestene is a beautiful bride and I believe she is going to make you a wonderful wife."

Slowly I began to pull myself together. She said, "I think you are worried about having to tell her about the real you. In my heart I believe you can trust her, sugar. She has shown me that she really loves and cares for you. She doesn't know that you are rich, and frankly she can care less. She just knows that you are a hard worker and she wants to do all she can to help you. She has been saving her money to help you get an apartment if you need it. I love that about her. She really loves you, honey, and she is always in your corner. That was my prayer for you. Now let's not keep her waiting like you told me."

Then there was a knock on the door. It was Mr. Crumpton. He came in and gave me a big hug and told me that he was proud of me and that I was going to be a great husband. He said, "Son, I know just how you feel because

I was the same way. Tehh, I was so sick at the stomach I didn't know what to do, but it finally passed over."

I said, "If it's makes you feel this bad, why do folks want to get married?"

He said, "I wouldn't take nothing in this world for your mama, son." They helped me pull myself together, and I went and joined Rev. Young and Toe Joe, my best man, and got ready to marry the girl of my heart.

The music started, and everyone walked in and took their places. Then came the ring bearer. It was the little girl dropping the flowers that caused my fears to go completely away, and I stood up straight like a proud man. At first she cried and didn't want to do it. She would start, change her mind, and run in the opposite direction. Her daddy caught her, whispered something in her ear, and gave her a big kiss. That little girl smiled and walked down, dropping those flowers like she was not afraid of anything. She had everyone's attention. If she could do that, then I could do this.

The moment had arrived, and everyone stood. Alicestene came out, and my eyes filled with tears. She was so beautiful. She looked like a queen, my queen walking down the aisle with her father by her side. She was simply breathtaking as the jewels sparked in her crown and her gown. I was glad to take this woman as my wife. I couldn't wait for Rev. Young to say, "You may now kiss the bride." I stood there, just shaking. When he did say it, I gave Alicestene the kiss of my life—the one I had been saving to give her for a very long time. Everyone applauded as we kissed. It was so long Rev. Young told us to come up for air. It was a beautiful wedding, and I never want to do it again. I thought it was going to kill me. I asked the Lord to hold us together like glue. We took pictures and more pictures while everyone left for the Weddings and Events Center at the Underground City. We even took pictures for the TV cameras and the newspaper.

All was done, and we finally left for the Underground City. It was a good thing we had parking spaces reserved for the wedding party because cars were parked everywhere. We went in, and there were hundreds of people standing around talking. We were presented as Mr. and Mrs. Thomas Hancock and escorted to our table, and everyone took their seats. Everything was just beautiful. I thought there were more people at the reception than there had been at the wedding. The food was out of this world, and the chefs brought all of our food to the table. They had also stocked both the refrigerator and the freezer at our new home as a wedding gift. As we were eating, the DJ played our special song, and we got up to dance. It seemed like the whole world froze in time as I pulled her close to me. It felt wonderful holding my wife in my arms, looking into her eyes, and her father couldn't do anything about it. She told me that she loved me so much and that she was proud to be my wife. I told her that I loved her and was so proud to be her husband. The music ended, and I motioned for them to play it again because the moment felt so right. It was our wedding, and we danced some more and then went back to our seats. The band struck a familiar tune, and everybody took to the dance floor. Alicestene just laughed as we watched everybody dancing. Our parents were really funny, and they were all having a great time. All I could think about was being with my wife on our honeymoon. I was like a rare bottle of wine ready to be opened. Finally we cut the cakes and shared our bites with each other. Before you knew it, we were saying good-bye to everyone. This was the happiest part of my day. In my mind I could see myself like a caveman dragging his mate by the hair to his cave. I was ready for my wife.

The limousine took us to the hotel on the other side of town, and we checked into our room. Alicestene went into the bathroom to change her clothes and put on the beautiful nightgown we had picked out together. I put on my PJs. All I could see in my mind were fireworks. When she came out, she was so beautiful. I quickly went to brush my teeth. I wasn't there but a minute. When I came out of the bathroom, Alicestene was asleep. I could have passed out. I couldn't believe it! I threw a little temper tantrum like a child saying, "How could you do this to me?" I wanted to pour cold water on her to wake her up. So many things were going through my mind. This was the night! This was my night, the right night! I tried to shake her, and she still wouldn't wake up. I decided to just go to sleep myself. I'd waited this long. Another night was not going to hurt anything.

I woke up first and called room service and ordered our breakfast so it would be ready when Alicestene woke up. I sat on the edge of the bed, just looking at her, smiling. She must have felt me looking because she opened her eyes and gave me a big smile and said, "Good morning, husband." I leaned over and kissed her, and that was all it took. It was fireworks time, and it was on and on and on. She made me feel like a real man, and I made her a real woman. I thought about our bedroom at our new home. I don't think we will ever want to come out. We had both saved ourselves just for that special moment. We were one in body, soul, and spirit, and I thanked God in my heart.

We were just lying there in each other's arms when there was a knock at the door. It was room service with our breakfast. We sat there enjoying our breakfast and looking into each other's eyes.

She said, "Tehh, I love you so much."

I told her how much I loved her. She told me she was sorry that she fell asleep, but she was so exhausted. I told her that was all right because she had made up for it. Then she frowned and told me that she didn't want to live with my mama and ask if it was okay for us to get an apartment.

She said, "There are some nice ones we probably could afford near Diamond Ridge. We never talked about where we were going to live. Living with my parents is definitely out of the picture, Tehh."

Her father was probably already a little upset with me because his daughter had no place to live of her own that he knew of. I smiled and told her not to worry and that everything was going to be okay. We would find something that I could afford. Then she just made me love her even more when she told me that she had asked Mama to let her work full-time to help us find a place sooner. She didn't have to worry about work because I made enough money at the Underground City to take care of us even without being a millionaire. Oh, but she had listened to her parents talk about their very humble beginnings and struggles as a couple. She wanted us to start at the bottom and work our way up life's ladder like they had. I smiled, took her into my arms, kissed her, and that was it. We were in heaven again.

We finally got up and drove around town to see what we could do. After we looked around, she told me she thought Box City was such a beautiful place now and wondered why she felt this place was better. I said, "Sometimes we can be programmed into thinking that what God has blessed us with is not as good as others. So He allows us to step away from our blessing and experience something else in order to appreciate what we have." There was no place more beautiful right then as the new Box City to me. She told me she only made reservations for two days because she thought that was all we could afford. She didn't want me to spend all of our money and have to ask our parents for something. I respected her wishes. I told her that was all right and everything was going to be okay. She was only concerned about where we were going when we checked out of the hotel and having enough money when we got there. I kept telling her not to worry and to trust me. Even though I knew she was scared, she was willing to take that leap of faith with me anyway.

The stores were closed since it was Sunday, so we just window shopped. She looked at the bedroom furniture and said, "We need a good bed if nothing else." We noticed a movie theater was open. We went in and watched one of those real scary movies. That really wasn't a good idea for me. Every time Alicestene held me tight, I was ready to go back to the hotel. I wasn't ashamed of how I was feeling because we were married. I made it through the movie and stopped by a burger shop and got us something to eat. Alicestene asked if she could order for me, and I said okay. She asked for a burger with fries and a large strawberry soda.

I said, "You got it, baby!"

She said with a big smile, "I know what my husband likes." We ate and took to the road again.

Then we both said at the same time, "Let's go back to Box City."

She said we could stay at the hotel there. After all the emotional drama she had put herself through, I decided there wasn't a hotel better than the home I had built for her. I prayed within myself and asked God to help me. It was now time for me to break my own rule and take my wife home. I was not going to wait any longer. Everything else in my life I had done for others, but Alicestene was God's gift to me. I was going to enjoy my wife and put her worries at ease.

We laughed and talked about everything going back home to Box City. Then she mentioned children again. The way I was feeling, she could have as many as she wanted. I smiled and told her if she wanted to start today, it was okay with me. Then I thought about what I said very selfishly because I wanted this honeymoon to last at least a year before our space was invaded. We agreed to wait at least a year and settle in somewhere. I just smiled as she talked about picking out a house and furniture one day. We talked about one of the new apartments not too far from Diamond Ridge again. She said she wanted a yard where the children could play if we bought a house. She went on and on, and I just let her talk. She said if we had to live with Mama that would be okay for a while. I knew she was looking out for our future with all of her heart. She was so happy and kept on talking. I just smiled because I knew she would be speechless when I got her home.

We saw a sign that said, "Open house today," and she wanted to go and see the houses. I pulled up to one of the houses, and we got out and looked around. She was so excited and told me how much she liked the house. We went to see a few more, and then we left. As we were driving, I noticed she was crying. I asked her if she was okay, and she said she was. I knew at that point that even though she loved me, she was a little disappointed in me for not providing her with a place to live. We finally made it to Wagon Trace when she said, "I thought we were going to the hotel."

I said, "I forgot just that quickly."

When I drove past Mama's house, she asked, "Where are you going?" Her face was full of question marks. I told her I just wanted her to look at a certain house on the hill.

She asked, "Why?" Then she said, "We can't afford any of those houses. Are you crazy?" She love to call me crazy. She is the only one I will take that from. Then she reminded me of what Rev. Young had told us about being realistic.

Her countenance changed as we drove around looking at the houses. She began to smile and told me all the homes were so beautiful.

Then she got so excited about one and said, "Tehh, look! Wow! Oh, my goodness. It is so beautiful. It's different from all the others. Oh, I just love that one."

Well, I pulled into the yard of "that one" and got out of the car. She really thought I was crazy then, especially when I asked her to come and look around with me. She was spellbound and wondered why I was looking around someone else's house. We walked slowly up to the door, and I felt her hand pulling back. I reached into my pocket and pulled out the key and opened the door, and she said, "Tehh, what are you doing?" She gave me that "I'm so afraid" look and asked whose house it was.

I told her everything was okay and not to worry about it. "Trust me," I said.

I took her by the hand and showed her around to help her relax. She was so excited about what she saw. Then I asked her to come upstairs with me for a minute because I wanted to show her something. I took her to the master bedroom.

She put her hands over her mouth and said, "Oh, my goodness, Tehh! This is the bedroom suite I wanted. I showed you the pictures of it, remember? Now these people have it too. Oh, it's so beautiful."

Then I opened the closet that was stocked with food and stuff and asked her to take a look.

She said, "I can't believe people live like this in Box City. This house is gorgeous. Whoever lives here has to be a very wealthy person."

I asked her to come out on the patio, and she said, "Oh, my goodness. I can't believe this. They have a complete private patio off the bedroom with flowers, trees, a fountain, and everything. Tehh, this house is like no house I have ever seen. I just love it. Maybe the Lord will bless us one day with a beautiful home of our own."

I must admit the house fit her like a glove. I took her in my arms, drew her close, and gave her a passionate kiss, and that did it. Those beautiful covers on that bed flew back in whoever house it was, and we were on our honeymoon for real. This time it was so perfect because we were at home and at peace ... for now. We fell asleep, and it was morning when we woke up. Alicestene told me the bed was so comfortable that she didn't want to get up. I told her we didn't have to. We could just lay there. Then she thought about where she was and suddenly became concerned about making sure everything was the way we had found it. She began to frantically fix the bed. I knew I had to tell her right then, but I had to pray hard and be very calm about it. I had had my episodes with Mama and Mrs. Collins, and I didn't want to go through that with her.

I sat her down on the bed. I got down on my knees, looked her in the eyes, and said as calmly as I could, "Baby, I love you so much. You know that if I could give you the world, I would, don't you?"

She looked at me, smiled, and said, "Yes."

I took a deep breath and said, "Alicestene, this is our house."

She said in shock, "What?"

I said, "I wanted to surprise you, honey. This is our home. I bought it for you. It's all paid for. Everything, including all the furnishings."

She looked at me like I was one of the biggest fools she had ever seen in her life again. She said, "Tehh, you need to stop playing with me like this now."

I said, "Honey, I'm not playing with you."

I asked her to take a close look at the deed. The girl nearly scared me to death when she read it and fainted. I didn't know what to do. I tried to revive her, but it didn't work. I put some water in a glass and threw a little on her, and that did the trick. That refreshment area really came in handy.

She sat up on the bed all wet and said, "Tehh, where am I?"

I told her she was at home. She looked around and fainted again. I couldn't believe the Lord would let me marry this girl and then kill her off like that. I shook her, and she came back to me. I thanked God and held her close to calm her down. Her heart was beating so fast. I asked her to go outside to get some air so we could talk. I took a blanket, and we went down to the lake just in case she got cold.

She was speechless and still couldn't believe that it was our house and asked, "How?"

She looked around, said the lake was so beautiful, and asked, "When?"

I asked her if she was okay, and she said, "Yeah."

Then she said, "Tehh, what bank did you rob?"

I said to myself, *Here I go again*. I told her I didn't rob a bank and that everything was all legal. As the wind blew through her hair, she looked at the lake, turned, and looked back at the house, brushing the hair out of her face. She did this several times very strangely. The last time out of the clear blue she looked and then took off running towards the house.

I picked up the blanket and yelled, "Where are you going."

She said, "I'm going to see my new home."

I thanked God and ran behind her. I thought she was going crazy. She got up to the house, stopped and looked around at everything. She was acting like a crazy woman, saying, "This is my patio. That's my swimming pool. That's my hot pool." She went into the house and did the same thing. "That's my kitchen. That's my dining room. That's my family room. That's my living room." Then she went downstairs and said, "Oh, my goodness! All of this is mine too." She came back upstairs and looked in the bathrooms. "These are my bathrooms." Then she went back upstairs, went into each bedroom, and said, "This is my bedroom, and this is my bedroom, and this is my bedroom, and this is my bedroom." She went into the master bedroom, looked in the closets and the bathroom, and said, "This is my bedroom too." She went out on the patio, opened the door, and screamed, "This is my house!" She closed the door, came back into the bedroom, and strangely said,

"I'm so tired now." She took off her clothes, got in the bed, covered up, and went to sleep just like that, snoring and all. I didn't know what to think after that. I watched her closely and let her sleep. I was afraid to leave her. I went out on the patio, turned on the television, and stretched out on the lounger. I was so glad we were alone because anyone else would have thought she needed to be committed.

Sitting there, I thought about the day I told Mama we were rich and how she fell asleep on the bus. She said it was peace. Maybe Alicestene was finally at peace with me. I must have fallen asleep because she woke me up and asked me to come to bed. This time it was different. She gave me a big kiss, and that was it. My passion was ignited. We were finally husband and wife, and she was finally at peace with me. We were in heaven all over again and didn't want it to end. As we laid there, she told me everything was just too much for her at one time. She was only hoping for a small apartment and not a mansion at all. I told her that the Lord will give you more than you can ask or think when you trust Him. Then she asked me if I was rich for real. I told her that I was rich for real, and she fainted again. She woke up and asked, "How long have you been rich?"

I said, "Since I was fifteen."

She said, "What?"

I asked her to not faint again because I couldn't take it anymore.

She said, "But you lived in the projects then. Your mama worked at Ricko's Bakery. You pushed your wagon and collected junk and stuff off the streets."

I told her I was rich then.

She asked, "Were you rich the first time you saw me in the store?"

I said, "Yes."

She said, "You mean you were telling the truth all the time and no one believed you, Tehh." I told her that had happened to me all of my life. Then I asked her if she was going to have a problem with being rich. So innocently she said she wasn't sure. She had never been rich before and didn't know how it felt. I told her if it would make her happy to be poor, we could be poor as long as we were together. However, it wouldn't last long. She asked me why?

I said, "Because the Lord just keeps on blessing me."

Then I said, "If we were poor right now, that would mean I couldn't give you your wedding gift."

Then she said, "Please, Tehh, let me be rich for a minute and think about it. I really want to see my wedding gift."

I said, "Okay, but if you want to be poor, you are going to have to give it back."

I smiled and gave her the gift. She shook the box before she opened it and said, "Oh, my goodness."

Then she fainted again. I took the gift and threw a little cold water on her again, and she came back. I didn't know what the limit for fainting was, but I thought she had exceeded it.

She said, "A million dollars! I have a million dollars in the bank, Tehh. I only have five hundred dollars saved in my account. Is it real ... for real?"

I said, "Baby, it is as real as real could be," and I asked her to please not faint this time. Softly, I asked, "What is the name of the bank, honey?"

She said, "The First Hancock Bank of Box City."

I asked her, "What is your name, baby?

She said, "Alicestene Hancock," and she fainted again. I just sprinkled some more water on her, and she was revived. She was the prettiest wet thing I had ever seen. I got her a towel to dry off, gave her a big kiss, and told her how much I loved her. After that episode I thought we were at a place where we could be husband and wife without any more fainting. I told her I was so sorry for throwing water on her, but I didn't know what else to do when she fainted.

I explained to her that she and Mama were the only ones who knew that I was rich. Benjamin, Diamond, and Mr. Crumpton didn't know. Even the guys didn't know. Mr. Crumpton thinks Mama is wealthy because of the restaurant, but that was their business. Then she asked me if I was rich when the guys gave me the jeep. I told her I was. She kept saying, "I just can't believe all this." I asked her to promise me that she would keep my secret and act natural. She told me she would, and we walked through the house together, looking at everything. She was so excited and told me her daddy was going to be shocked. He thought the only place we could afford to live was the projects. I thought, *Some of those buildings I owned weren't bad.*

My wife came to herself and said we had the rest of the week before we went back to work and we were not leaving the house for anything. We were officially on our honeymoon. We went out and played in the pool and had lots of fun. We sat in the hot pool and talked, and then it hit her.

She said excitedly, "You mean we could have been in Paris for real ... right now, Tehh?"

I simply said, "Yep!"

Then she said, "I can just kick myself."

I smiled and said, "Don't do that because I don't want my merchandise damaged." I proudly assured her that we could go to Paris anytime she was ready.

She grabbed me and held me so close and said, "I am so sorry for not believing you. Even Rev. Young didn't believe you because of me. It was you that gave the church all that money, wasn't it, Tehh?"

I told her it was and asked her to not let the church know that we are millionaires. I wanted her to understand that they would be expecting us to do everything. I only moved when the Lord told me to and not before. I smiled and told her to tell them if they ask that we were just blessed because I worked at the Underground City.

I said, "Baby, if people knew that we were millionaires, we would have no peace. People would be at our door begging and looking for handouts or even trying to rob us. I have come this far by being humble and acting natural. Nobody believes I'm rich because I don't act that way. I'm just Tehh. And you know what else, honey? With the whole city progressing at the same time and people enjoying a better quality of life now, no one will ever suspect us of being millionaires."

All of the excitement had worked up an appetite. My wife went into her new kitchen and looked in her refrigerator to find us something to eat. I told her the chefs filled our refrigerator and freezer with everything.

She just smiled and said, "Man, I'm going to love this. I'm telling you."

She fixed our plates. She got enough food and snacks for three days, and we went up to our bedroom and locked the door. We went out and ate our dinner on the patio off the bedroom and continued to talk. She asked me if Mama was rich. I told her Mama was a millionaire too.

She said, "But she don't dress or act like it."

I explained to her that was what being humble would do for you.

She said, "Now don't get me wrong. She always looks good, but not like the rich people we see on television."

I tried to make it as clear as possible by saying, "The less people know about you and your money, the happier you will be."

She smiled and said, "You know what, Tehh? My mama and daddy are going to faint when they see our house."

I told her my family will be shocked too, because I wanted her to be the first to see it. I was going to need a big bucket of water for all of them. We spent the rest of the week in heaven and enjoying the comforts of each other and our new home. We were in a world of our own in our bedroom for three days. We didn't have to come out for anything.

It was the morning of the fourth day when we emerged from the Hancock bedroom like hibernating bears and went downstairs. We looked around the house again and went out on the patio. Excitingly Alicestene said, "Let do something we have never done before."

I said, "What is that?"

She said, "Fish. We have a lake. Let's do it."

I looked in the storage closets, and there were fishing poles and equipment. The decorator had thought of everything. We went down to the lake and tried our hands at fishing. We used the little rubber things that looked like worms. I cast my line, and Alicestene cast hers. We sat on the bench, kissing and waiting to see who would catch the fish first. The book on fishing was one I had never read, but I was certainly going to start. Ignorance was not one of my pleasures. We were just talking when there was a jerk at Alicestene's pole, and she screamed. "Help me, Tehh. Help me." We pulled the fish in, and it was a whopper. She was so excited she didn't know what to do, watching the fish jump around. We took it off the hook, and then there was a jerk at my pole. She got all excited again. "Pull it in, Tehh! Pull it in!" It was another whopper. Two big fish were more than enough for us. I told her we were having fish for dinner. I cleaned the fish and prepared them, and she did the sides with dessert. She looked so good cooking in her kitchen. We had a great fish dinner. Then Alicestene smiled and said, "See, Tehh, ain't nothing wrong with being poor because we went down to the lake and caught our own fish dinner."

I smiled and said, "Baby, if we were poor, we would have gone to jail for fishing in a rich man's lake."

She said, "Ah, shucks," smiled and gathered up the dishes.

CHAPTER 34

The honeymoon was over, and we went to visit our parents. We went by Alicestene's parents' house first, and they were so glad to see her. For some reason her dad wasn't too thrilled to see me, his only son-in law. It seemed like he wanted her to marry a man who had something to offer her. My life really didn't measure up to his expectations anyway. All he knew was that Mama owned a restaurant and I was riding on her success. I knew his main concern was where we going to live. *Did he think we were going to be homeless or something?* I could just feel something brewing. I asked the Lord to help me through whatever was going to happen.

We were sitting around talking when her dad asked, "Are you living with your mama, Tehh?"

Alicestene was so excited about our new home said, "No, Daddy, Tehh found us a place to live." He was absolutely shocked.

He frowned and asked, "Where? In the projects?"

He wanted to know where I was taking his baby, but he had just struck a nerve in Alicestene. I sat back and let Alicestene have it out with her dad. I knew it wasn't good to argue with a man in his own house. She proudly put her hands on her hips and told him that it was in Wagon Trace. He got up out of his chair and told her that he just didn't believe it. Then Alicestene started crying and asked him why he didn't like me, and what had I ever done to him. He told her it wasn't that he didn't like me. It was the idea that I couldn't afford to take care of her. Then he got the nerve to asked Alicestene why she was lying for me, and that did it. They were having it out verbally. She told him that she was not lying and that she had never lied to him. It was like I was invisible again.

Then he said, "You know he can't afford a house in Wagon Trace. You got to be rich to live there."

Man, he was upset, and so was I. The veins were popping up in his head. It seems you don't know the truth about some folks until you marry into the family. I didn't expect our first family feud so soon. I hoped he didn't have a heart attack when he found out the truth. He actually thought we were lying. This man thought he was so bad that he grabbed his hat, jacket, and car keys and said,

"Y'all going to show me this house in Wagon Trace right now. Come on! If you got a house in Wagon Trace, I will eat my hat and shave my head."

I said to myself, *You want hot sauce or mustard with that?* Alicestene looked at me and smiled. Her mama, sweet as she could be, never said a word. She just got in the car with him.

We backed out of the driveway, pulled off, and headed back to our house with her parents following us. Alicestene said, "Honey, I am so sorry. I never expected anything like that to happen. What are we going to do? They are going to know that you haven't been on your job long enough to afford this kind of house."

I said, "Let's just tell them the truth. They won't believe it anyway. You didn't believe me. Just tell them I make very good money working at the Underground City." I was just tired of lying. Maybe the Lord was saying this was the time. I swallowed all of his insults like a good soldier. Now it was time for him to eat his hat and shave his head. Not only that, daddy or not, he had insulted my wife.

I pulled into Wagon Trace and drove up the hill to our house and got out of the car. Her dad quickly got out of his car looking like a pit bull, asked me to wait a minute. I stopped and turned to see what he wanted. He had the nerve to say, "Boy, are you sure this is the right house?"

I didn't think anyone could be that stupid. I overlooked his stupid remark, took a deep breath, and asked them to come in. He walked in, grabbed his chest, and almost fainted. I caught him before he hit the floor and sat him down. He sat there, looking around.

Then he said, "Boy, where in the world did you get the money to afford a house like this? Are you dealing drugs or something?" Then he stood to his feet, pointed his finger at me, and said, "You'd better not have my baby in no mess like that."

I thought, *Man, you are in my house now, and you are working my last nerve. I don't have to take this from you.* I really wanted to kick him out, but the voice inside of me said it was going to be okay.

Alicestene was so upset with him. With a sharp tone in her voice, she said, "Daddy, now listen here. We don't do drugs. Why would you say something like that? I have never seen you act like this before in my life. Tell me please what's wrong."

He just said, "This don't make no sense to me."

Alicestene said, "Daddy, I am telling you the truth, but you don't believe me, your very own daughter. Now I know how Tehh feels when people don't believe him."

Then she pointed at me and said, "I didn't marry this man for us to fight with you, Daddy. I married one of the best men in this world. I thank God for him. If you don't like it, please feel free to leave our happy home, and you will never see us again. Mama, you can stay." Her mom looked at her and smiled. I was so proud of my wife. She really stood her ground by standing up to her father.

That really got to him though. He started breaking, and tears ran down his face. His voice cracked as he walked over to her and told her that he was sorry. He gave her a big hug and asked her to forgive him with tears in his eyes.

He said, "Alicestene, honey, I have worried myself almost to death because I was afraid Tehh couldn't take care of you. It seemed like all the other guys were doing well for themselves except him. I just couldn't figure him out. I am so sorry."

Alicestene's mom said, "I told you there was something special about Tehh and to stop worrying so much. Oh no, you just had to keep on."

The moment of truth came when he looked me straight in eyes and told me that he was sorry for the way he had treated me and Alicestene. He asked me if I could find it in my heart to forgive him. As tears fell from my eyes, I gave him a big hug, called him Dad, and said I would. But, it was Alicestene who put the icing on the cake, bringing him his hat on a silver platter with hot sauce and shaving cream.

She said, "Daddy, how do you want to eat your hat?"

He flopped down in the chair, looked at her like he had forgotten what he had said, and smiled.

He said, "Well, I done put my foot in mouth, and now I got to do something about it."

Of all things, he took his teeth out of his mouth and started gumming on his hat. We all laughed so hard we started coughing. Alicestene got everybody something to drink, and we all felt better. He was a funny sight. Her mom was so proud of her. Tears were running down her face. I didn't know if she was crying because Alicestene had stood up to her father or because she was glad her daughter had married me. She gave her a big hug and said, "Sugar, this house is simply gorgeous! I am so proud of both of you. Tehh, I thought your mama's house was beautiful, but this, I must say, can't compare."

Peace finally came over everyone, and we started acting like a real family.

Her mom said, "There is one other thing we have to do. Can we all go into the kitchen? Alicestene, get me some scissors so I can have the pleasure of shaving your father's head."

He was stunned. She sat him down in the chair, and he said,

"Oh, my goodness. Woman, wait a minute!"

She cut off most of his hair and then took the shaving cream, covered his head, and shaved it completely bald. He was really hurt. He went over and looked in the mirror and came back. He looked kind of sad with no teeth in his mouth and no hair on his head. He was one funny sight to see. However, I enjoyed every minute of it. He said as we were going into the family room, "I will tell you something. This experience has really taught me to be careful how I judge people from now on, especially you, son, especially you."

They asked us to show them around. I asked them to wait while I went back into the kitchen for a minute. I leaned on the counter to clear my head. Alicestene's father only pretended to have confidence in me. He didn't really want me to marry his daughter. He was only looking at me through what my mama had. Physically to him I had nothing he could see. You would have thought he would have focused on all I had accomplished—getting my GED, getting a car, finishing college, and getting a good job in the Underground City. That should have made him proud. This incident taught me that no matter what a person does, some folks will never see them for who they are.

I got over that moment, thanked God, and rejoined them. I thought we would start upstairs and work our way down. They loved all the bedrooms and how they were decorated, but when they got to our bedroom, they just couldn't believe it.

Her dad said, "Good gracious, boy. I didn't know people lived like this in Box City. This room got everything, including the kitchen sink. I ain't never seen or heard of a bedroom like this before."

I said, "That's because you have never been in Tehh's world before." Alicestene felt better, and she was so proud now that we had worked out our differences with her father.

Her mom said, "You can live in here and never come out for anything." Well, we knew that for sure. We had already stayed there three days and nights. We never left the room, not even for our breakfast, lunch, dinner, or a midnight snack. I told Alicestene to show them around while I called Mama and asked them to come over to see the house. We would just make a celebration of it.

A little while later the doorbell rang, and it was Mama, Mr. Crumpton, Benjamin, and Diamond. They were shocked out of their senses. They looked at the house and almost fainted too. I had the water ready just in case. They couldn't believe their eyes. This was the first time Mama had seen the house. She said that she wasn't sure about it, but the house had my name written all over it. They were so glad to see us. They gave us so many hugs and kisses and continued to look at everything. They asked, "Where did you go for your honeymoon?"

We told them we just went to the other side of town. I said, "It turned out that it didn't look as good as Box City. Alicestene wanted to come back to one of our hotels. I decided I would surprise her with what I had for her here."

Mama smiled and said, "Girl, what did you do?"

Alicestene said, "Mama, I fainted." Mama told her she would have done the same thing because the house was magnificent. Oh, the family was so proud of me and Alicestene. Mama and the ladies were so excited about seeing the house that they all took off and left us men alone. All of us guys were just standing there. I told them that Alicestene and I had caught two big fish out of the lake and how good they were. The next thing I knew, her dad was saying, "Y'all got a lake too?" He just had to see it.

Then Mr. Crumpton looked at Alicestene's father and asked, "What happened to your mouth and head, man?"

He smiled and said, "It's a long story," and then put his teeth back in his mouth.

We all went outside. I looked in the storage closet and asked them to take fishing poles just in case they want to fish. We got our stuff and some refreshments and went down to the lake.

Mr. Crumpton said, "I haven't fished in years, and now my son has them in his own backyard. You can't beat that with a stick."

Benjamin said, "Man, I have never seen a house like this one. All of the houses are pretty over here, but none of them looks like yours. This is awesome. I'm going to get me a house like yours one day, Tehh. If you can do it, I can do it too." Then he said he wanted a lake too.

I thought to myself, *You can afford it all right now.* He and Diamond were just about millionaires but didn't know it yet.

Alicestene's dad said, "I still can't see how you can afford a place like this." He just wouldn't let it go.

I smiled and said, "You could if you owned the bank." They all thought I was being funny, but I was telling the truth.

Mr. Crumpton cast his line into the lake first, and then the rest of us joined in. We all sat there on the bench, eating and drinking sodas and waiting for our catch.

Alicestene's dad said, "Man, this is the life. I've been living here all of my life and never thought I would ever see anything like this in Box City. Colored folks having houses like these—never!"

Then Benjamin said, "Ain't no white folks got a house like this one in Box City. Whoever thought this place up had to be some kind of genius."

Alicestene's father looked around and said, "This place was nothing but a field, and I never even saw a lake. Look at it now with all of these mansions, and my baby lives in one. Here I was worried, and God had everything already worked out. Tehh, I must admit, you had me scared to death. I saw your determination, but nothing else. I just wanted the best for my daughter. I thank you, son," and then he asked me to take good care of her.

Mr. Crumpton told him that he didn't have to worry about nothing like that. He knew that I was going to be a good husband one day from just watching how I treated Mama, Diamond, and Benjamin. Now that was something.

"This is one young man who didn't want his family to want for nothing," he said. Mr. Crumpton, my dad, was standing up for me. He told Alicestene's father to stay on my good side because everything I touched turned to gold.

Benjamin said, "You know it's good to see so many good things happening to colored folks in Box City, especially to our family. We have really been blessed all because of Tehh." Then he told us how he was beginning to see more and more colored folks owning businesses now. He had never seen that before. One day he wanted to own a business too. Mr. Crumpton told us that it seemed like when Mama opened her restaurant and he opened his store, it gave the people of our city hope. Now that was something.

While we were just sitting there and having a good time, the girls came down to the lake with more food and poles. They told us they were going to catch the big one, and it was on. All of a sudden Mr. Crumpton's pole started shaking, and he jumped up to get his fish. Then Alicestene's dad pole started bending, and he jumped up. Then Benjamin's and mine started, and we were all jumping up, trying to bring in our fish.

Alicestene cheered me on, saying, "Bring it on in, Tehh. Bring it in." Then Mama cheered Mr. Crumpton on. Alicestene's mom cheered her dad on. Diamond was the loudest thing out there, cheering on Benjamin. It was a lot of fun, and we all caught some nice fish.

Then the ladies said, "This time the ones who catch the most fish will sit back and watch the losers clean and cook them."

It turned out that the ladies caught the most fish, so we had to clean and cook them. The ladies decided to take a dip in the pool and make fun of us. We were just about through cooking everything and decided to play a trick on them. We fixed our plates and sat down to eat, leaving the ladies in the pool. We piled most of the fish on our plates, leaving them tiny pieces of scraps. You should have seen them laughing and tussling with us for the fish. I thought about how blessed we were. When you can have fun and enjoy being with your family without the fussing and arguing, that makes you rich in a way you can't imagine. We all sat around the patio, eating that delicious cat fish and talking about our wedding and going back to work.

CHAPTER 35

The honeymoon was over, and we both went back to work. As time went on, Alicestene developed a different attitude about work and saw it as something to keep her busy since she didn't have to work anymore. She enjoyed working at the restaurant. She told me that if Mama could do it and be a millionaire all those years without anyone knowing, she could do it too. Mama would go to the restaurant one or two days a week and helped in the office because she was lonesome at home. She later developed some complications as the result of her pregnancy. The doctors took her off of her feet completely. Mr. Crumpton had gotten her a maid to take care of the house, but later hired another one to help take care of her. He didn't want Diamond and Benjamin to stop working when he could afford to do that. Alicestene could always leave work and check on her if needed. I never noticed Mama when she was pregnant with Benjamin and Diamond. I was so young then. Even though she had put on a few pounds, she was still beautiful to me.

The Hancock Bank and the Underground City were doing great business and drawing people from everywhere. In fact, all of the businesses in Box City were very successful. One day while I was at the bank taking care of some business, I saw my daddy (not Mr. Crumpton) standing in line, and he saw me. He smiled and waved at me, and I waved back. He finished his transactions, and I went over and met him at the door.

He said to me, "How you doing, son?"

I almost fainted. He remembered that I was his son. I asked him if he was in a hurry, and he said he wasn't. I invited him to join me for lunch. I quickly went over and told my staff where I was going. We went to his favorite restaurant. He said they cooked the best soul food in the Underground City there. We ordered our food, sat down, and just talked. He said he heard that Mama had gotten married and wished her well. I told him she was having a baby in a few months.

He said, "Wow, Meyel's having a baby. I know her husband must be proud."

He congratulated me on my graduation and marriage and said he wished he could have been there. He told me he clips the articles about me from the newspapers and shows them off to his friends. He had every article they had ever written about me in the newspaper.

I ask, "How have you been doing, Daddy?"

He said, "I been doing ok."

He told me his life had not been the same since the last time he saw me. He only remembered me as the little boy crying when he left us. He was shocked when he saw that I was now a grown man. With a heavy heart he told me that he was sorry that I had to do what he should have been doing all those years.

I asked, "Why did you leave us the way that you did?"

He simply said, "Son, I had no choice."

He cleared his throat and said, "Me and your mama fought and argued all the time. As I look back over my life, most of the time it was all about nothing." He took a deep breath and continued to talk. "Nobody ever taught me how to love a woman. I treated your mama the way my daddy treated my mama. One day I had gotten into a big fight with a guy for cheating at a card game. He took all my money and ran. I was so mad after that. Son, to tell you the truth, I was so mad I could have killed somebody that day, anybody. Your mama didn't know that. If she had said one thing out of the way to me that day, I would have killed her dead. That was just how mad I was."

After that, I had to get myself together. I realized he could have killed us too.

He said, "But something told me to leave town. I went and looked under the bed where your mama kept the money and took it all out of the jar. I went and bought me some whiskey, hopped a train, and left town. Son, I am so sorry, but I was messed up that day. When I finally came to myself, I was in Detroit. Oh, I cried for days when I realized what I had done. I got a job at the motor company there and made good money, but I drank and gambled it all away."

Then he looked me in the eyes and said, "I thought about y'all when I was sober and hated myself for what I had done. So I drank to forget what I had left behind. After ten years of misery I decided to come back home. I knew your mama didn't want to see me again after I had hurt her so bad. As time went on, I met a nice lady who helped me get back on my feet. She had two children already, and we got married. Later on we had a son and named him Jimmy, Jr."

I sat there listening to my father with tears in his eyes as he rubbed his hands together. He answered most of my questions about him. I knew he was truly sorry. He asked me if I could find it in my heart to forgive him, and I did. God had been too good to me to hold anything against him.

He said, "One day, I hope to meet Benjamin and Diamond so I can apologize to them too."

We finished our lunch. As we were heading in the direction of the bank, he said, "Son, do you like the Hancock Bank?"

I smiled and said, "Daddy, I really do."

He said, "I like it too because it has the same name as ours."

I gave my daddy a big hug and asked him to stop by and see me the next time he came to the bank. I watched him walk away with a little pep in his step. It was like a burden had been lifted off of him. I thought to myself, *Daddy, God took the mess you made of our lives and turned it into a miracle.* I went back to the office, did a few things, and called it a day.

One day while I was driving home, I felt there was something else the Lord wanted me to do, but I didn't know what. I was driving, but I didn't know exactly where I was going. Finally I pulled to the side of the road and stopped. I got out of my car and looked around and didn't see anything. Then I looked again and saw an old red and white sign in a field and went over to see what it was. It was a piece of Box City's history that had gone unnoticed. The worn and rusty sign read, "Box City Textile Plant built in 1949." I went back to the car, thinking about the sign and what the Lord was trying to tell me. When the colored folks burned down most of the city, they must have destroyed this plant too. I decided to go to the library and see what I could find out about this company and who owned the land.

I discovered that it was owned by Joseph Turkell and his family. It turned out that in the fifties nearly half the colored folks in Box City worked in this plant for very low wages. The white folks made five times more than the colored people did. They made blue jeans, shirts, skirts, and other garments. The merchandise was shipped throughout the country. The owners made hundreds of thousands of dollars each year. Now it seemed like more and more people were coming to live in new Box City and looking for jobs. I wasn't sure if the Lord was telling me to build this plant back up or what. I got in my car and drove off, looking around to see what Box City didn't have. A lot of people still caught the bus to the other side of town to work and shop. Those dollars sure could be used right here in Box City. I called the real estate office to see if the land was still for sale, and it was. I thought I would contact a few textile companies to see if they wanted to start a company here in Box City. I had to do my homework before I ventured into a textile plant.

CHAPTER 36

It was the day of our eighth month wedding anniversary, and I felt so good about it. I decided I would go home and fix a surprise dinner for Alicestene. Living with her made my life worth living. She was such a joy. I looked forward to going home every day with no regrets. I pulled the car into the garage and went in the house. To my surprise, I smelled food and went into the kitchen. There she was cooking.

I smiled and said, "Hi, honey," and went over and looked in one of the pots. It smelled so good. I gave her a big kiss and told her how much I loved and appreciated her saying, "Happy eighth month anniversary."

She smiled, gave me a big hug, and said, "Happy eighth month anniversary to you, honey." I went to the sink and washed my hands, put on an apron, and helped her finish cooking dinner. She fixed my favorite—fried chicken, turnip greens with onions, her delicious sweet potato casserole, macaroni and cheese, cornbread, and strawberry shortcake. We fixed our plates and went out on the patio to eat. It was so good.

I was enjoying my dinner when she smiled and looked at me with those big, beautiful puppy dog eyes. I began to wonder, *What is she up to?* Then she told me she had some good news to tell me. I got excited and thought she had finally made up her mind and was ready to go to Paris or something.

I was really excited and asked, "What is it, honey?"

She said, "I had to go to the doctor today because I have not been feeling too well lately."

That flew over my head, and I didn't get it. I asked her if she was okay now, and she said she was. I thought something may have happened to her at work. Then she asked me to not get upset with her for not waiting. I still didn't get it.

I said, "Waiting for what, honey?"

Then what she told me hit me like a ton of bricks. She smiled and said, "Tehh, honey, I'm having a baby," and I fainted.

That was all I remembered. When I came to myself, I was as wet as a rat. She paid me back for throwing all of that water on her that time. She said it was the only way she thought she could wake me up.

Then she said, "The doctor said we are having twins," and I fainted again. When I came to myself, this woman had a big pitcher of water, getting ready to drown me with it. It would have been better if she had pushed me in the pool.

She said, "Tehh, are you okay, honey?"

I said, "Yes, I'm okay for now."

She said, "Please don't die on me now, honey, because me and these babies really need you."

I gave her a big hug and thanked her with tears in my eyes. I said, "Honey, I need you and these babies. I am not upset at all. Of all the things God has blessed me with, this is the greatest thing that could ever happen to me."

She was so relieved. After that, she became so happy about becoming a mother and began to glow. My baby was having two babies, and I thanked God in my heart.

I sat her on my lap and said, "No more work for you, baby. You are going to have a maid and whatever you needed to help us through this." I told her to go and get some rest while I dried up all the water she had thrown on me and cleaned up the kitchen.

Later we walked down to the lake and just talked. The fresh air was just so peaceful and relaxing. I told her how I thought the Lord wanted me to do something else for Box City.

She looked at me and asked, "What do you mean something else? Tehh, what have you done already? Please tell me."

I took a deep breath and told her that no one but Mama knew all that I had done for Box City. I pleaded with her not to tell anyone. So as the birds flew over our heads, the fish jumped in the lake, and the clouds rolled and formed all kinds of shapes before our eyes, I opened up and told my wife all of my secrets regarding Box City. I told her I own fifteen apartment buildings, ten old and five brand-new ones. Three of the new ones were buildings where she once wanted us to live. They were near Diamond Ridge.

Then she looked puzzled and said, "Wow!"

I told her I owned the antique shop where I worked.

She jumped up and put her hands on her hips and said, "What? You mean to tell me you worked part-time at your own store as a stock boy? Did they know it?"

I said, "No one knew. That way I could keep an eye on things."

Then she smiled and said, "No wonder I got such great discounts. This is just amazing, but it's still so hard to believe."

I told her I owned the Ricko's Bakery building, both bank buildings, Johnson Hardware Store building, Mr. Crumpton's building, the Underground City, the Hancock Bank, the training school, the technical school, and several other buildings throughout Box City. I had even built Wagon Trace subdivision where we live.

She said, "Tehh, tell me the truth. Did you have the house built for your mama?"

I said, "Baby, I sure did."

She smiled and said, "I had a feeling something was up with that. I couldn't figure out how a rich white man was going to trust his mansion to some poor colored folks who lived in the projects."

She had a point there. I smiled and continued talking. "I built Diamond Ridge, and the Benjamin Heights subdivision was 50 percent complete, not to mention the Crumpton's Villa." I told her that I couldn't name everything because there was so much.

She said, "Tehh, you mean to tell me you had all those beautiful signs put up about a new Box City on the rise, yourself?"

"Yep! You got it right again, baby," I said.

She told me how beautiful they were. Then she asked in amazement, "Are you trying to tell me you rebuilt Box City all by yourself?"

I said, "I actually did it with the help of the Lord. I was just following His lead."

She said, "Wow," and then she asked, "How did you do all of that without an education? You weren't even twenty years old!"

I told her I didn't know. Maybe it was because I was a genius. She just smiled. I told her that I had an awful lot of help from Mama. She had been the adult who had to sign the papers with me.

My wife made me so proud when she told me that she was learning a lot about my mama, especially her humble attitude. She said, "Tehh, all of what you have told me would be hard for anyone to believe just looking at you. That's the kind of stuff good books are made of."

She made this startling discovery about me saying, "But you are a colored man, Tehh. Ain't no colored man never done anything like this before, young or old."

I just smiled and said, "That's because I wasn't here before until now."

She got a little upset, stood up, and said, "Everybody was thinking that some white folks were doing of all of this, Tehh."

I told her that I knew it and that it always made me mad, but that was life.

Then she smiled and said, "One day everybody is going to be shocked when they realize that the boy pushing the wagon and collecting junk off the streets rebuilt the new Box City."

I just said, "Yes, you are so right."

I spent the rest of the evening telling her the story of my life, and she couldn't believe it. She kept saying, "This is just too amazing." Then she asked me if I was behind everybody getting their GEDs and going back to school. She wondered how I did it. I told her I was, and I did it one person at a time, beginning with me. I couldn't encourage others to do what I wasn't willing to do myself. I told her about my Finang Gang, how I had trained all of them to get their GEDs, go to college, save their money, and invest in the city among other things.

She said, "If I didn't know you and closed my eyes, I would think you were a sixty-year-old man just listening to you."

I smiled and said, "I really look good for an old man, don't I?"

I told her the gang went out and recruited others to join us and now many of them are employed in top positions. Educating the people would be the key to the success of the city. They all worked for me, but they don't know it. She took a deep breath and finally admitted that I was truly a genius. She thought about all the times she didn't believe me. She gave me a big hug and told me that she was so proud of me and hoped that our children would be little geniuses too.

Then she said very seriously, "Tehh, it seems like after what you have told me, honey, whatever the Lord has for you to do, it's going to be something great. Whatever I can do to help, you can surely count on me. I want to be able to tell our children I helped their daddy rebuild the new Box City too." That woman just made me so proud of her that I just couldn't help myself. I just couldn't stop kissing her. We walked on back up to the house to enjoy the rest of our evening.

I woke up early one Saturday morning and left Alicestene sleeping in the bed. I went down to the pool and sat down on the lounger with my strawberry soda, looking up at the ceiling. I began looking back over my life and this incredible journey I was on. I thought about where God had brought me from and how He had allowed me to rise above all of my circumstances to get to this point in my life. I saw the little, fatherless boy with a tumor who had been put out of school for having a severe learning disability, emotional problems, and all the pain associated with those hurdles. I thought about my daddy leaving us and Mama working four and five different jobs a week to keep food on the table and a roof over our heads. I saw myself at thirteen, collecting junk off the streets to help Mama take care of us. I thought about how as a little boy I prayed to God and asked Him to help me make my mama happy if I could and make Box City a better place for us. I thought about all the people who had mistreated me in my life and asked the Lord to forgive every last one of them. People like Ray James, who said there wasn't any money in junk and that I didn't know what money was, and that I would never have any, those who called me dumb and stupid and said I was a waste of time and a burden on society, those who thought I should just be institutionalized or locked away somewhere. I thought about how they said I couldn't read, write, or understand anything and how they never tried to seek the truth. I thought about how I was friendless, and how God had given me Toe Joe, Mad Dog, Brock, Jason, and the Finang Gang. I thought about my daddy, who left us penniless, and how he apologized to me. I thought about Mama finally forgiving him and how Mr. Crumpton had replaced him as a father. I thought about the baby Mama was having. I thought about the money the Lord allowed me to find to rebuild our lives and this city and how the interest I received from it made us multi-millionaires. I thought about all the lives He had allowed me to change for the better. People who had no hope found hope at last—people like Mrs. Collins and the children who had no one to turn to. People who saw life in shades of gray can now see it in brilliant color because life was worth living now. I thought about the bankers' words, which gave me the motivation and determination to prove them wrong. I thought about the day I fell asleep at the wheel and almost lost my life. I thought about so many things. I laid there thinking with tears running down my face like a faucet. I thought about receiving my GED and graduating from college. Then I thought about this great gift of a woman God had given me as my wife, and now she was having twins. The tears just kept coming because I was so happy, and yet I felt so undeserving. I don't know why God had chosen to bless me the way He has, but I am so grateful. I thought about the new Box City and how God said yes to everything I had asked him for. Then I remembered to thank God for coming into my life and for the voice inside of me that He taught me to listen to and obey. The tears were still falling. I decided to hop in the pool to wash them away. At that moment I was just too emotional.

My baby, my precious Alicestene came and stood by the pool in front of me in her nightgown with that beautiful smile on her face. Her gown was open, and I thought I saw her stomach move. It was so weird. She was four and a half months pregnant, and for some strange reason I felt like these babies knew I was their daddy. She hopped in the pool with me and held me closed and told me how much she loved and appreciated me. Then she gave God thanks for me and bringing us together. Looking back, it was my sister, Diamond, who taught me the true meaning of love and how to genuinely show it. You can never say, "I love you," too much to those you really love.

After the good news about the babies, I couldn't hold it any longer. I decided to call and invite all the family, Miss Emma and her husband, and the guys and their wives over to tell them the news. My nerves were shocked, and I was still in no condition to prepare the food, for thinking about the babies and Alicestene. I did the next best thing. I called my favorite chef, Andrew, who did most of catering for the Weddings and Events Center, and asked him to whip me up something for about twenty-five or thirty people for Friday evening, and he did.

We both got ready and waited for our guests to arrive. The doorbell rang, and I went to answer the door. It was Mama, Mr. Crumpton, Benjamin, Diamond, and their friends. We all hugged one another, and Mama asked me what was going on. She was just as pretty as usual, and as round as she could be. I asked them to wait until everyone arrived and said that I would tell everybody at the same time. Alicestene's parents arrived. Then Miss Emma and her husband and finally the guys with their wives and some of the members of the gang showed up. Everyone wanted to know what was going on. We went out to the patio to eat. Andrew did a fantastic job with the food. Everyone was so excited and talked about how good the food looked and smelled. We all got our plates and sat down. I had wine for this occasion, and the server filled our glasses.

Toe Joe said, "Man, this got to be some good news for wine."

Mad Dog said, "He probably made a lot of money in the stock market or something again."

I stood up and said, "No, nothing like that."

I asked Alicestene to stand up. Her mom just looked at her, smiling. I was so excited and said, "Alicestene is pregnant. We are having babies, and they are twins."

Everybody jumped up, shouted, and congratulated us. They all just hugged Alicestene and kissed her and gave me some love too.

Mama said, "That is so wonderful. The babies can grow up with their aunt or uncle and have fun too."

Alicestene's mom just held her with tears in her eyes, saying, "I'm going to be a grandmother … not of one, but two. We are going to have to turn Alicestene's room into the baby's room now." Her dad appeared shocked by all of this.

I thought, *This man can't be mad with me for getting my wife pregnant.* He really wasn't.

He said, "I never thought I would be a grandfather of two babies at the same time. God will truly give you more than you ask for sometimes." He held Alicestene and kissed her and said, "My baby is having two babies." Tears were running down his face.

Then he came over to me and said, "Congratulations, son. I am so proud of you."

We all went back to our seats and finished our dinner as we talked about baby stuff. The ladies quickly got up and left us men alone again.

Alicestene's father stood up and said, "Son, I guess we have to go to the men's retreat down by the lake and have us some fun too. How about a little fishing?"

We had a few hours before dark, and everybody was okay with that. We all grabbed snacks, drinks, and fishing poles and headed down to the lake. Benjamin brought the music, and it sounded good. Everybody found their favorite fishing spots and cast their lines hoping for the big one. Mr. Crumpton said that Mama had a couple of months to go and that she was doing well. He just couldn't wait for the baby to hurry up and come. She looked like she was going to pop in a minute. Mama wanted a junior if it was a boy, and if it was a girl, he would choose the name.

He said, "Here I am an old man, and now I am going to have to learn how to change a diaper."

Then Alicestene's dad said, "At least you won't be like Tehh. He's going to have to change two at the same time."

Mr. Crumpton laughed and said, "Yeah, wait until you have them at your house. You are going to have to clean those butts." We all laughed till tears ran down our faces.

Jason said, "Wait until they keep you up all night because they want you to play with them."

Smiling, Brock said, "Man, that ain't nothing. Wait until all the mess in their diapers starts running out everywhere. You clean them up real good and put baby power on them, and you still smell stuff. You check everywhere trying to find that smell. Then you reach in your pocket, and there it is. It's all over your hand, change and stuff. Don't ask yourself how it got there because you can't figure it out. Just take everything out your pockets. Wash it off and take the pants to the laundry quick. That stuff is like battery acid. It will change the color of your clothes, man. I'm telling you."

We were all falling all over the place, laughing. A little later the ladies came and joined us, and we all sat around and talked and had a good time.

CHAPTER 37

After a few months, I was still trying to figure out what the Lord wanted me to do. It was getting the best of me. I got off work a little early and found myself driving down by the old textile plant location. The land was for sale, and I decided to buy it at a very good price. In fact, I tried to buy up as much land as I could before investors started moving in. That way they would have to buy it from me and the Hancock Bank. Everyone wants to get on the bandwagon when thing are going well and you have done all the work. I went back over where I saw the sign and looked around again. I noticed there was another sign a few yards away that I didn't notice before. I walked over to see what it said. "Get in a hurry. Jesus is coming soon," is how it read. I smiled because I thought the Lord had a great sense of humor. I kept looking and saw another sign. It was for an expansion of that textile plant. They were going to make baby clothes back in the early sixties.

I left and went by the post office to check the mail. I had three letters from textile companies. I went and sat in my car and began to read them. Two said they were not interested in building a plant in Box City. The other one said they might have an interest and for me to contact them. That was wonderful news.

I decided I would stop by and check on Mama before I went home since it was close to her time to deliver. I drove over and rang the doorbell, and she opened the door. I gave her a big hug, and she asked me to come on in and sit down. She had some fried chicken and pound cake in the kitchen, and my strawberry soda was in the refrigerator. My mama knew me all so well. I fixed my plate and came back and sat with her. She asked me how Alicestene was. I told her she was doing fine and gaining a lot of weight.

Then she said, "Tell me about it. I didn't get this big with y'all."

She said Mr. Crumpton would be in a little later because he had to make a stop. She had been a little restless but not in a lot of pain. Her back had been hurting a little most of the day.

She looked at me with tears in her eyes and said, "Tehh, I am so tired. I am just too old to be having a baby."

I told her God knew what he was doing and she was too close to turn back now. The baby is just about ready to pop out. When I said that, she jumped up and asked me to excuse her because she had to go to the restroom. She told me she couldn't remember when she peed so much.

She started walking toward the restroom, and I noticed water falling on the hardwood floor. I got up and said, "Mama, did your water break?"

She looked down and saw the water on the floor and said, "Oh, my goodness, Tehh. My water just broke. Get me to the hospital quick!" I told the maid to tell Mr. Crumpton to meet us at the hospital and to call Diamond, Benjamin, and Alicestene for me.

I got Mama into the car, and we were off to the hospital.

I pulled up to the hospital screaming, "My mama is having a baby. Her water just broke. Somebody help me please!"

Someone came with a wheelchair and rushed her on in. I was a nervous wreck as I went up to the desk. The lady asked me a few questions and asked me to fill out some papers, and I did. A nurse took me to the waiting room until they checked Mama out to see what was going on. I sat there wondering, *Where is everybody? I don't want to go through this all by myself.* I was so scared this time because it was my mama and I couldn't help her. *Where in the world is Mr. Crumpton. What's taking him so long?* It seemed like minutes were turning into hours as I paced the floor. Then I would ask the first nurse passing, "How is my mama?" They would go and check. The last message was, "They are getting her ready, and then you can see your wife before she goes to delivery." They keep saying I was the father, but I was the son. I kept telling them she was my mama. I sat there, waiting for somebody to come through that door.

Suddenly Alicestene came in holding her stomach with Benjamin and Diamond all out of breath. I asked her if she was okay, and she said she was. She gave me a kiss, held me close, and told me everything was going to be all right. I told them that Mama's water had broken and that I brought her here.

Now they were getting her ready to go to delivery. Finally Mr. Crumpton came rushing in all out of breath. I didn't want him to have a heart attack.

I said, "Please calm down, Mr. Crumpton, and get yourself together because Mama and that baby needs you."

He finally pulled himself together and went back to be with Mama. We all just sat there waiting to hear from somebody, anybody. A nurse came and told us that she was in labor and delivery and that we would know something soon. We all sat there with our eyes fixed on the door waiting for the news. Suddenly the door opened, and it was Mr. Crumpton. We all jumped up and ran to him like little children who were glad to see their daddy.

Before we could ask, he said, "It's a girl! She weighs eight pounds and six ounces, and she is twenty-one inches long."

Diamond smiled and said, "That is how much I weighed when I was born." He told us Mama was doing fine, and we could see her as soon as they put her in a room.

Then Diamond said, "What you gonna name her, Pop?"

He smiled and said, "Heavenly. I think I'm going to name her Heavenly because God answered my prayers." He said that because he thought he would never be able to father a child of his own.

The nurse came out and told us we could go in and see Mama in room 118. We all marched down the hall as fast as we could to her room. We slowly opened the door and peeped in. She was laying there with baby Heavenly in her arms. We all went over and gave her a big kiss on the cheeks or forehead. We told her how much we loved her and how beautiful little Heavenly was. She looked like a little angel in Mama's arms. We counted all of her toes and fingers to make sure she had everything, and Mama just smiled. She didn't have to tell us because we could look at her face and tell that she was still tired. We all left so she could rest. We went back into the waiting room for a while to talk about the baby, and then we left. Mr. Crumpton told us later that it would be about five days before Mama and the baby could come home. We spent that time getting the house ready for the baby since Mama didn't know what she was having. I thanked God for making my mama and Mr. Crumpton happy again and keeping her safe during her pregnancy.

It was the big day for Mama to come home, and everything was ready. Little Heavenly's room was right next to theirs. I never anticipated a baby in the picture when I had the house built for Mama, so a nursery was never part of the plan. Mr. Crumpton and I had a door cut from their room into the next bedroom for the baby. It was truly beautiful with the French doors. I had never seen so many diapers in my life. Mr. Crumpton ordered fifty boxes of diapers, various sizes and everything else a baby would need. That means I would have to order one hundred boxes when the twins arrive. Then I got the brilliant idea to open up a baby store in the future for all of those children Alicestene and other folks wanted to have. We had every store except a baby or infant store in Box City.

The doorbell rang, and we all went downstairs. Mr. Crumpton and Mama were coming in with our little bundle of joy. The first one to go for the baby was the one who said he wasn't going to clean any baby's diaper, Benjamin. Diamond and I couldn't believe our eyes. He took the baby, went over and sat in the chair with her like we didn't exist. He and Heavenly were in their own little world. I was jealous. Here I was a grown man, and I was jealous of my little brother because he had gotten to the baby first. Mama sensed something and took the baby from him and gave her to me. I held her close and sniffed her. She smelled so good. I handed her to Diamond, and she did the same thing. We followed Mama upstairs to her room. She was so excited to see the French doors. She went and opened them to see the baby's nursery.

She just couldn't believe it and said, "This is so beautiful. Thank y'all so much."

Since the baby's name was Heavenly, there were clouds, rainbows, and angels everywhere. Mama was very pleased with the room and told Mr. Crumpton that she had never seen so many diapers in her life. We also had a bassinet by her bed to make it easy for Mama to care of the baby until she got stronger. Mama said she wanted to try to care for the baby the first week before she gave her to the babysitter. Mr. Crumpton took the baby from Diamond, kissed her, put her in the bassinet, and helped Mama into bed. We all stood there looking at her, smiling. Then she told us to get out and let her get some rest because she was so tired. Mr. Crumpton loves my mama and does everything he can to make her happy. That was one thing I was so grateful for. There was no fighting or arguing or disrespect like there had been with my daddy when I was younger. I could go home to my own family and not worry about someone hurting my mama.

CHAPTER 38

Several months later while I was at work, I got an amazing phone call from a man named Mr. Thornton. He was the man who was interested in starting a textile plant in Box City. He said he was in town and wanted to take a tour of the place if I had the time. He liked unscheduled visits so that he could see places untouched. People tend to spend a lot of money for nothing trying to impress them. That interfered with their vision for the place. He asked me if I could meet him at the hotel if it wasn't a problem. I told him it was no problem. I was so excited that a major corporation was interested in coming to Box City. I had been the public relations person for Box City for a very long time, and nobody knew it. I told my assistant that I was leaving for the day to meet a client and that I would see her tomorrow.

I drove over to the hotel to pick up this Mr. Thornton. I had no idea what he looked like. It turned out he was standing near the desk. I knew he wasn't expecting a colored man by the way he looked past me. I went up to the desk and told the clerk that a Mr. Thornton was expecting me. He cleared his throat, turned quickly with a cigar in his mouth, and said that he was Mr. Thornton and shook my hand.

He politely said, "I thought Mr. Hancock was a white man, son."

I smiled and said, "Sir, I get that a lot."

We drove around town, and he was very impressed with what he saw. He said, "Box City is a clean, homey little town with a big-city appeal."

I drove over to the old textile site, and we looked around. We walked over the whole place. I told him the history of it and showed him some of the old signs nearby. He told me that they had done some research on the place and that it did pretty good business back then.

As the smoke from his cigar circled his head, he said, "It's a pretty large building site with lots of potential, and I just might be interested."

He was pleased to hear that the city promoted education. Most of the young people were getting an education, and those were the ones he would employ. He said he also wanted to look at the homes in the area. If he did decide to build the plant here, the people he would send down needed a permanent place to live.

We drove all over the city. He wanted to look at Diamond Ridge and Benjamin Heights. He was very impressed with the standards of living and said they were really nice communities. Then he looked at my newest ventures, Crumpton's Villa and Emerald Cove subdivisions. Finally he wanted to look at the one with the mansions, Wagon Trace.

He said, "I noticed them when the cab brought me to the hotel. They really got my attention."

We entered the gate and drove through the community.

He was in awe, and said, "For a small town to look like yours, it would probably be wise to invest in it."

As we drove, he kept saying, "The houses are just beautiful."

I was getting ready to turn in the opposite direction when he saw my house, not realizing it was mine.

He said, "That house is simply magnificent. I wonder what it looks like on the inside and who lives there. If I didn't know any better, I would say it looks like the owner of a bank," and then he laughed.

You got that right, I said to myself.

Well, I pulled up into the driveway of "that house", and he said, "No, son, I didn't mean for you to go to the folks' house."

I said, "Well, Mr. Thornton, that's the only way you are going to see inside, sir."

He looked at me like I was crazy with a frown on his face. I said, "Relax, Mr. Thornton. It's okay. You are at my house. I hope you don't mind, but we don't smoke inside."

He politely put out his cigar, and we went in.

I heard Alicestene say, "Honey, I'm in the kitchen."

I wondered why she was up because she was on strict bed rest. I told her we had company and she said, "Okay, come on in."

I asked Mr. Thornton to follow me to the kitchen so that I could introduce him to my wife. I told him she was expecting twins and that they were due any day now.

He said, "You don't say. Congratulations."

She turned with that beautiful smile, gave me a big hug and a kiss, and shook Mr. Thornton's hand. He was very impressed. I must admit that she was one big, beautiful sight. I explained to her that Mr. Thornton was the man who was interested in building the textile plant.

All of a sudden, he started sniffing and said, "Something really smells good in here."

Alicestene smiled and said, "The maid and I were preparing dinner. You are more than welcome to join us."

She fixed us a snack while we waited for dinner and told me she was going to the family room to lie down and watch television. Mr. Thornton and I went out on the patio by the pool and the maid brought us our snack. We ate and talked about the textile plant as we neared an agreement.

He said, "Mr. Hancock, do you mind showing me around. I just love this house." He told me I had a beautiful home and asked me how old I was. I told him I was twenty-two, and he couldn't believe it. We went outside first and looked around, and then he noticed the lake. He told me he never had the time to fish even when he wanted to. He was always too busy. I had the maid pack us a few more snacks with drinks. Alicestene asked us to not eat too much because dinner would be ready soon.

We grabbed a few poles and headed for the lake. He took the cigar out of his mouth and said, "What do you do for a living, Mr. Hancock?"

I said humbly, "I managed the Underground City Shopping Mall and Entertainment Center, sir.

He said, "They must pay you pretty good to live like this?"

I just said, "Yes sir, pretty good."

We made it down to the lake, took off our jackets, rolled up our sleeves, and began to fish. He cast his line, and I casted mine. We sat on the bench and continued our conversation. He got up and took off his shoes and walked around in his socks. He said he liked the way the grass felt. Then his pole began to move, and he forgot that he was a businessman. He jumped up and grabbed his pole like a big kid and began to bring in his fish. It was a beauty. He took it off the hook, put it in the fish pail, and cast his line again.

He said, "This place is like heaven to me. I remember when I was a young boy fishing with my daddy in a creek. We had a lot of fun." Then his pole moved again, and he jumped up to pull it in, just laughing. "Dat blasted. It's a beauty," he said and put it in the fish pail. Then he said, "You know Mr. Hancock, if I catch another fish, you can consider the textile plant a done deal here in Box City." He cast his line, and before it was in the water for a moment, a fish took the bait. He was so excited, and brought it in. It was the biggest of them all. He said laughing, "Now that has never happened to me before in my life. That's a good sign."

I thanked God for giving us the textile plant, which would employ several hundred people. All he had to do now was submit his plan to the city. There wasn't any alcohol, night clubs, strippers, or anything like that involved in sealing the deal. It was just a few beautiful fish shaking their tails. He told me he had never had so much fun.

He laughed and said, "Mr. Hancock, I can't believe you didn't catch a fish out of your own lake."

I said, "Mr. Thornton, I believe this was your day."

I cleaned the fish and took them back to the house. I told him we could have them tomorrow if he wanted. He thought that was a great idea. We went on back to the house and washed up for dinner. The maid had everything ready in the family room so that Alicestene could be with us. She said upstairs was so far away from everything. She couldn't climb the stairs like she once could because of the weight of the babies. We had chicken and dumplings, turnip greens with fresh onions, sliced tomatoes, glazed candied yams, corn bread and rolls, fried chicken, ice tea, chocolate cake, and my strawberry soda.

Mr. Thornton was blown away and said, "It's been a long time since I had food that tasted this good. Folks just don't cook like this up north. Not only that, but I have never had such hospitality extended to me. I know it's not because of the textile plant." He said even though he had just met me, he sensed there was something special about me. He put some more food on his plate and continued to talk. He was really enjoying himself among us colored folks. I remembered what the banker said, "Low-class people will never have a high-class mentality."

We were getting ready for dessert when the doorbell rang. I went to see who it was. It was Mama, Mr. Crumpton, baby Heavenly, Diamond, and

Benjamin. I didn't know they were coming over. It turned out that they had come to check on Alicestene since she wasn't feeling well. I took everyone in the family room to be with her. Mama gave Alicestene the baby, and she was so happy. I introduced everybody to Mr. Thornton and told them he was going to build a textile plant here in Box City.

Alicestene said, "If you are hungry, there is plenty of food in the kitchen, help yourself."

I told Mr. Thornton that Mama owned Meyel's Bakery and Family Restaurant in town. My father, Mr. Crumpton, owned Crumpton's Big and Tall Men's Clothing Store. My sister, Diamond, and my brother, Benjamin, were in high school and college.

He was very impressed with our family and said, "Y'all are business people like myself."

I took the men out on the patio to hang out and enjoy our dessert while Mama and Diamond stayed with Alicestene. Benjamin was hungry, so he stayed behind to eat.

Mr. Crumpton asked Mr. Thornton, "What kind of business are you in, sir?"

He told us that he owned ten textile plants across the country. His grandfather started the first plant in Kentucky, and when he died, his father took over and built five more. When he died, the business went to him. He said he built three more and was now looking to build another right here in Box City.

Mr. Crumpton was so excited and said, "That's great, Mr. Thornton. Your plant is certainly going to be a welcomed sight to our city."

We sat and talked for hours, and then it was time for Mr. Crumpton and Mama to go home. Alicestene hated to let baby Heavenly go, but she had to. She told me she couldn't wait for the twins to come. We all said good night, and everybody left. Mr. Thornton felt like he was at home. I told him that he could spend the night if he wanted to. If he wanted to get up early and go fishing, he knew where everything was. He was so excited about that.

I drove him back over to the hotel to get his things for the night. The man went on and checked out of that hotel completely so he could enjoy my lake. He came back with all of his luggage, and we went back to the house. When Alicestene started having trouble going up the stairs, I converted our offices downstairs into bedrooms and moved our offices upstairs. We allowed Mr. Thornton to stay in the bedroom across from us downstairs. He said the room was better than the hotel. I showed him where the restroom and refreshment bar was. I told him if he wanted to relax in the heated pool, he could. He smiled and thanked me. Then I helped Alicestene into bed, and we went to sleep.

I got up early and started breakfast. I went to check on Mr. Thornton and noticed the door was partly opened. I peeped in, and he was not there. I went and looked out the kitchen window, and there he was at the lake, fishing away. I took him a pot of hot coffee and told him to enjoy himself. Breakfast would be ready shortly. He looked at me with a big smile and said, "Thank you, son." I went on back to the house and finished breakfast.

I went in to check on Alicestene, and she was grunting in her sleep like she had some discomfort. I asked her if she was okay and she said she was. I told her I would bring breakfast to her and not to bother about getting up. I went on back to the kitchen and finished up everything and set the table for Mr. Thornton. He came in the house like a little boy excited about the fish he had caught.

He said, "Being with y'all has allowed me to air out my mind. I feel like I'm on a real vacation and not a business trip at all. I tell you. I don't know how you did it, but I feel ten years younger."

I smiled and told him breakfast was ready. He was just amazed at how things were set up. I took Alicestene her breakfast, gave her a big kiss, and went back to join Mr. Thornton.

He asked, "Were you ever a chef, Mr. Hancock?"

I said, "No, sir, but I read a lot of cookbooks, and I've cooked most of my life. I just got better at it."

While he was chewing, he said, "I saw a vacant lot on the other side of the lake. Is it for sale? If so, tell me who I need to contact about having a house built there." I told him that I didn't know, but I would find out and let him know. For some strange reason I left a few vacant lake lots available.

CHAPTER 39

While we were finishing our breakfast, Alicestene called me and I rushed in to see what she wanted.

She said, "Tehh, I accidently wet the bed. Help me get up so I can change my clothes."

In a panic I said, "No, you didn't, baby. Your water just broke!"

I told Mr. Thornton that her water broke and we had to get her to the hospital quick. I had the maid call the hospital to let them know that we were on our way and gave her the list to call everybody. You should have seen us trying to figure out what to do. I helped Alicestene change her clothes, and we helped her into the car. Mr. Thornton had to drive us to the hospital because I was a nervous wreck.

I rushed into the hospital, screaming, "My wife is having a baby. Her water broke. She's having twins. Help me please!"

It seemed like everyone came out to help her. They put her in a wheelchair and rolled her away. One strange nurse who remembered me from the time when Mama had her baby said, "Mr. Hancock, you are having another baby?"

Mr. Thornton parked the car and came in with me. I was a nervous wreck. I had to fill out the paperwork, and I barely made it through that. I went back to check on Alicestene, and I saw that she was in a lot of pain.

She took one look at me and said in an evil voice, "Get out! I never wanted to see you again as long as I live. Get out!!!"

I said, "But, honey, it's me."

She screamed, "Get out now!!!"

The nurse told me she didn't mean it. She asked me to leave so I wouldn't stress her out. I couldn't believe she would do me like that. My mind went back to the days when people mistreated me on the streets. I sadly dropped my head, turned and walked away with tears in my eyes. The woman I loved with all of my heart for some strange reason now hated me. Mr. Thornton saw the tears in my eyes and asked me what was wrong, and I told him.

"She said she never wanted to see me again and told me to get out, Mr. Thornton. What did I do to make her feel like that?" I asked him?

He took me over to the waiting area, and we sat down. He said, "She didn't mean it, son. She was just in an awful lot of pain at the time and blames you for it. Two babies means twice the pain. My wife did that to me several times. When the babies were born, she didn't even remember telling me those horrible things. Everything is going to be okay."

I finally pulled myself together. I called Mama and told her that we were at the hospital. In my heart I prayed and asked the Lord to let Alicestene and the babies be all right. *Let her love me again.* I couldn't bear the thought of her hating me for any reason. I went back over and sat with Mr. Thornton. I was glad he was with me because I couldn't have made it alone.

I use to see men pacing the floor when their wives were in the delivery room on television. Now I was doing the very same thing. Mr. Thornton decided he would walk with me because I was making him dizzy. We walked back and forth, talking. Whenever the door opened and a nurse came out, I would ask, "Is my wife okay?" Mr. Thornton finally got me to sit down.

I looked up, and Mama was coming through the door with the baby, and asking, "How is Alicestene?" I told her I didn't know because she didn't want me back there.

She said, "Baby, that's because she was in a lot of pain. She didn't mean it. When the babies are born, she won't even remember it."

Then Mr. Thornton said, "I told you."

We all sat there, waiting. Mama said, "I left a message for Harold. Benjamin and Diamond are on their way. I had them stop by his store just in case he didn't get the message."

Mama asked me to hold the baby. She thought it might calm me down, while she went to check on Alicestene. Little Heavenly looked at me like she was trying to tell me everything was going to be okay, smiling.

Mr. Thornton said, "She is a beautiful baby. Can I hold her?"

I gently gave him the baby. He began to make all kinds of sounds, and the baby just smiled at him. I noticed a tear forming in the corner of his eye. I wondered what he was thinking.

Mama came back and told me that the babies should be coming soon. She was so excited, and I was about to have a heart attack. Mama took the baby from Mr. Thornton and sat between us. He asked me if I was okay, and that was all I remembered. They told me later that I fainted and one of the nurses checked me out to make sure I was okay. When I came to myself, everyone had made it to the hospital. The doctor came out and told me that I was the proud father of two beautiful baby boys and that I could go back and see my wife. I was so relieved. I slowly stuck my head through the door.

She said, "Hey, honey, come see our sons."

I couldn't believe it. She wasn't mad at me anymore. I took a deep breath, went over, gave her a big kiss, and looked at our beautiful sons. In my heart I lifted them up to the Lord and thanked Him for keeping them and me. The nurse told me they were taking her to room 125 and I could see her in a few minutes.

I went back out with tears in my eyes, and I said, "I have two sons, and they are so beautiful. They are taking her to room 125. We can see her in a few minutes."

The nurse later came out and told me that we could see her. We were so excited, and piled into her room to look at the babies. Alicestene told me to pick out the names because she had done the hard part, and everyone laughed. I knew she was tired. We left so she could rest.

I called the maid and told her that we had two beautiful boys for her. She was so excited. Then I asked her to fix the fish Mr. Thornton caught yesterday for lunch because we were on our way home. While we were driving home, Mr. Thornton told me that I had a wonderful wife and two beautiful boys. He thanked me for allowing him to share in my happiness. He said he and his family were not close at all, and it was partly his fault. He was so busy making money that he missed out on some of the best times of his life.

He said with a big smile on his face, "For a few minutes I felt more like family than a business partner."

Driving home, all I could think about were my beautiful sons God had given me, and eating some food. We were both very hungry.

We pulled up to the house, and Mr. Thornton said, "Son, I need to take a good puff from my cigar before I go in."

I went on in the house, and the maid came and gave me a big hug and congratulated me on the twins. She said, "What did you name them?"

I smiled and said, "Thomas Edison Hamilton Hancock two and three."

She said, "Something told me that you would do something like that, Mr. Hancock." She just smiled and continued, "Lord, have mercy. Your food is ready on the patio."

Mr. Thornton finished his cigar and came on in the house. He was just amazed that colored folks could have a maid in a place like Box City. We washed up and went out on the patio to eat. The food smelled so good.

He lifted up the tray and said, "Got dog it! There's my catfish! It's on now!"

We pile the fish on our plates and sat back and enjoyed ourselves. We didn't even talk. We just ate. Then Mr. Thornton asked me if he could have some of that chocolate cake from yesterday. I told him Ms. Mable may have something else for us today.

I got up and went to see what she had and said, "Homemade apple pie with ice cream today, Mr. Thornton."

He said, "That's my favorite."

He came and got a slice of pie and put two scoops of ice cream on top. We decided to go down to the lake and enjoy our dessert. I called Ms. Mable and told her we were going down to the lake. Mr. Thornton gave her a big hug and thanked her for the delicious lunch. She was as happy as a bee making honey.

While we were sitting by the lake, Mr. Thornton told me that he would be leaving in the morning, and wanted me to know how much he had enjoyed himself. He told me he was definitely interested in the lot across the lake and wanted to bring his wife down to see it. He said he had traveled the country and had never been to a place quite like Box City. It was a jewel of a place. He wanted to know if it would be okay if they could stay with us when he came back. I thought it was a blessing that he considered that. He said he wanted to come back and spend some time with his twins. I told him that they were welcome anytime. I wanted to take a nap and get back over to the hospital to check on Alicestene and the twins. I told him to make himself at home. He said he would probably go in and take a nap too, pack up his clothes, and then take in a little fishing later on. We headed on back up to the house. I explained everything to Ms. Mable and went to bed.

I woke up, grabbed a bite, and left for the hospital. I walked into the room, and Alicestene was still asleep. The nurse told me they had given her some more medicine to ease her pain. I sat in the chair next to her bed and just watched her, thinking about how much I loved her. The nurse came in with the babies. I was so proud to see them. She told me they were some beautiful boys, and they were identical. They were so tiny and still asleep. I looked at them with tears in my eyes, thanking God again for His blessings. Thank God for baby Heavenly as well because I got a little practice before the twins arrived. A little while later Alicestene woke up with that beautiful smile on her face.

I gave her a big kiss and asked, "How you feeling, baby?"

She said, "A little sore, but other than that I'm okay after delivering two big-headed boys." She smiled and said, "I want you to know that's your head on those boys. Look at them."

We laughed and talked until she fell asleep again. I stayed with her until after midnight and finally went home. Mr. Thornton was out like a light. He must have worn himself out fishing because he didn't make a sound. We got up early and had breakfast. I took him to the airport after we closed the deal on the property.

Alicestene had to stay in the hospital for seven days. It seemed like those were the longest seven days of my life. Diamond and Benjamin went with me to the hospital to discharge her. I needed them to help with the babies. I got my family, and we were going home. I was so happy. I left mama and Mr. Crumpton at the house to get things ready for their arrival. She was still not able to climb the stairs, so we set up the nursery in the spare bedroom downstairs.

We walked in, and everybody said, "Welcome home." She went to the bedroom and got in the bed because she was still a little weak. She talked a little, and the next thing we knew she had fallen asleep. Diamond and Benjamin continued to hold on to the babies, and Mama held little Heavenly. Ms. Mable had prepared snacks for everyone in the family room across from Alicestene. She was waiting for her chance to hold the babies, and Benjamin brought one over. She was so happy and took the baby and put him in his bed. Then she took the other one from Diamond and put him in his bed.

"I don't want y'all to spoil these babies now," Ms. Mable said smiling.

Diamond asked, "Which one is number two," looking from one to the other, "and which one is number three?"

I said, "I don't know right now. We are going to have to look at their name tags until we can find some noticeable difference."

We all sat around eating, and talked about how our lives had changed. Mama and Mr. Crumpton were proud grandparents. Our family like Box City's had expanded greatly. We had gone from four to nine members of our family—ten if you counted Ms. Mable. She had agreed to be our live-in housekeeper and babysitter to help us raise our children. She would get to travel with us wherever we went in the world. This was a woman who had never been outside of Box City.

CHAPTER 40

The twins are nearly two years old now, and little busy bodies. They are into everything. We can finally tell them apart. Thomas #2 has a mole on his right ear. Other than that, they can make us cross-eyed because they look so much alike. For some strange reason Thomas #3 loves to take off baby Heavenly's shoes and play with them. It's a beautiful sight watching my little baby sister play with her nephews. Alicestene is doing very well and enjoying motherhood. She told me she wants a little girl because I have the boys. I told her that whatever made her happy made me happy. She even told me that she might want to open up a daycare center that would give the children of Box City more learning opportunities. She said Mama had her restaurant, and I owned most of Box City. She wanted a business too.

I asked her, "How are you going to care for the babies and run a business too?"

She put her hands on her hips, smiled, and said, "I'm going to do like the genius and hire qualified people to run the business for me. I will just show up to make sure everything is okay, and the money makes it to the Hancock Bank." Alicestene is a very smart woman. I know she will have no problem getting it off the ground.

Mr. Thornton lives across the lake from us now, and fish all the time. While crews were building the plant, he and his wife came and stayed with us for three weeks until their home was completed. Mrs. Thornton is a very beautiful woman and fell in love with the twins and Alicestene. She took one look at the lot and said she loved it. We now visit each other often. The thing that I'm proud of the most is that Mr. Thornton claimed us as his family. He said Box City saved his life and his marriage. He has gotten his passion back for his wife, and they really enjoy each other now. The Thornton clothing manufacturing plant is awesome and is bringing in big bucks. They are shipping merchandise all over the country. The building is huge, and it has brought more than two hundred jobs to Box City. Mr. Thornton wanted a good finance manager, and I told him about Brock. Brock applied for the job there and became one of the finance managers. That was a major step up for him. Mr. Thornton said that out of all the people who were tested, he was the second highest. He said since Brock was a friend of mine, he knew he was getting a good man for the job.

I went into my office one day, and there were beautiful roses on my desk. They were not from Alicestene. Brock had sent them along with a card. The card read, "Thanks, man. I could not have done it without you." Tears just ran down my face. Like me, he has spent a lot of time thinking about where the Lord has brought him from. He told me he was grateful that Mr. Thornton brought his plant to Box City.

The funny thing is that Mr. Thornton's company has caused many other companies to establish headquarters right here in Box City. I believe Mr. Thornton had something to do with that. There are skyscrapers and five-star hotels going up on land they purchased from the Hancock Bank. We have a theme park and our own movie theater. No more driving way over to the other side of town. I also opened up several baby stores for all the children Alicestene wants to have. The good thing is the clothes are made right here at Mr. Thornton's company. The Hancock Bank was doing so well that I opened up another bank on the other side of town, and to manage the location, I promoted one of those bankers who said, "Low-class people will never have a high-class mentality." That was years ago. Today he is singing a new song about the new Box City.

Box City is now a place where everyone is proud to live. When I moved up, I allowed others to move up as well. No one was deprived of success unless they just wanted to be. People are proud to live in a nicer apartment or a new home because it was better than what we all had before. There are still several people with that low-class mentality who want to live on the streets. If they're caught, they have to pay fines or go to jail. Now they are glad to go to the shelters where they can get a bath, a bed, clean clothes, food, and training. Several have gone on to get their GEDs.

I realize my life story may not be as interesting as others, but it's my life in ten short years. With prayer and hard work, your dreams can come true too. I am grateful that the Lord allowed me to rewrite my life's story. It started off kind of rocky, but who would have ever thought my life would have turn out like this.

Right now there is one other thing I want to do by the time I'm twenty-six. I want to see Paris in person. I heard the best time to go to Paris was in the spring. After I had postponed because of a third baby, I thought it was time to go before Alicestene brought me some more good news about another baby. Yes, I'm the proud father of three for now. Baby number three is a little girl. Her name is Tomasene Edison Hamilton Hancock, and she looks just like Alicestene. She asked me if I was going to name all the children after me. I told her if she could find a better name, a stronger name, a more powerful name here in Box City than mine, then I would call that baby by that name.

She looked at me and said, "Don't forget, I'm a millionaire too with a strong and powerful name."

I said, "If the next baby is a girl, I will name her after you. Alicestene Edison Hamilton Hancock."

She smiled and said, "I just can't believe you, Tehh. Even the girls have to have Edison Hamilton in their names?"

I said, "If it worked for me, it will work for them as well."

I got all of my affairs in order one day and went home and surprised Alicestene. My heart was bubbling over. I went in the house and told her to start packing because in five days we were all going to Paris for a month. Do you think she gave me any trouble or told me she was having another baby? She started screaming and jumped into my arms. She gave me a big kiss and told me that she would be ready. The boys started jumping up and down too. I was so excited, I started shouting, "Paris, here we come!"

The maids came running to see what was going on. I told them we were going to Paris for a month.

They both said, "That's wonderful, Mr. Hancock. We are going to miss you."

When I told them they were going too, they both fainted. They were revived and didn't know what to do.

Everybody started asking, "What are we going to wear?"

I said, "Clothes, people! Please wear some clothes."

I asked them to not take a lot because they just might want to buy a few Paris originals. Ms. Mable told me she had never been in an airplane before and she was afraid. I told her not to worry because everything was going to be just fine. I knew how she felt because I had never flown either. I drove to most of the places I went that were out of state. This was going to be a wonderful experience for all of us. I told Ms. Mable to let go of her fears because there was a lot to see in Paris. There was no telling where we would all go next year.

She began to pat her chest and said, "My goodness, Mr. Hancock. I never thought something like this would ever happen to me. Let me go and start packing right now. Oh, my Lord!"

The guys gave us a nice surprise going-away party at the Weddings and Events Center. We had a great time. It was like everyone thought we were never coming back. I told them we were just going to be away for one month, thirty days.

"There is no place in this world that could keep me from coming back. This is my city, my home, the new Box City. I've got to come back to it." Then I said, "There is nothing that says, I can't bring a little bit of Paris back to new Box City."

That Saturday morning we got up early and went over to Alicestene parents' and to Mama's house to say good-bye. I asked Mama, Benjamin, and Diamond to keep an eye on the house and gave them the keys. It was really hard. I had never been that far away from my mama that long before. She had gone to Hawaii, but this was different. As we got ready to leave, my little sister Heavenly started crying and reaching for me. I turned, went back, and took her in my arms. I gave her a big kiss and told her how much I loved her. She just smiled as I gave her back to Mama. I told her I was going to bring her back something very special.

I left them, and we were off to the airport. I had to be strong for everyone, but I was shaking in my boots as I thought about flying. Then I thought, *If I have never flown before, how do I know I'm going to be scared? Where did I get that idea from?* I was sabotaging myself mentally. I tried so hard to think of something positive. I asked the Lord to ease my heart and calm my fears so I won't be afraid. Alicestene noticed that I was sweating and thought it was because we were rushing. We boarded the plane and took our seats. I didn't want to show it, but I was scared. I couldn't believe the Lord would let me get on the plane and kill me dead. I took a few deep breaths to calm down. I think Alicestene knew something was wrong because I squeezed her hand tighter than usual.

She looked at me and said, "Baby, are you okay?" I lied and told her I was.

As the plane took off, it was like all the air was going out of me. I couldn't breathe for a second, and then the horrible feeling went away. The Lord came to my rescue again and told me everything was going to be all right.

He said, "Sit back and enjoy the ride because there will be many, many more to come."

At that moment I was liberated. It was like all of my fears just went out the window. I leaned over and gave Alicestene a kiss and told her I was okay. The maids were sitting across from us with the boys, and they looked like they were okay too. In my heart I thanked God for this new experience in my life. I didn't really know why I wanted to go to Paris, but I will certainly find out when we get there. Our tour guides would meet us at the airport, and they would assist us the whole month.

As the plane flew through the clouds, I looked out and thought, *How close am I to God's house?* I thought perhaps I could get a glimpse of His mansion. I wanted to wave at Him just in case He was looking out of His window. I could even see myself going up to His door, ringing His doorbell, and letting Him know that I stopped by because I was just in the neighborhood. A smile came over me, and I continued to look out of the window. The sky was simply magnificent. It was like another world—a world I had never seen before. Looking up at the clouds was one thing, but flying above them was another. In my calm I thought about all that the Lord had allowed me to achieve in ten short years. Then to top it off, He allowed me to rise to the heights of the heavens. I thought, *If I died right now, I would have no regrets because He allowed me to do more than most people in a lifetime.* I don't know what the Lord has in store for the next chapter of my life. All I can say is I want to be ready for it.

After all of those hours in the sky, the plane finally landed, and we got off. My feet touched the ground of a new country. A place that had only existed in my imagination, and it felt wonderful. The sky was still blue. The grass was still green, and there was still a sweet breeze that I could feel. At that moment I knew God was right there with me in Paris. I collected my family, and we went to find our tour guides. All I could say was, "Paris, here we come!" Then I heard the voice inside of me say, "You haven't seen anything yet."